Hope you enjoy —

Alan Ketchum

THE VANISHING A-list

ALSO BY DIANE KETCHAM

Long Island: Shores of Plenty

The VANISHING A-LIST

a novel by

DIANE KETCHAM

Tidelow Press

Cover design by Janet Long

For information contact:
Tidelow Press
Book #228
300 Fifth Avenue South, Suite 101
Naples, Florida 34102

Or visit www.tidelowpress.com

FIRST EDITION

ISBN 978-0-9797555-3-8

Library of Congress Control Number: 2007904849

PRINTED IN CANADA

To Terry, my rock.

Without you, none of this would have been possible.

PROLOGUE

She was a woman who invited stares. But on this summer night she didn't notice the someone staring at her. She had left the cocktail party later than planned. With the top down on her black Mercedes convertible, and Billy Joel blasting from the Harman Kardon speakers, she never saw the van pull in behind as she left a mansion by the sea in Southampton.

"*WE DIDN'T START THE FIRE*," she and Billy sang as the Mercedes zigged and zagged down hedge-bordered lanes. What had Billy told her about that song? She knew Joel. She knew everyone who was anyone in the Hamptons. Because she was someone too.

The week before in East Hampton, the paparazzi swarmed like yellow jackets at a picnic. So many celebrity-seeking photographers descended upon a private party at Nick and Toni's restaurant, they had to be roped-off on both sides of the entrance. To gain entry, partygoers walked a gauntlet of flashing lights. The husband of a fashion designer arrived just ahead of her.

"IS HE ANYBODY?" a photographer shouted.

"NO, HE'S NOBODY," another shouted back.

Well here comes somebody, she thought, starting down the walkway. Flashes popped. Sound swelled from the crowd.

"It's PAINE!"

"You look gorgeous Paine!"

"Look this way Paine!"

1

Daughter of a billionaire father and actress mother, Paine Hayes was born to the A-list.

As she approached the highway, she hit the brakes. Eastbound traffic was at a standstill. No left turn tonight. Fortunately she was going right, towards East Hampton. Or was it fortunate? On this Friday in August, everybody seemed to be heading east. She nervously tapped her forefinger on the leather steering wheel. She was going to be late to the dinner party.

"*UPTOWN GIRL*—." She would have to wait until someone let her in. It didn't take long. With her lion mane of hair, the color of the bicolored corn sold at local farm stands, eyes always turned in her direction. She was 28 and simply stunning. The long hair framed perfect cheekbones, which were set off by a golden tan that accentuated a perfect size 4 figure. Much of it was on display as she sat in her convertible. A man in a Green Range Rover saw bare thighs and jammed on his brakes. He motioned for her to pull in front of him. She waved a thank-you and headed east. She never heard the horn blasts as a gray van darted in a few cars behind, nearly sideswiping a BMW.

She was thinking of the party she had just left, a fundraiser for the environment. For which group? It didn't matter. They all became a blur. Billy had been there along with Steven Spielberg, Charlotte Ford and Martha Stewart. What fun watching Charlotte and Martha interact. But she would have to hurry if she was to change for dinner. She turned down Georgica Lane. The V-12 engine roared as she made a left, then a quick right, then another right. She had turned into her driveway when she felt the bump. A van with tinted windows hit her from behind.

"Damn!" she said out loud.

A man in a gray polyester shirt and brown pants jumped out of the van and raced toward her. Instinct warned her to lock the car door, but she had already opened it. As she reached for the handle, he grabbed it first." My wife is in labor. Do you have a car phone?"

"Yes—." Still wary, she kept her eyes on him as she reached for the phone. But as she grabbed for it, the phone hit the steering wheel and dropped to the floor. She turned to pick it up. He was on top of her before she could react. A cloth came over her face. She panicked. What was that smell? Gasping for air, she tried to shove the cloth away. "Oh God, fight it, fight it,"her mind screamed as her body, as if in slow motion, struggled from a growing grogginess. She felt the man's breath in her ear. She smelled body odor. This could not be happening to her. He pushed her half onto the passenger seat. With one hand he tried to hold the cloth over her nose and mouth. With the other he pulled down the top of her black dress. "He's going to rape me,"she thought.

He turned her towards him. "What beautiful breasts,"he said.

She wanted to scream. But she couldn't form a sound.

"Oh I see such fear,"he said. "You think I am going to attack you. But I am not allowed to handle the merchandise."

One last attempt to fight, to cover her breasts. "And what mer-chandise you are. They will be very pleased. But you—no."She was asleep now. "No, I do not think you will be pleased with what they will do to you."

CHAPTER 1

"I'm late. I am always late, which is why, damn it, I have just goosed a congressman." A.J. Billings silently swore as she waited for the Capitol elevator. Waiting next to her was the startled congressman, an aging Dapper Dan from Mississippi. He eyed her as if the contact was intentional. Perhaps this attractive brunette with the sparkly eyes and that nice set of legs desires me, his smirk suggested.

You have got to be kidding, A.J. wanted to say, all the while keeping her eyes riveted on the closed elevator doors. This is not some type of journalistic foreplay. I accidentally rammed my reporter's notepad into your posterior because I am late to a press conference. Even when I start early, I am always late.

The doors opened and the congressman bowed, gesturing for A.J. to enter first. "Ride this often?" he asked. She offered her best "How-nice-of-you-to-ask-me-to-dance" smile, learned in seventh grade at Miss Reed's dancing school. "Ladies are always polite," Miss Reed had said. "Even with assholes?" Trudy Polansky had whispered. Trudy did not graduate from Miss Reed's. A.J. did.

She rode in silence to the second floor, Mr. Mississippi staring at her, she staring at the door. It finally opened on another hall of congress. "Excuse me coming through," she shouted to a gaggle of aides milling in front of the elevator. Half walking and half running, her heart began to race. "This lateness thing is going to kill me. I still have dreams that I'm late for college classes and that was 10 years ago."

Down another corridor, then another, trying to arrive at the press conference before it started. But of course it already had. The lights of the television cameras had turned the small hearing room into a sauna by the time A.J. barreled in. A few reporters nodded in recognition. What was the number one features reporter from the *New York Tribune* doing at a Washington press conference on the Everglades?

Most eyes were focused where the cameras were, on a sea of microphones placed before a tall man whose back was to the crowd. He was listening intently to a blonde woman with large blue-rimmed glasses. "Is that Congressman James Fennimore Whitman?" A.J. asked the photographer next to her. "Yeah, but he's no Mohican," the photographer answered.

It was an odd name for a congressman from Florida. From the back he looked fairly conservative, dressed in the standard congressional garb—a navy blue pinstriped suit. His sandy-colored hair was cut chez house barber, which meant just a few inches away from being scalped. She didn't know much about Whitman except that he was squiring around Armando Guyera and she had orders to ask about the connection. Why was she even there? She didn't cover government. She wrote human interest stories for *The Trib*. She had won a Pulitzer for a series on homeless children living on the streets of New York.

She rifled through her reporter's pad looking for the few questions she had jotted down. Unfortunately she jotted them down at the end of another interview. Turning page after page she couldn't find the right one.

"Betty informs me the number is 25 not 29," the congressman

said turning once again to face the crowd of reporters. "Sorry for the error. I'll take another question."

A.J. glanced up. The voice sounded familiar. Then the blood in her face did a free fall. This was the man whose belly button she had probed with her tongue. Her only one night stand. The only time she ever had sex with a man she hadn't officially dated at least three times. It was a rule she and her college roommate had devised. It kept her practically chaste in college. Her career had kept her fairly chaste since.

Her mind raced back to last April. She rarely visited Washington. But she was working on a story about a former nun who won $50 million in the State lottery. The ex-nun was the daughter of a U.S. senator. She needed to talk to the senator. After the interview, she headed for the Delta Shuttle and the quick flight back to New York. But a freak snowstorm started and wouldn't quit. The airport closed. She took the last room at the Hyatt. After she checked in she headed to the hotel bar. This was something else she rarely did. But a night in Washington without even a toothbrush demanded drastic action. He was sitting at the bar. The only seat left was next to him. They talked; they laughed. He said his name was Wit. She said her name was Annie. Well, was she really going to tell him her real name—Agatha Jasmine?

It was her mother's invention. Delilah Cordelia Billings of Decatur, Georgia tended towards the dramatic. She named her daughter after a spinster aunt, Agatha, who lived in Mobile. "She has money up to the rafters," Delilah said, "and she will think most kindly of you when she kicks the bucket." It turned out Aunt Agatha thought more kindly of Sidney, her Persian cat. When the aunt died, the cat got the money, or technically the animal hospital owner who assured Aunt Agatha that Sidney and other homeless cats in Alabama would want for nothing. A year later he and Sidney were living in Palm Beach.

Jasmine was because her mother felt so badly about the Agatha name, and Jasmine was Delilah's favorite southern flower. Only A.J. grew up on Long Island where she endured the taunts of classmates who called her Jasmine-schmazman, or worse, Aggie.

To save her sanity, she became A.J. at school and later in the professional world, and Jazz to her family and close friends. Jazz was what her father had called her. Her mother always called her Agatha Jasmine. Delilah was not fond of nicknames, which made for a challenging childhood. Nothing like riding bikes with your friends, and hearing, "AGATHA JASMINE—time for dinner!"

With a southern-bred mother and Brooklyn-born father, life was never dull for Jazz. When she was born, her father, Jack Billings, was stationed in Viet Nam. After the war, he worked in the newspaper business as a pressman. Delilah told everyone he was an editor. He never corrected her. Jack doted on his wife and daughter. He worked overtime every week to put money in his only child's college fund. A year after Jazz entered Northwestern, he died of a heart attack.

She hadn't told Wit about her complex name, or anything about herself. But then he didn't go into details either. They avoided specifics. For one night it was just sexual attraction and later gratification. Yes, and that one moment, when he whispered "Oh Annie, you could steal my heart." How her own heart had soared. They had been so free with each other. She had never done half the sexual things she did with him. At 32, her relationship scorecard was still in single digits. The last beau, as her mother called them, was David, the doctor. But David was gone. And the next morning so was Wit. He left before she woke up.

The only male in her life now was Willie, her black Labrador retriever. A show dog and soon to be stud dog, Willie would probably have more sex than she ever had.

Whitman hadn't noticed her yet, but he would. The Washington editor, Ed Towstin, had ordered her to ask him some questions. She was in D.C researching another story. She could have told Towstin she was too busy. But she didn't balk at his command because it would help another reporter and friend, Joanne Meltzin. It was Joanne who encouraged Jazz to expand her writing by doing longer pieces. If it hadn't been for her, Jazz probably wouldn't have written the series that won the Pulitzer.

Before a bus rear-ended Joanne's Honda and put her on sick leave, she had been working on a story about stolen artwork being smuggled into the United States. Armando Guyera, an Argentinean, owned a large importing business based in Miami. There was talk he might be involved in the smuggling operation. Joanne learned that his business was under investigation by the FBI. She also discovered that Whitman had met with Guyera on several occasions. What was the connection? Towstin ordered Jazz to find out.

Questions were being shouted. What were they all asking? How much more time was left in the press conference? She had to do this. There had to be some comment before the paper's deadline. Suddenly, a lull in the jumble of noise.

"Congressman Whitman!" she shouted. Was that her voice? Was this her nightmare? Eyes turned towards her. He looked in her direction. Was there recognition? She didn't know. She just stumbled on. "Ah, Congressman, could you tell me what your relationship is with Armando Guyera?" He stared at her, saying nothing. "Oh God, make this be over soon," she thought.

"I barely know him," Whitman finally answered.

"Then why have you met with him at least three times?"

Now he was glaring at her. "I don't think this is the time to go into that."

"Thank you, Congressman Whitman, that's all." Betty Norris, the press secretary with the big blue glasses hurriedly ended the news conference. Jazz had gotten nothing except sick to her stomach. Get out of here, her mind screamed.

"A.J. what was all that about?" a network reporter asked as she charged past him.

Behind her, the room slowly emptied. As the last straggler left, Whitman turned to his press secretary. "Find out who she is," he said. "Find out what she knows."

CHAPTER 2

The message light on the telephone was blinking when Jazz returned to the borrowed desk in the Washington bureau.

"Ed's been asking for you," a copy editor said. The phone would have to wait. Might as well get this over with. Towstin was not one of her fans. She decided that the first day they met. Their paths had never crossed before this week, at least not that she remembered. She worked in New York. He was based in Washington. Maybe it was the Pulitzer. Winning the Pulitzer had been the most exciting and yet divisive event. Her life was B.P. and A.P. And the way people treated her A.P.—after the Pulitzer—was not always with affection. At least not from colleagues.

She walked into Towstin's office. He was on the phone but quickly hung up.

"What did you get?" he growled. "We've left a space in the story."

How to tell him she had nothing. That James Whitman was— was what?

"It was basically a no comment," she said. "When I asked what their relationship was, he said 'I barely know him.' When I asked about their meetings he said 'Now isn't the time to go into it.' And then they ended the press conference."

"Did you stay after? Did you push him?"

"He —. Look I said I would try to help Joanne. And I did. I went to the conference. I asked the questions. He wasn't going to answer them."

"Call his office."

"It won't help if I call his office. He's not going to respond by our deadline."

"Well, we don't know that unless we try, do we? Call the office. Tell them you have a deadline in two hours."

"Right." She left his cubicle. Why argue? Whitman would never return her calls. Back at her desk she noticed the flashing light. She dialed her code to play the messages. There was only one. "Jazz, it's Joe. How is it going there? Call me. I've got something for you."

Joe Nemond was her boss in New York, the deputy national editor who steered her articles through the maze of administrative editors *The Trib* employed. Since the Pulitzer, management had given her free reign to find subjects, and only Joe to report to. But it had been several months since she had something really exciting to report about. She dialed his number.

"Nemond."

"Hi, it's me. Say something that isn't going to depress me more."

"Well the computers are down here. It's got to be better there."

"It's not. What's up?"

"I got an interesting call from Mancox, our esteemed leader. He had dinner last night with Charles Hayes—you know the owner of Mirose Cosmetics. Hayes's daughter is missing. He's not certain that she's not on some romantic adventure. She's disappeared before for a few days, even a few weeks. She's about 30, and been linked with rock stars and playboys. Takes off with them at a minute's notice. But this time there are some odd circumstances. He said he'd be willing to talk to one of Mancox's reporters.

"I remembered you mentioned wanting to do something on the A-list—the trials and tribulations of the elite—as if they had any—and I thought this might be an interesting angle. Is the daughter really missing? Probably not. But she will definitely make good copy. I've got a picture of her here from the style pages. This is a young lady I would like to be missing with. I know you have to be back here this weekend when Willie loses his virginity. I thought maybe you could go out to Long Island and see Hayes. He'll talk to you. And I already got the okay from Mancox."

Why not? Maybe there was something there. At least it was a way to get out of Washington. She told Joe yes, she would do it. She had a few calls to make, a little packing to do, and she would be on the 9:00 p.m. shuttle.

"Want to talk about what's happening there?" he asked.

"No. I'll see you tomorrow."

Around the room, fingers feverishly tapped on keyboards and phones rang and rang. Deadline was growing nearer and the bureau was busy. She looked up Whitman's number. His receptionist transferred her to Betty Norris who said the congressman was on his way to Miami. An interview today would be impossible. Perhaps she could schedule something next week?

So much for this deadline. She dialed Towstin. "Whitman is on a plane to Miami," she said. "There's no way to get more than we have."

"Right Billings, thanks for nothing." He hung up.

Jazz made a face at the phone as she hung up. A copy editor caught it. "I've had it," she said to him. "I'm out of here. Anybody wants me, I'll be in New York tomorrow."

After a quick taxi ride to her hotel, she packed and checked out via the express option on the television. In less than 30 minutes she was on her way to the airport. She grabbed the last seat on the 8:00 p.m. shuttle. Wedged between the window and an overweight businessman, she watched as Washington disappeared below. "No happy memories here," she thought.

Back at the hotel she had just left, a bellhop approached the desk clerk. "Did Miss Billings get the letter that man asked me to give her?" he asked.

The clerk took out a room folder. " No, It's still here. Looks like she checked out without coming down."

The bellhop shook his head. "The guy said it was really important. But it was for her eyes only. If she didn't get it, I was to tear it up."

"Well she's gone. Here it is. Maybe we could read it before you throw it away."

The bellhop took the sealed envelope and turned it over several times. "You know, he gave me a real good tip." He turned it over one more time. "Sometimes you've got to do the right thing." He tore the envelope into little pieces and dumped them into the wastebasket.

CHAPTER 3

Willie loved his morning walks by the sea. It was all he could do to keep from barreling through the door as Jazz looked for her shoes, then the leash. She had chosen this apartment in Brooklyn because of its nearness to the water. She knew Willie wanted salt spray in his face. She did too. A quick jaunt from the brownstone led woman and dog to an asphalt path with panoramic views of sea and sky.

Tomorrow was to be Willie's first sexual encounter—at least with a living creature. Since reaching dog puberty, he humped a favorite lime-colored throw rug on a daily basis. Hopefully Willie would accept sex with something that wasn't inert or colored green.

Labrador bitches were lining up for the newest stud dog. In less than eight weeks in the show ring, Willie had become one of the top labs in the country. For two years he had just been the family pet, content to give Jazz his sole affection. But then Willie's breeder, Larry Hogan, happened to visit a neighbor in Jazz's building. He hadn't seen Willie since he was a six-week-old bundle of black fur. Jazz met Larry on the front steps and asked if he would like to see her "baby." He took one look at the now big baby of 90 pounds and said "This dog has perhaps the best head in the country. You must show him."

And so it began. Larry found a trainer. Willie took to the circuit. His beautiful head, body, and zest for life made him the talk of the show ring. The first month he won his American championship. The next he became a Canadian, then an international champion. Larry convinced Jazz his genes had to be passed on.

"Tomorrow is sex day, Willie." The dog wasn't paying attention. The smells of the sea were too much. He pranced away, heading for the tall meadow grass and the thrill of the unknown. "Get it out of your system," she called. "It's going to be a long day in the apartment before Carrie can walk you."

Her neighbor, Carrie Farley, was wild about Willie. Carrie loved animals and since she was usually at home with her toddler, Jamie, Willie was a diversion as well as a source of a little extra income. Carrie would take only a few dollars a day for caring for the dog. He was almost a part of her family. As was Jazz. Although the two women led different lives, they had become close friends. Carrie loved to hear all the exciting things Jazz did. Jazz envied the sense of home and family her neighbor had.

After a quick morning walk, Jazz was to take off for Southampton and the meeting with Charles Hayes. But Willie wasn't on schedule. It took a bribe of the dog biscuit Jazz always kept in her jeans' pocket to make him come back from his wanderings. It took another bribe of a big white chewy bone to get him to settle down in the apartment.

At 9:30 she backed her beige Toyota Camry out of the garage she rented and headed for the parkway. Less than two hours later she turned onto Main Street in the village of Southampton. The drive had been easy. Late September was a time to enjoy the eastern end of Long Island. The summer crowd was back in the caverns of New York. It was a beautiful day in the Hamptons. The air held a hint of coldness, and the sun was shining.

A huge privet hedge hid the Hayes home from curious eyes. White wooden gates barred any view of the driveway. Entry could only be obtained via an intercom box by the road. Jazz pushed the button.

"Yes?" an aloof voice said.

"It's A.J. billings from the *New York Tribune*. I have an appointment with Mr. Hayes."

"He's expecting you," the voice said. "Please park your car to the right of the house."

The gates opened and Jazz drove in. Huge sculptures adorned the lush green lawns that bordered both sides of the driveway. The house looked like a French country estate, only larger, much larger. Jazz parked next to a silver Mercedes and walked to the door. She was about to knock when a woman in a gray uniform opened it.

"Miss Billings, please come in."

They walked down the hall to a sunny room with a wall of glass overlooking gardens and a swimming pool. The sounds of crashing waves could be heard from behind dense shrubbery. Although wealthy Hamptoners lived by the ocean, Jazz had learned most were more concerned with privacy than view.

"Miss Billings, I'm Charles Hayes."

Jazz turned to see a thin man in tennis whites. Aristocrat seemed printed on his face. "Please have a seat," he said. "I'm sorry, I have a match scheduled in a half-an-hour. So this will have to go quickly. You should know that I've already contacted the FBI and they are not happy that I'm talking to you."

Jazz smiled, ignoring the comment. Taking a seat on an oversized yellow sofa, she opened her purse and took out her reporter's pad and a pen. "Have you heard anything new regarding your daughter's disappearance?" she asked.

"No, not a word. That's why I finally decided to bring in the authorities. It was not an easy decision. Paine has dropped out of sight before. But she always returned, once engaged to a rock star from—what's that group—Metal Soul? Thank heaven that ended quickly.

"Another time she and a friend decided to join a captain on a schooner heading for Rio. She has always been a free spirit. But this time, things seem different. She owns a home in East Hampton. Her car was left in the driveway. Not the garage, but the driveway. If she were going away for any length of time, you would think she would put the Mercedes in the garage. And she had a dinner to go to that night and never showed up, never called the friend who arranged it. Well, she's done that before too. My daughter has so many invitations she sometimes forgets what she has agreed to attend."

"Has there been any contact with any friends?"

"Not that I know of. Her best friend is Megan McCarthy, the model. You might want to talk to her. She has a place in the city. But she also owns a house in the Hamptons. I think she may be here this week. These girls travel a lot you know. They're always going to L.A. for some party, or St. Barts, or Europe. And you worry about them because they are—. Well, I don't know if you've ever seen my daughter, or a picture of her. Paine is a stunning young woman. Just like her mother was. I suppose you know that Paine's mother was Sally Woods, the actress. She died in a car crash about twelve years ago. Paine was 16. She was very attached to her mother."

"Are you two close?"

"Not anymore. We don't talk that often. We haven't been close since the accident. She blames me for her mother's death."

"Why?"

"Because I was driving. It was an accident. It was raining when we left a party. But Paine couldn't deal with it." He looked away, towards the sound of the hidden ocean. Jazz waited.

"I'm telling you much more than you need to know," he said, finally turning back. "Paine is missing and I am now concerned. It's been a month or so since Megan or I have spoken to her. Perhaps an article about her disappearance might trigger

18

something. The police think I shouldn't go public but—."

Jazz had stopped writing. "A month? She's been gone a month. What do you think has happened to her?"

"I don't know. I'm hoping it's not the worst. I'm a very wealthy man, Miss Billings. No one has contacted me about any ransom."

"To write about her, I would need to know everything about her and her lifestyle."

"Then call Megan. I'd prefer people not know that I talked to the press about this. Now I'm sorry. I have to go."

As if by remote control, the maid in gray popped into the hallway. "Miriam will get you Megan's address and phone number." Hayes shook Jazz's hand and was gone.

Strange, Jazz thought. She turned to the maid who handed her a piece of paper with a phone number and address on it. Obviously this part of the meeting had been planned. Back in the car, Jazz dialed Megan's number. The model answered on the second ring.

"I'm doing a story on the disappearance of Paine Hayes, "Jazz told her.

"Oh thank God," Megan said.

"I'm here in the Hamptons. I just finished talking with Mr. Hayes. Can I see you so we can talk?"

"Sure," Megan said. "I've got about an hour before I head back to the City. Do you know where Sagaponack is?"

"I don't even know what it is," Jazz answered. "But I'll find you."

CHAPTER 4

The home of Megan the model, as the tabloids dubbed her, sat on land that once grew potatoes. Now the crop was the young and wealthy. Although each of the million-dollar houses around hers looked a bit different, all shared a common scenery—flat fields leading to the ocean. Megan bought the house in Sagaponack, a community in the Hamptons, after signing a contract with Mirose Cosmetics. A dark-haired supermodel, whose face was as recognizable as Christie Brinkley's or Claudia Schiffer's, Megan was known simply by her first name.

Cheekbones to die for, Jazz thought, as the model opened the front door. The body, however, looked like it had been put through a pants press. In jeans and a form-fitting black tank top, Megan was so thin, Jazz wondered how she had the strength to dance the night away, as she did every night according to the gossip columns.

"Come in," Megan said. "I'm a fan of yours."

Jazz was stunned. "A fan of mine? You're the superstar."

"But you're the writer. A really good writer. I was going to major in English in college. I wanted to write. But greed got in the way."

"There's something to be said for greed," Jazz replied, as her hand swept the keys of the black baby grand in the living room.

"Please sit," Megan said. "Can I get you anything?"

"No, thank you." Jazz took the nearest seat, a black leather chair. Megan sat next to her on a black leather sofa. Black seemed to be Megan's motif. "Thanks for seeing me," Jazz said. "Mr. Hayes told me that you and Paine are very close."

"We became good friends about two years ago. We met at a party on St. Barts. We really hit it off. We were laughing about something, I don't remember what. We couldn't stop. Mick—Jagger, that is—said if we didn't stop laughing he'd throw us both in the swimming pool. Of course we didn't, and he did. Which made us—sopping wet— laugh even harder.

"Paine and I were supposed to both be at a dinner party the night I think she disappeared. I called the next morning, and when she didn't answer I got nervous. I called her father but he said I shouldn't worry. She's disappeared before. And he's right. But I can't imagine that she wouldn't call me eventually. I had to go away on a shoot later that day. Several times I tried to reach her. But I was in Aruba and the connections weren't so good and I'm afraid I just got too busy. When I got back, there still was no word from her."

Megan had been sitting cross-legged. Now she shifted her position and leaned forward. "Something is definitely wrong. I called the police but they said a family member would have to report her missing. I called her father several times."

"He finally contacted the FBI," Jazz said. "It's hard to believe he waited so long before calling anybody."

"Yes, I think it was about two weeks after that night she didn't show up that he finally relented and called the FBI. I think he truly thought she was just off doing something wild, and she has done that many times. Plus you have to realize he and Paine were never very close. She hasn't had much of a family life."

"I want to learn more about her and the way she lived. Can you help me?

"Sure. Better yet, I can show you. I'm going out tonight in the city. Why don't you come with me? Do you party much?"

"I don't party at all."

"Well tonight's your night. We'll meet at midnight."

"Midnight? I guess I better go take a nap."

"Oh you are funny."

"I'm not kidding."

CHAPTER 5

"I'm stepping out tonight," Jazz said as she and Carrie sat on the couch in Carrie's living room. Jamie was on the floor playing with blocks. Willie sat beside him watching every move. The dog had already been warned not to touch any of the blocks. But the movement of each was making him salivate.

"Do you have a date?" Carrie asked. "Did that Wit call?"

"Please don't mention him again."

When Jazz returned from Washington, she finally confessed to Carrie about the one-night stand and how it turned out the "standee" was a congressman. She even told her about the humiliating day after the greatest sex in her life when she waited in her hotel room watching *The Price is Right* and every other game show, waiting for him to call. Carrie, ever the romantic, said he would definitely call now that he found who she was. Jazz tried to explain that he would definitely *not* call now that he found out who she was.

"I am going out tonight as part of the story I'm working on. You know I can't tell you everything about it, but tonight I've got to go out with the A-list crowd and see how they party."

"Oh sounds like real hard work."

Carrie was not usually sarcastic. Jazz looked closely at her. "Hey, actually it will be for me. They don't go out until midnight. You know me. I fall asleep in front of the TV by ten. I figure I'll take a nap after dinner so I can stay up with them."

"You sound like you're eighty. Try having a baby and you'll be up all night, and day too."

"Someday I just might." Jazz stood up. "Help me pick out something slinky to wear—not that I really have anything slinky. Come on."

Carrie shook her head no.

"Are you okay?" Jazz asked, sitting back down. "What's wrong?"

"I don't feel in a slinky mood today. I don't know when I'm ever going to feel slinky. Oh Jazz, I think I might be pregnant again."

"Carrie! That is so exciting. Does George know? Are you sure?"

"No I'm not sure so I haven't told him and I don't know how he's going to react if I am. We thought we would wait a few years and I might even work for awhile. I don't know if our finances can handle it."

"Everything will work out. You are such a good mother. It would be wonderful to have two Jamies or maybe a Carrie junior too. Oh don't be upset. Find out for sure and then tell him. I know he will be ecstatic."

"I hope you're right. But—let's change the subject. Tell me where you're going tonight."

"I'm going with Megan, the model. I don't even know the names of the places we're going. I guess the in crowd doesn't always go to just one place. They see who's there and if not the right people, they move on. She said we would probably be out until four." She looked at her watch. "I better go downstairs and fix dinner for Willie and me." Hearing the word "dinner," Willie leaped up and looked expectantly at each woman. Who was going to feed him?

"Yes my boy, it's din-din time," Jazz said. "Is it okay to leave you Carrie? I hate to see you upset. Another baby, this is a good thing, not a bad thing."

"I know, I know. I'll be okay. Have a good time. I want to hear everything that happens. Bye Willie."

Willie didn't hear. The front door had opened and he was racing down the stairs to his own front door and the food bowl that waited behind it.

☆ ☆ ☆ ☆ ☆

Eight hours later, attired in the one basic black dress she owned and sipping a club soda, Jazz stood by a bar in a club whose name she had already forgotten. The nap hadn't helped much. It was 2:00 a.m. and she was dragging. The music was loud, the lights low and this was the third club of the night. Where had she been? She would have to go over all these club names tomorrow with Megan. She had brought a small notebook to write some notes in. But so far, she had taken it out only once. Megan would leave her for awhile and then come back with a drink in her hand and ask how she was doing. Every once in awhile she would bring somebody over. She could barely hear what they had to say. This was not working. She wasn't getting anything except a headache.

And then it happened. The moment every reporter lives for, when you hear or see something, and realize this could be the start of the biggest whopping story you ever had. Megan had left again but this time came back with the young actress Mary Anne Lowdron who was known to her friends and fans as Mallow. She was wearing a low-cut white dress with a slit on the side that seemed to go up to her waist.

"Mallow, I want you to meet A.J. Billings," Megan said. "She's a reporter but she's really a good reporter. She's doing a story on Paine and her disappearance." Megan whispered to Jazz, "Mallow idolizes Paine. She thinks of her like a mentor."

A mentor? An A-list mentor? She would have to remember that. Mallow offered an air kiss and Jazz took hold of her shoulders, not knowing quite what to grab. The girl weighed at most 90 pounds.

25

"I can't believe something's happened to Paine," she said. "People are always comparing us, but she is so much more than me."

The music had grown even louder. "WHAT DO YOU MEAN?" Jazz shouted. "Could I call you to talk about Paine? It's really hard to hear in here."

"Sure, do you have a piece of paper? I'll write my cell phone number on it." Jazz tore out a page from her reporter's notebook. At the same time, a man leaned over and kissed Mallow on her neck. She smiled at him as she kept writing. The music pounded through Jazz's chest. Tomorrow, she thought. Maybe I can learn something tomorrow after I sleep. Mallow was saying something to her.

"AreyoudoingastoryaboutJeffAnkiss too?" She seemed to say.

Jazz wasn't sure what she heard. "Jeff?" she asked. "Who is Jeff Ankiss?"

"JEFF and CHRIS," Mallow shouted in her ear.

She pulled Jazz into a nearby alcove. Megan followed. "I was at a party in L.A. last week and someone mentioned that Jeff Worthington, the television actor, was missing. I think his family or Moira—Megan you know Moira, his girlfriend—one of them contacted the police. It's all very hush-hush but then somebody else mentioned Chris Whitman, you know she writes those books about the X-generation. She's from Miami. Well no one has seen her for awhile either. People thought maybe she was in rehab. I mean people are always dropping out of sight and going into rehab. I heard her mother got a letter from her postmarked from Europe, So maybe she's there, but still for no one to see her?"

"And now Paine," she added. "Weird isn't it?"

Jazz was stunned. Could three prominent people be missing? Suddenly the noise didn't matter. She had so many questions.

But someone had grabbed Mallow's arm and they were headed towards a table of A-listers partying up a storm.

"Mallow, WAIT!" Jazz shouted.

"Sorry got to go," she shouted back. "Call me. We'll talk. Bye Meg." She blew Megan a kiss and headed off.

Jazz grabbed Megan. "Did you hear that? Do you know these people?"

"Sure, everybody does. But I don't know that something's happened to all of them. Mallow can be dramatic, you know."

"Please can we walk outside so we can talk? I've got so many questions."

"Okay, let me get my drink." She picked up her Cosmopolitan and followed Jazz.

They stood by the front door. Jazz's mind was rushing. She couldn't wait to talk to Joe about what she had. But what did she have? "Tell me about the three," she said to Megan. "Is there a common denominator?"

"Well, they all are young, good-looking and well-known, at least in our crowd. You know about Paine. And Jeff—he's about the same age and I guess so is Chris, whose really adorable and bright. Come to think of it, I haven't seen her in a few months."

"But how could three well-known people be missing and nobody in the media know about it?"

Megan took a slow sip of her Cosmo, and sighed. "Okay if they are all missing and we don't know they are, here's probably why nobody has the story. Have you seen what they've written about me in the tabloids? If someone I knew had a problem, do you think I would call the press about it? Nothing personal but contacting the media is not everybody's answer. For many of us, it's the problem, not the solution."

"Okay, but these are prominent people, surely someone would leak something."

"Well Charles finally got in touch with you about Paine. I suppose you could call that a leak."

"But what about Jeff Worthington, and Chris Whitman?"

"I don't know why there hasn't been a story about Jeff. You'd have to check that out. But Chris Whitman? She comes from old money and her brother's a congressman—James Whitman from Florida. These are not people who want their private lives in the *National Enquirer*."

Jazz never heard the last comment. Her mind had tuned out after she heard Wit's name. His sister might be missing too. To do the story right, she would have to talk to the family, maybe even to him. Her stomach churned. She could research Jeff Worthington. And she could keep working on Paine. But it was inevitable. She would have to go to Florida and talk to the Whitmans. And they would have to meet—again.

CHAPTER 6

The fiancée of Jeff Worthington, Moira Wayne, was an actress working on a film in Hawaii. Jazz's expense account went just so far. She set up a phone interview.

From her hotel room in Maui, Moira said she had been in Hawaii a week or so when she began worrying that Jeff was never home when she called him. They had fought about something. Moira wouldn't say what, but that's why she wasn't surprised he hadn't called her. After two weeks of not speaking, Moira grew concerned and contacted his parents, who immediately called the police. There were no leads. He just vanished. The only clue to when was his last log-on on the computer. Just like Chandra Levy, Jazz thought, remembering the story of the Washington D.C. intern who disappeared after using her computer, and became a page one story for months.

Jeff's agent advised Moira and the family not to contact the press. Jeff was on hiatus from his television show. The agent was in delicate negotiations with the show's producers for a new contract. He didn't want it to appear that there were any problems. So the family let the police handle the disappearance. Now, Moira decided, not contacting the media may have been a mistake. She said she was glad someone was doing a story about Jeff and to please mention how distraught she was.

In fact most of the conversation was about how she felt and what Jeff's disappearance was doing to her life. She asked if any photos were needed. She had quite a few of Jeff and herself.

After the conversation, Jazz realized she knew a lot about Moira but little about Jeff. She decided to interview his parents in Lake Tahoe. That's a lot cheaper then flying to Hawaii she told her editor. "Just don't stay at the Ritz," Joe replied.

Since she wasn't a skier, snow and mountains held little appeal for the girl from Long Island. But the lake—"oh this is so beautiful," Jazz said as she and the Worthingtons watched the sun sparkle on blue water. They sat on the front porch of a rustic cottage, one of the few at sea level. Most Tahoe residents prefer chalets high up in the mountains surrounding the lake. "But I like to be near the water," Jeffrey Worthington senior said.

"I do too," Jazz said. She immediately liked this couple. They were so excited when she told them she would be visiting. They wouldn't hear of her renting a car or staying in a hotel. They picked her up at the Reno airport and drove her to their home in Tahoe. Hours flew by as they talked about Jeff. Barbara Worthington brought out the family albums and proudly displayed pictures of her son at every stage—from childhood to a successful acting career.

He is one good-looking guy, Jazz decided, and fun too. In a home video, he playfully picked up his mother and plopped her in a snow bank. Then he laid down beside her. After flinging handfuls of snow at each other, they lay there and waved their arms making snow angels. You could hear Jeff's father laughing in the background as he shot the footage.

"We have always been so close," Barbara said. "I know he would contact us if he could. His agent didn't want us to say anything to anybody. He's so afraid for Jeff's career. We are afraid for his life. Please help us find him."

Jazz casually asked about Paine and Chris. The Worthingtons didn't know them. Moira had said she wasn't sure if Jeff knew them.

Were the three disappearances related? Is there a connection, Jazz kept asking herself as she flew back to New York. Her research had found that a hundred thousand people are reported missing each week in the U.S. But three from the A-list? That was a story even if the disappearances had nothing to do with each other.

The next week Jazz spent finishing her interviews on Paine. It was hard to believe they both lived in New York. "I feel like a nun compared to the life she leads," she told Carrie.

Jazz continued to frequent the clubs Megan had taken her to. To research Paine's life, she had to live it. The bouncer at the High Cloud, Manhattan's top club of the moment, even knew her by name. "Who is that?" people in line whispered as she was quickly ushered through the doors.

Club-goers, in between dancing, drinking, and taking who knows what in the bathroom, told her that Paine "always looked like a movie star, but acted liked she owned the studio." Bitchy was often the word of description.

But Megan told her that Paine could be different. She might snap at a slow waiter but on the way out leave him an exorbitant tip.

There was a sensitive side to Paine Hayes, Jazz discovered. Only she rarely revealed it. Why bother? The Mirose Cosmetics heiress was spoiled as a child and continued to be spoiled as an adult. The A-list and all its trappings consumed her, keeping her isolated from the social graces demanded in the real world.

"And what world are you in now, Paine?" Jazz wondered out loud as she transcribed her notes. The research was making for an interesting profile, but leading nowhere in finding out what happened to Paine, or Jeff. "Where am I going with this story?" she typed on her laptop. "Where are they?"

CHAPTER 7

It had been a difficult month all around, even for Willie. The dog's first sexual encounter had not gone well. He was willing. Actually that was the problem. He was too willing.

At four years of age, Champion Sirena of Princeland had never been mated. But then neither had Champion William by the Sea. He, Jazz and Larry the breeder traveled to Connecticut for the sex act, which was to take place in the fenced-in backyard of his designated paramour. Willie took one sniff of a female in heat and tackled her as if he was a Green Bay Packer and she the opposing quarterback. Foreplay was not in his repertoire. Rough sex was not in Sirena's. She howled and bit his face. Shocked, Willie jumped back. He tried again, this time more gingerly. He never had this problem with the green rug.

Sirena would have none of him. Larry tried putting a sock over the bitch's face to protect Willie. It didn't stop Sirena's growling. Willie started rethinking this whole sex thing. Watching from the dining room window, Jazz wondered if the incident would cause Willie to have a sex phobia. Larry offered another solution. Sirena, a yellow lab, was one of the top show dogs in the country. So was black Willie. The offspring from their mating would be worth thousands. He said artificial insemination might be the answer. Jazz thought he was joking. He wasn't. He took out a jar and proceeded to stimulate Willie by hand. Willie got so excited he never made it near the jar. Sirena's owner said "Maybe some other time."

On the way back to Brooklyn, Larry told Jazz he could mate Willie with a younger bitch the next week. The problem hadn't been Willie's, he assured her. A younger female would be more receptive.

"I thought with animals it came naturally," Jazz said. She looked at Willie in the backseat. Exhausted from trying to lose his virginity, he was fast asleep.

★★★★★

Two weeks later, Willie was still a virgin and Jazz realized she could put off Palm Beach no longer. It was time to call Chris's mother. But Doris Whitman refused to speak to Jazz. On the telephone, her maid said reporters must talk to her son, Congressman Whitman. That meant she had to call Wit.

Calm, be calm, she said to herself as she picked up the phone. This is so stupid. He probably won't even remember me.

CHAPTER 8

J ames Whitman hadn't forgotten the reporter whose body he
had explored. After security checks and research by his staff, he
knew more about Jazz's current life than her mother did. He studied the reports numerous times. Had he been made a fool of in
that hotel room? Had it been a set-up? How much did A.J. Billings
know about him? Or Guyera and his sister?

A reporter! He kept saying it over and over as he drove his white
Corvette down 41 in Naples, Florida. How could he have been so
stupid? To have sex with a reporter? It wasn't as if he had committed adultery. His marriage had ended three years ago. But he never
let himself go like that. He was always so cautious.

It was the weather that night. It was so bad, he decided to stay
in the hotel after he and a businessman from his district had dinner there. He stopped in the hotel bar. She sat down next to him.
The brown eyes, the freckles on her nose—freckles. Most women
he knew had those removed, as well as any lines on their face. They
used Botox and Restylane and who knows what else. But she—she
seemed so natural. She made him laugh, something he hadn't been
doing much of lately. As the hours went by, their heads moved
closer, first to hear over the din, then just to be nearer. When their

thighs touched on the bar stools, he felt an adrenaline surge. He had finally taken her hand, and she looked at him, and all he could think of was how much he wanted her. He couldn't even remember who said 'let's go.' They just did. They were in her room and on the bed and touching and moaning and he couldn't get enough of her.

After he watched her sleep, he wanted to tell her how much the evening had meant to him, how much she could mean to him, but his Blackberry caught his attention. "Urgent, call me," the message read. He didn't want to wake her. So he dressed and went to his room to use the phone. It was his mother, telling him that his sister was missing. His mother pleaded with him to return to Florida immediately to help look for Chris. The snow had practically disappeared. There was a plane leaving at 7:00 a.m.. It was 6:15.

No time for good-bye, no time for an explanation to Annie. He didn't even know her full name. It turned out he didn't even know her first name. He called the hotel later that day. They had no Anne or Annie registered on the fourth floor. He didn't remember the room number. He had thought about her often. And then there she was, asking him a question. A reporter, for God's sake.

It had all been a set-up, he was sure. Well, he would keep his distance from A.J. Billings. The Guyera connection was his only lead. And the Argentinean was waiting for him at the Ritz.

The FBI frowned on him trying to investigate on his own. Agents kept telling him and his mother they were working on the case. But there was no news on Chris. And it had been five months. Five months! How could nobody have found her in five months?

The first few weeks after her disappearance had been the hardest. When she worked on a novel she would go off on her own. But he always knew where she was. Ever since their father died and he hadn't been able to find her, she made sure he knew how to contact her.

While her friends suggested she was just off working on the book, he knew something was terribly wrong. Then the letter came from Europe. She had met someone, she wrote. They were traveling. She was fine. It had been her handwriting. That he was sure of. But when the letter was written, and under what duress, he didn't know. The FBI still had no leads. He discovered the Guyera connection on his own after a chance conversation with a friend. The friend, who owned a private plane, had been at the West Palm airport when he saw Chris getting on Guyera's jet. Actually being helped on the jet, he said, "like she had too many martinis. She looked wasted."

His sister loved to party. But to be drunk getting on a plane, that was not Chris. She was so into image. She might go a bit crazy with her friends. But to be falling down drunk—during the day? No, something was wrong.

He made a point of meeting Guyera at a charity function in Miami. When he casually brought up his sister, Guyera told him he had never met her. A dead end. But then he found out that Jeff Worthington, the nephew of a major Republican fundraiser, had dropped out of sight, and several times he had attended parties at one of Guyera's homes. He felt there was a link. Ron Graham, the FBI agent assigned to Chris's disappearance, said it was a coincidence. People who travel in certain circles share acquaintances. Graham said he had questioned Guyera about Chris being on his plane, and Guyera told him he was crazy. He didn't know her. Nor had he been in Palm Beach the day she was supposedly seen getting on the plane. He was in New York at a meeting. That checked out. Graham moved on. Wit didn't. He decided to learn more about Guyera.

Research had been one of Wit's passions at Harvard Law School. He grew up splitting his time between family homes in Palm Beach and Boston. Preferring the warmer weather, he started a law practice in Naples. With his money and intelligence, he was soon asked to run for office. The Republicans needed a congressional candidate. He won on his first try.

Now he was in the middle of his third term. Married at 30, he divorced at 35. She didn't like Washington. He eventually realized he didn't like her. Fortunately there had been no children, although he wouldn't mind children. At 38, he was starting to think more of having a family, a home life, someone to come home to—like Annie—A.J. Billings. Yeah, right.

Why had she asked the questions about Guyera? What did she know about the disappearances?

Guyera was waiting in the lobby of the Ritz Carlton. Casually dressed in a open-necked shirt and Armani pants, he sat next to the grand piano. "This is a lovely place, yes?" Guyera said as they shook hands. "I had some business to take care of here, in your district. I am delighted you can have lunch with me. I thought it would be nice to eat outside. Do you mind?"

"No, that would be fine." They headed towards the beach bar. Wit wasn't sure what he was going to get from Guyera. But he was the only tie to Chris. Wit's researchers had found that the Argentinean businessman had been involved in several shady import deals. But kidnapping, or worse? And why Chris? And possibly Worthington? It all seemed such a long shot.

"So I am having a party at my Palm Beach home next month," Guyera was saying. "It is for charity. We raise money for the group that shelters victims of domestic violence. Is that how you say it? I would love for you to come. There will be people there you know—Donald Trump, Ron Perelman, maybe Jennifer Lopez. That would be fun, yes, J-lo? And all those pretty friends of your sister—have you had any word from her?"

"No." Here was an opportunity. "Have you heard anything more about her disappearance?"

"Nothing, but that you are worried. I would not be. These girls, they like the intrigue. She will show up. Do you think you can come to my party?"

"I'll have to check with my scheduler. But I would like to."

"Good, you will meet my son, Sebastian. He has not been to visit me for a while. I bought him this small island in the Florida Keys. He was going to develop it like Jumby Bay. But so far he just stays there with his friends. I tell him you must come to the mainland. So he has promised he will be at the party."

"Well I hope to be there too." His cell phone rang. "Excuse me." It was Betty, his press secretary.

"Senator Warther called. He needs to talk to you about an article the *Washington Post* is working on. And you got a call from your mother who said a reporter tried to contact her about Chris's disappearance. The reporter was told to call you. And she just did. Guess who it is!"

He didn't have to. He could sense it. Annie, A.J., Jazz, whatever she called herself, was back in his life.

CHAPTER 9

The call to Wit's office was one of the hardest Jazz ever had to make. She knew once she mentioned his sister he would talk to her. The only relief was he wasn't in the office to talk to her that moment. When she hung up, her body was shaking. Oh this is good, she thought. If I'm like this on the phone, how am I going to be in person?

Waiting for the callback, she tried keeping busy by looking at newspaper and magazine stories on the three who were missing. Her desk at the Trib had become a sea of clippings.

She wasn't required to go into the paper. After the Pulitzer, management assigned a desk assistant to answer her phone and forward messages to wherever she was. It wasn't the most creative of jobs. Which was why Jazz was now on her third assistant, a young man from Detroit named Roger Barron. Roger, a graduate of Yale, had dreams of becoming another Russell Baker. When the *Tribune* hired him, he thought he was on his way. Before the column, however, came the copy. Besides helping Jazz, he was required to check the calendar guides for the regional sections. It took much of his time. Jazz felt sorry for him, and asked if he would like to do some research on the A-list story. He dove in.

He's like a junior G-man, she told Joe. He thinks intrigue looms with every phone call.

"Jazz, I found some really good stuff." His hands full of clippings, Roger entered her small corner office in the city room. The glass-enclosed cubicle was another perk of the Pulitzer. But the office made her feel isolated. Roger's visits always cheered her. He dumped the clippings on the desk.

"How's my Perry Mason?" she asked.

"Who's Perry Mason?"

"Roger, don't you know old TV? Perry Mason was a lawyer who always solved crimes. Raymond Burr played him."

"Who's Raymond Burr?"

"Forget it. What's up?"

"I found a good story on Paine Hayes in an old People Magazine. It's right after her mother died."

Jazz preferred doing her own research before finding out what others had done. But now it was time to check the competition. She took the clipping and put it on top of the stack. Paine's face smiled up at her.

"She looks like Claudia Schiffer," Roger said.

Jazz usually described people by comparing them to celebrities. Roger had picked up on it. But his celebrity knowledge was more limited. "I think she looks like a young Catherine Deneuve," Jazz said. "And don't ask who that is. Now Chris is kind of Cameron Diaz." She picked up a photo from the Whitman pile. "She's cute and vulnerable looking. Both are blonde. I wonder if that is important. What else do they have in common?"

"Well, they have different tastes in men," Roger said. "Chris dated an art dealer, Gary Dire, who owns galleries in London, Palm Beach and Southampton. There's a picture of him somewhere. He's not very good-looking. I guess you'll talk to him. Paine seems to prefer male rock stars. Do you think she was rebelling from a conservative father?"

He took another clipping from the pile he had just brought in. "Here's a good story about Jeff and Moira. Looks like they've been together for over two years. Didn't you tell me one of Jeff's friends thought Moira might be cheating on the side with her new co-star? Was that why she waited two weeks before calling his parents? Or could it be more sinister? Could she be involved in his disappearance?"

Roger's questions were interrupted by the phone ringing. He started to pick it up but Jazz waved him off. She could still answer her own phone. It was Wit's press secretary. Her tone was ice. The congressman would talk to Miss Billings, Betty said, but only in person. He was in Naples. Could she get down there for a Friday afternoon appointment? Jazz asked Roger to check her schedule. He ran out to his desk, then hurried back.

"Friday's clear," he whispered. She had planned to go to the East Coast of Florida to talk to Chris's friends. Naples was on the West Coast. But she could fly into Fort Myers, see Wit, then rent a car and drive across the stretch of Interstate 75 called Alligator Alley.

It was do-able, and necessary, she decided. She had found out how close Chris was with her older brother. She told Betty she could be there Friday. They set an appointment for 2:00 p.m. in the Congressman's district office.

No longer in the mood for work, Jazz popped a Tums in her mouth, and told Roger she would take the articles and read them at home.

The next few days she spent sorting clippings, taking notes, and taking care of Willie. He would stay with Carrie while she was away. But first he had to go to the veterinarian. He had developed an ear infection after chasing a duck into the water. At least that's how Jazz thought he got the infection. The water off Brooklyn was not the best for bathing—for man or dog. After a few days of scratching his ear, Willie was now walking like a drunken sailor, cocking his head to the side. "He just needs drops," the vet told her. "He'll be fine."

be fine."

"He's supposed to have sex next week," she said.

"Excuse me?"

Jazz explained that she had agreed to another attempted mating for Willie the following Tuesday, this time with Champion Wilhemina by Riverside. Wilhemina was a woman of the world, she told the vet. She already had a litter. Willie could learn from her. Ever since the fiasco with Sirena, he was boycotting his green rug.

"I probably told the vet more then he needed to know," she told Willie as she packed for Florida the next day. "But I don't want you to be a sexually frustrated creature." She thought of her visit to Naples and the old ratty T-shirt she had packed for sleeping. "One in the family is enough," she said.

CHAPTER 10

Less than a mile as the pelican flies from the warm green
waters of the Gulf of Mexico, Jazz sat in a traffic jam.
Mercedes and BMWs surrounded her. Naples reminded her of a
palm tree version of East Hampton—chic shops, well-manicured
lawns and people. It had a natural setting that knocked your socks
off. Not that anyone in Naples wore socks. Feet were encased in
the most expensive sandals and boat shoes.

"The natives call it Paradise," Jazz wrote in her reporter's pad as
she sat at a traffic light. "And the tropical scenery makes you think
of Eden. But to live in this paradise, Adam and Eve would have to
take a second mortgage."

"I'll have to work on that," she decided, turning onto Fifth
Avenue from 41. She had arrived early to get the feel of the city
before meeting with Wit. That morning she checked into the La
Playa Hotel on Vanderbilt Beach. It was just down the street from
the Ritz-Carlton, one of the highest-rated hotels in the country. As
the Ritz was barred from her expense account, La Playa would
have to do. It shared the same beach and it was running a special.

When Joe, her editor, heard that she was driving across
Alligator Alley, he warned her not to go at night. The four-lane

44

highway was a desolate stretch of road "and women shouldn't drive it alone," he said. Having toured the Amazon with only an Indian guide who didn't speak English, she wasn't worried about an interstate. But she had heard what a lovely spot Naples was, and it was another location the A-list often frequented. So she decided she might as well stay there for the night, then get an early start.

Although parking appeared to be at a premium, a spot opened up just as Jazz approached Wit's office building, a three-story white structure wedged between a chic boutique and a bank. A Jaguar pulled out and she pulled in, her rented Ford Escort taking about half the space.

The congressional office was on the second floor. Elevator doors opened onto a large foyer with mosaic tile. In the center stood a modern sculpture made of metal. Pretty plush congressional digs, Jazz thought. I wonder if the General Accounting Office requisitioned this.

"May I help you?"

A male receptionist sat behind a large desk. He looked more like the greeter for a fashion designer than a congressman.

"Is this Congressman Whitman's office?" she asked.

"Yes it is. May I help you?"

"I have an appointment to see the congressman. I'm A.J. Billings from the *New York Tribune*."

"Won't you have a seat?" He picked up the telephone and Jazz plopped on a beige leather sofa. She prepared for a long wait. There always was one. Politicians seemed to love to keep reporters waiting. It was a mind game. But waiting for this politician guaranteed her stomach would keep spinning like the rinse cycle on an old Maytag.

In the wee small hours of the night before, when she couldn't sleep, she decided she would say nothing about their previous encounter. She would be the serious reporter. She was sure he would be the serious congressman. It would be as if they were meeting for the first time.

"Ms. Billings?" She looked up to see a young man in a beige linen suit. "I'm Jed Furrows, Congressman Whitman's district administrator. Please follow me."

Now the adrenaline was really pumping. Think of why you're here. You're working on a story. A big story.

They walked past a maze of desks. Wit seemed to have a large local staff. Everyone they passed took a look at the Pulitzer Prize winning reporter. At the end of the hall was a closed door. Jed knocked, then walked in. She followed.

Wit sat behind a large mahogany desk. Behind him, a window overlooked the street and the shops below. He had been writing when the door opened. He stopped and looked up. For a second she saw emotion. She wasn't sure what it was.

"Miss Billings," he said.

"Congressman Whitman," she answered. He stood up and they shook hands.

Jed walked out. They were alone. "Please sit down," he said. "I understand you have some questions about my sister."

What was she worried about? He was acting as if he had never met her.

"I'm working on a piece about people on the A-list. Your sister is one of those I'm focusing on. I'd really like to know about her and her disappearance."

"The FBI would have a file on her disappearance. I can give you the phone number of the agent in charge of the case. He's Ron Graham. He's based in Miami. I haven't found him very cooperative. Maybe you will. As for Chris's life, I'm uncomfortable talking about that."

"But perhaps an article about her might bring out somebody who knows something. Nothing seems to be happening without the publicity."

Wit weighed that comment. His mother had been adamant

about not speaking to the press. But maybe Guyera would have to talk if people around him started doing the same. "What kind of information would you need?"

"I'd like to really know Chris—her likes, her hopes. How she felt about being in the in crowd, and who she was involved with. I have so many questions. I'd like to see her home. I'd like to meet her friends. Do you know any of them?"

"Some. Chris is nine years younger. Her good friend, Eva Long, and I were—well, we're good friends. Eva is an interior designer. She spends time traveling between L.A. and Palm Beach. She could help you with Chris's personal life."

"Does Chris know Paine Hayes?"

"I don't know Paine Hayes. Is that a man or a woman?"

Jazz looked at his face. He didn't seem to be lying. If he didn't know Paine, he certainly didn't know she was missing. She decided not to bring up Jeff Worthington. Perhaps there was no connection between the three disappearances. And why give him added information. Focus on Chris.

"Paine is a female, the daughter of Charles Hayes—Mirose Cosmetics. She's another person on the A-list. I'm just trying to find out who knows who. But Chris is the reason I'm here. Could I ask you some questions about her?"

"Not right now. I just got word of a conference call coming in that I have to be part of."

"Could you at least tell me about her disappearance? What made you think she hadn't just gone off somewhere? "

"My father died two years ago. He had been in a car accident. He was in intensive care and I tried reaching Chris. She was off working on her novel. She didn't tell anyone where she was. He died and still we couldn't find her. She finally came back two weeks later. She missed the funeral. I don't think she will ever forgive herself. From then on, she calls and tells me where she is going and for how long.

"Last April my mother called me frantic that she couldn't reach Chris. She'd been trying for two days. I used to see my sister about once a week. I felt this need to watch over her. She is so bright, but she likes to party with her friends. One day she is working on the great American novel. The next night she's dancing on a table in some club. It's as if she can't decide who she wants to be.

"After mother called, I went over to her place. The property manager said he received a note from her asking him to stop the paper and hold her mail. I wanted to see the note. He said he had thrown it away, but it was definitely from Chris. In it she said she was going off to finish her novel and would contact him in a month or two. I called the FBI right away. As a favor to me they started an investigation, even though there was no evidence that something had happened. They found nothing. Two months later, my mother gets a note from Chris, from Europe. It said she was fine, had met someone and would be in touch. It also said to say hello to Witty. Chris knows I hate the nickname Witty. That was a signal. I told that to Graham, the FBI agent. But I got nothing from him. So I've started doing my own digging. I pray she is still alive. If she is, she is not free. So I also pray that all this is not too painful for her. She puts on this bravado but she has a vulnerable side. I hate the thought of her suffering—." He stopped talking.

Jazz didn't speak. She was having a problem with him showing so much emotion. "Have you found anything?" she finally asked.

"No," he lied. "But I won't stop until I locate her. I even considered taking a leave of absence from Congress to spend all my time looking for her. But then I think the congressional work is keeping me sane. Now that's an interesting paradox, isn't it?"

The more he talked, the more Jazz wanted to comfort him. One night with this man and he already possessed a chunk of her heart. But she had to protect the remaining parts.

"I'd like to learn more about Chris," she said. "Is there some time that we could talk?"

"Why don't you talk to Eva first," he said. "And there is Gary Dire, Chris's last boyfriend. They broke up about a year ago. I suspected him at first but he had an alibi for when she disappeared. He was in New York with an art show. He's in Palm Beach now. I think Eva is there too." ·

"I'm heading over to the East Coast tomorrow," Jazz said. "Maybe I can see them both. Do you have their phone numbers and a number for Graham?"

"Jed will get them for you." His phone rang. "I'm sorry I have this conference call." He got up. She did too.

"Good-bye, Jazz," he said.

"Good-bye." She started for the door, then turned. "How did you know my nickname was Jazz?"

"Would you have preferred I call you Annie?"

For a moment their eyes locked. Then Jazz opened the door and walked out.

CHAPTER 11

Gary Dire was out of town but Eva Long agreed to an interview. Driving across Alligator Alley, Jazz knew she should be thinking of what questions to ask. Instead she was thinking of all the things she could have said to Wit when he brought up the name Annie. She had said nothing. Perhaps it was for the best. What good would it have done to discuss that night? Sleeping with someone was a big move for Jazz. Obviously it meant little to the congressman. It was time to focus on the career and leave the sex to Willie.

✯ ✯ ✯ ✯ ✯

White is the predominant color of Palm Beach. White sand, white buildings, and white people. Which is why Eva Long was such a shock to Jazz. She was black, an African-American surrounded by D.A.R. offspring.

"Come in, Come in." She greeted the reporter in bare feet, her toenails painted a bright red.

This was a woman who Wit made love to. The "we were—are good friends" meant they had an affair. How serious an affair, Jazz would probably never know. Eva was some good-looking woman. Brown hair cascaded down shoulders attached to a lean but shapely body. She looked like a young Diahann Carroll. Jazz felt like an old Annette Funicello. She was dressed like a mousketeer in a dark skirt and white blouse, New York standard garb. But she was in Florida.

I've got to get into this pastel thing, she thought, as Eva, in a flowing pink and white tunic, escorted her to the living room.

They sat overlooking the ocean. Eva was gracious, offering iced tea, water, "something for this hot spell." Jazz wanted to get right to the interview. "How did you and Chris become friends?"

"We were college roommates. At Brown. I was majoring in art, Chris in English."

"Did you have much in common?"

"Well both our families are well off. But Chris comes from old money, ours is newly made. My father runs an agency representing sports figures. Chris's father was a banker. We had different backgrounds, but we just really liked each other. And we stayed roommates for four years. I remember that during our sophomore year, she wanted me to come visit her family in Palm Beach for spring break. They had never met me. I told her it would be a shock to them. She said the color thing wouldn't matter. So I showed up on their doorstep on Easter morning. I don't think her mother ever got over it. Her father couldn't have been more gracious, and Wit, well, I know you've met him, so you know what a love he is. My first real love, actually. But I'm afraid I fell for him a bit harder than he fell for me. We dated when I was a senior. He had finished Harvard Law. I thought I would marry him. He let me down easy. He's that way. We're still friends. And Chris and I have never stopped being good friends."

"Then she would have contacted you if she went away?"

"Eventually. She liked to 'escape' as she put it when she got into one of her books. She was so good at turning out these philosophical books of what it was like to be part of the X-generation. Her publisher loved them because no one was speaking for the

20-something group. She was scared that when she turned 30 next year it would all fall apart. But we're all getting older I told her. Her readers would stay with her."

"What do you think has happened to her?"

"I don't know. I think maybe someone abducted her. I can only hope that she is still alive. But she wasn't kidnapped for money. There have been no demands. I wouldn't tell her brother or mother this, but it's not a good sign, you know. Why would someone be kidnapped and kept alive if not for money?"

"Do you know Paine Hayes?"

"Of the Mirose Cosmetics Hayes?"

"Yes."

"I've seen her at parties in New York. I do quite a bit of interior design work in Manhattan."

"And Jeff Worthington?"

"The name sounds familiar. Jeff Worthington. Jeff Worthington—the actor? I know his girlfriend, Moira. We all travel in the same circles, although they spend more time in L.A. than I do. Why are you asking about him and Paine?"

"Jeff is missing. So is Paine Hayes."

"You're kidding. Three of them? Is there a link?"

"I don't know. I was hoping you could help me with that. I'm working on profiles of the three. Chris is the last to do if you'll help me. Then I'll go to the FBI and see what they've got. Wit doesn't have much confidence in this agent, Graham. But I need to talk to him. After that, we'll publish the piece on the three and the news that they're missing."

"Well, I'll tell you whatever I can. Most of Chris's friends and her ex, Gary, will be at a party in a few weeks at Armando Guyera's. He's hosting it at his place down the beach."

That name again. Could there be a connection? Was that why Wit was so quick to cut off the press conference? She would have to call Joanne Meltzin and find out more about Guyera.

"I'd love to go to the party," Jazz said. "Can you get me in?"

"Oh sure. I know the family. I've done work on just about everybody's house here in Palm Beach."

"Good, well if you have time now, let's talk about Chris and what she's like."

Three hours later they were still talking.

CHAPTER 12

Jazz spent the next few weeks learning about Chris Whitman. What she discovered, she liked. Wit's sister seemed a feisty and fun female. In her twentieth-floor penthouse apartment overlooking South Beach, Chris kept a trampoline. Its use—Jazz could only imagine.

The apartment was full of surprises. A telescope pointed into a bedroom of a neighboring high-rise. A poster of a naked Al Gore hung in the bathroom. Her library of books featured the same irreverent humor. Even the plants she kept were unusual, not your standard potted palms. Jazz hoped Wit's sister was still alive and that someday they would meet. She seemed to possess all the joie de vivre her brother lacked. Their mother, however, remained an enigma.

Mrs. Whitman still refused to meet with Jazz. She hated reporters, Betty Norris told Jazz, again and again. All inquiries regarding the Whitman family were now going through Wit's press secretary. Not that Jazz yearned to talk to the congressman. The Annie comment completely unnerved her. But it seemed stupid to call Washington to contact people in Florida. That, however, is how Betty wanted it. And Jazz knew not to question the power plays in a congressional office.

To find out more about Chris, she needed to talk to Chris's friends. Eva said most of them would be at Guyera's party. The day before returning to Florida for the event, Jazz spent two hours in the newsroom with Joanne Meltzin. The topic was Guyera. He was an importer of artwork, Joanne said, mostly sculptures. There appeared to be more money in the Guyera household, or more accurately households, than an importing business could produce. The family jet ferried Armando between homes in Argentina, New York, Palm Beach, St. Barts and London. Plus, there was the island he bought for his son, Sebastian. It was called Reef Key because of a large coral reef bordering three-quarters of it. The island measured approximately four miles long by two miles wide. It had to cost at least forty million, Joanne told Jazz.

Guyera had married only once. His wife, Sylvia, was wealthy, Jewish and from Manhattan. She died twenty years ago in a freak skiing accident in Aspen. That left Armando to take care of their only child, Sebastian. Joanne had done a lot of research on him.

Sebastian was fourteen when his mother died. From that time on he became the most spoiled teenager in the Western Hemisphere, according to Joanne's sources. Whatever he wanted, his father bought. He was given a Ferrari when he was fifteen and still not of legal age to drive it. At least in the United States. So he drove it on the family's ranch on the Argentinean plain.

When he was seventeen, his father gave him a 40-foot Fountain powerboat, which he used to race around Miami waterways. It was important to Armando that his son learn American ways. Which is why Sebastian spent much of his youth in Miami. He attended the best private schools in Florida, but didn't do well. For all the things a father's money could buy, it couldn't buy a normal teenage life.

Sebastian was not handsome. The dark good looks of the father were lost on the son. The eyes were too wide apart, the nose too big, the height too short. No matter how much he ate, he was always thin, giving him a birdlike appearance. When he was young, he tried to make himself look taller by styling his hair in a pompadour. When the wind blew, the mass of hair shot straight up. Classmates named him Ibis, after the bird.

At thirteen, his crooked teeth were imprisoned in braces, which made him develop a slight stutter that grew worse when he was excited. Around girls, he was excited the most. The teenage girls he knew were not kind to a skinny boy who took a long time to say what was needed. Girls in his school had money too. There was no incentive for them to treat Sebastian well. So they didn't. It was a lonely adolescence. And a bitter one.

College was different, Joanne told her. He overcame the stutter, slicked down his hair and found out that he could buy friendships at Penn State, his alma mater. He collected a small group of male friends who enjoyed having all their pleasures paid for. So did many women. As the years passed from his twenties to early thirties, he attended the right parties, often accompanied by beautiful women. Few knew they were prostitutes. To the outside world, Sebastian seemed to have overcome his solitary teenage years.

In many ways his father's life had been just as lonely. Although Armando was romantically linked with dozens of models and actresses, he had no permanent relationships after his wife died.

In his Florida home of glass walls and panoramic views, not a single personal item was on display. There were no pictures or mementos showing happy times with family, only posed photos of Guyera with celebrities. That was the first observation Jazz made after arriving at the party in Palm Beach.

Eva said to get there around 10:00 p.m. That's when dinner would be served. As was her custom, Jazz arrived late, a little after 11:00. No matter, she soon discovered. Most of the guests hadn't begun the buffet dinner set up on long tables near the pool. Beyond the tables, torches lit a path to a dance floor overlooking the ocean. A three-piece combo performed a mix of Jimmy Buffett and Creedence Clearwater. The younger crowd at the party loved it. Jazz waved to Eva who was on the dance floor with some actor. Jazz knew she knew him. She just couldn't think of his name. She was never good at remembering names, which often made for a challenge, given her choice of career.

Although members of the A-list surrounded her, she couldn't recall who they all were. Yes, she recognized Donald Trump and his wife. And there was Jennifer Lopez and Rosie O'Donnell sitting at one of the candlelit tables. But all those young tanned bodies in designer clothes. Who knew their names? Eva would. She sought her out. "Will you be my guide?" she asked.

Eva pointed to a dapper-dressed man with gray hair taking pictures. "That's Jay Warrens," she said, "He's a pretty famous photographer who specializes in society weddings and celebrity photos. I think Armando gives him some special kickback for taking pictures at his parties. He always seems to be wherever Armando is. And that's Gary Dire." She pointed to a stocky man dressed all in black. "He used to be involved with Chris. You should talk to him. And that crowd sitting at that table in the corner? They're all from Palm Beach. They certainly know Chris."

"Where is Guyera?" Jazz asked.

"He hasn't made his entrance yet. He waits until the booze and the music get everybody in a frenzy and then he appears. It should be soon. He can't take a chance that a guest like Jennifer Lopez will leave before he greets her."

Jazz headed for Dire. He was engrossed in a conversation with two men in their 30's, both of whom looked Latin. One was tall, the other short. As she approached, the taller man made eye contact. He smiled, an absolutely contagious smile. She found herself smiling back. "I am going to dance with this beautiful woman," he said to the two other men.

"It is all right?" he asked her. She nodded. He grabbed her arm and steered her towards the dance floor. "Do I know you?"

"No," she replied. The music was slow—*The Lady in Red*. He took her in his arms.

"Well, I will soon enough. You have a lovely smile."

"You do too," Jazz said. What was happening to her? She couldn't take her eyes off his face.

"I'm Ben Luvana," he whispered in her ear. Their bodies grew closer as the dance floor became more crowded.

"I'm Jazz Billings."

"Jazz—a strange name."

"It's a long story."

"Names often are. My first name is really Reuben. I don't normally tell people that. So you must confess to me. What is your real first name?"

"Agatha—Agatha Jasmine, that's why Jazz."

"Agatha—I didn't know any Agathas still existed in the world. It is an old-fashioned name. You are young and vibrant. Your secret is safe with me."

The music stopped. They stayed together a fraction longer, then smiled at each other. What is happening here? Jazz wondered.

The same question crossed the mind of the man watching them dance. Congressman James Whitman didn't know what he felt as he watched Jazz and Ben finish dancing and walk back to the other two men. He knew Jazz would be at the party. Eva told him. But she was supposed to be working, not playing. Was it play? She had looked at him like that once, too.

Maybe she used sex to get all her stories. That seemed the only plausible reason why she would be flirting with Ben Luvana, the best friend of Sebastian Guyera.

CHAPTER 13

Jazz didn't notice Wit across the dance floor. She was being introduced to Gary Dire and Sebastian Guyera. "Sebastian is like a brother to me," Ben told her, "and Gary, he is our art dealer. He sells us things of beauty, but Sebastian buys more. You are much more into beauty, aren't you my friend?"

Sebastian studied Jazz as if she was a filet mignon he ordered. The leering disturbed her. She was about to cut it off by telling him who she was and why she was there when a man rushed over and whispered in his ear. The licentious look disappeared. "Excuse me," he told the group. "My father would like to see me. Ben come with me."

Ben turned to Jazz. "I will look for you later. Please stay."

She smiled. She really didn't know what to say. He took it as a yes and headed off. She turned to Gary.

"I'm a reporter for the *New York Tribune*," she said. "I'm doing a story on Chris Whitman. I was hoping I could talk to you."

"Does Sebastian or Ben know you're a reporter?" he asked. But then he didn't wait for an answer. Chris's name released a torrent of emotion. "I'm really worried about Chris. What happened to her? I don't know what I can tell you, but sure let's talk. Let's sit over there." He motioned to an empty table.

A half an hour later, Jazz and Gary parted. Now I know why she broke it off, Jazz thought. Gary talked about Chris as if she were an appendage. It was "I love to sail. Chris went with me." "I love old movies. Chris would watch them with me." The only interesting fact she learned was that Chris had ended the relationship, and Gary was not happy about it. "I couldn't believe it," he said. "I gave her everything and she tells me that she doesn't love me and wants out. It had to be because of the money, you know. She's richer than I. She and Eva and their friends, they think they're so much better, because they've got millions."

Definite hostility, Jazz noted as she walked back towards the house. But enough to kidnap, or even kill Chris?

She saw the group that knew Chris and sat down with them. She had just begun her interview when a surge of activity erupted by the glass doors leading from the dining room. A pack of people were jockeying for position. It was as if the bride and groom were about to leave the church.

"What's going on?" Jazz asked the woman next to her.

"It's Armando making his grand entrance."

Suddenly the sea of glitterati parted and Jazz saw Jay Warrens walking backwards snapping photos of Armando, who had his arm around Sebastian. The contrast between father and son was startling. Tall and relaxed, the elder Guyera was dressed casually in a beige silk shirt and white pants. Short and rigid, the son was dressed formally in a dark suit with dark shirt. The more Armando laughed and greeted each guest, the more uncomfortable Sebastian seemed.

Finally a guest pulled Armando aside and he lost his grip on Sebastian. The son scurried away as if he was a mouse released from a lion's paw. He ended up next to Eva. Jazz hurried over, catching the end of Sebastian's comments.

"It's time to leave Eva, I want to party." He possessively put his arm around her waist, then lowered it until his hand rested on her buttocks. Eva would have none of it. She pushed the hand away, then him. "I'm not interested," she said. "Why don't you find someone your own size?"

"What is this? You do not like my son?" Armando Guyera had approached from the other side. He, too, possessively put his arm around her waist. Eva was now wedged between two Guyeras. Jazz didn't know what to say. No one acknowledged her.

"Your son needs to learn manners," Eva said to Armando. She did not try to remove his arm.

"And what do I need?" Armando said pulling her closer. "Maybe both the father and the son are interested in this beautiful black woman." Sebastian glared at his father and Eva, then slinked off. Armando began massaging Eva's back. She didn't look as if she was enjoying it. But she didn't move away. She noticed Jazz.

"Have you met A.J. Billings?" she asked the host.

Armando turned towards Jazz. "Are you a friend of Eva's?" he asked. "She does not seem happy with me tonight."

Maybe if you'd stop pawing her, Jazz thought. But she said only "We're getting to know each other. I'd like to talk to you—."

But before she could finish, a couple appeared alongside Armando. "We just wanted to say good-night and tell you what a wonderful party it was," the man said. Armando grinned. "I am so glad you came," he said, letting go of Eva. The wife gave her most inviting smile. "You must come to visit us the next time you're on St. Barts. You know who will be with us next month? The duchess."

With his attention on the couple, Eva was free. She pulled Jazz aside. "I've been looking for you," she whispered. "I've found out something about Chris and the last day she was seen. I think you'll find it very interesting. Meet me by the front door in 15 minutes." She quickly turned back to Armando whose arm was once again around her waist. "Have you met Eva Long?" he asked the couple.

Jazz hurried away. She would try to speak to Armando later.

What had Eva found out? Jazz decided to wait for her in the house. But as she approached the pool, a man barred her way. "Leaving already?" It was Wit.

"I've probably seen enough," she said.

"And have you learned anything?"

"Not much. Just that millionaires must spend millions on parties."

He took her elbow and began walking her away from the pool and down the torch-lit path. "I talked to Ron Graham of the FBI. He said he has an appointment to see you this week." Jazz stared at him. How much was Wit monitoring her movements? She hadn't expected him at the party. But then it was Guyera's. What was their connection? "I'm going to the FBI on Thursday."

"Could I ask you to tell me if they have anything new?"

"You could ask. But then you never tell me anything. For instance what are you doing here tonight? You never answered me about your relationship with Guyera."

Wit paused for a moment. Maybe two could play her game. "I should tell you," he said. "God knows I could use someone to talk to about all this. But I'm not sure I can trust you."

"You have to trust someone," she said.

"This coming from a reporter?"

"I'm also a person, with feelings." They stared at each other. "Dance with me," he said.

Her whole body tingled. She felt like she was attached to an electric charge machine. She took a step towards him.

"Ah, but she is dancing with me." Ben Luvana grabbed Jazz and pulled her out on the dance floor. She looked for Wit. He was already heading back to the house.

"You didn't want to dance with a politico, did you?" Ben asked. "We must make plans to have dinner. Where are you staying? You are not from here, are you?"

Jazz could barely speak. "Give me a phone number," he said, pulling her closer. He started talking about—what—she wasn't listening. The dance was taking forever. Over his shoulder Jazz looked at her watch. How much time had gone by since she talked to Eva? And where was Wit?

"Tell me how I can reach you," Ben was saying.

"I'm staying at the Hilton by the airport," she answered. Finally the music ended. "I've got to be going. I have an appointment later this evening."

"Ah a lady of mystery," he said. "I like that."

She rushed from him, and into the house. There was no one by the front door. Wit was gone. No sign of Eva. She stood and waited. Ten minutes went by. People were leaving. Twenty minutes. She felt like the doorman. Where was Eva? After a half-hour she decided to go back to the party and see if she was there. *Hot, Hot, Hot* the band played. Two young women danced by doing their own conga line. She saw Gary Dire at a table draped over a blonde with smeared eye make-up. "Have you seen Eva?"

"I think she left hours ago," he said.

"And Armando, is he around?"

"He's gone upstairs with someone very young and very beautiful. You won't see him for the rest of the night."

Well Armando would have to wait. And whatever Eva wanted to tell her would also have to wait, until tomorrow. She would call Eva. No, she would go to her house. This could be a major break in the story. Jazz wanted to get it as soon as possible.

CHAPTER 14

E va didn't answer the phone the next morning. And she didn't answer her door. Jazz tried both numerous times. For two days, she called and stopped by the house. Who should she tell that Eva might have disappeared? There had to be someone who would be concerned that something was wrong. As she headed towards the FBI building in Miami, she decided she would mention Eva to Ron Graham.

This was deadline day. She promised Joe that no more than 24 hours would elapse between the time she spoke to the FBI and her story was filed. Once agency officials learned that she was writing about a possible link between the disappearances, they might release information to their favorite reporters, or worse, call a press conference. So she had left the FBI interview for last.

She had spent the week after the party in Florida, writing and calling back sources. She had spoken to the local police investigating the disappearances in New York, Miami Beach and Malibu. All said they had nothing new. She spoke to relatives and friends of the three. The national editors wanted to see the piece as soon as possible. With important families involved, they were anxious to check the facts. It was decided the story would run Sunday. Today was Thursday. To deliver the piece by the next morning, Jazz would have to "pull an all-nighter" as they called it in college. But she didn't mind.

She was happy with what she had so far. Three of the beautiful people missing in action. Their stories were intriguing. So were their disappearances. Were they connected? Her gut instinct said yes. Paine, Jeff and Chris all knew each other. She had found that out from mutual friends. They had all disappeared in the last six months. And they all had sent notes to loved ones after they were reported missing.

A letter from Jeff to Moira had arrived two days earlier. In it, he called the engagement off saying he needed time alone. He asked that she tell his parents not to worry. The postmark was from Greece. Moira was furious. She asked that the story not run. Nobody had ever dumped her before, she told Jazz. What would her public think?

Jazz couldn't believe her reaction. What if the letter was written under duress, she asked. Moira didn't seem to care. She kept talking about her reputation. Jazz decided to trim her part in the story. This was not a woman she wanted to give publicity to.

Paine had e-mailed a message to Megan.

"It could have come from anybody," Megan said. "You've got to keep working on this, A.J."

And so she did. What would the FBI say about all that she had? She would soon find out.

Graham's office was on the sixth floor. He was out of the room when she was escorted in. That gave her a few moments to look around. Not that there was much to see. There were no pictures of family, nothing personal, not even a plant. She understood the FBI's concern about criminals learning of agents' personal lives. But not even a plant? Were they afraid someone would take a fern hostage?

In the few times she dealt with FBI agents she thought they

must have graduated from the school of sternness. None cracked smiles, or ever acted silly. These were not men or women you'd expect to dance the night away.

Especially Ron Graham. As he walked into the room, Jazz mentally wrote a description. He was an older agent. Probably 55 or so. About her father's age, or what her father would have been had he lived. The belly hung over the belt in typical middle-age male fashion. The hair was short, almost a crew cut. He looks a bit like Gene Hackman, Jazz decided.

Was he happy spending the twilight of his career in Miami? In the media, you were judged by the market you worked in. A reporter knew that he or she arrived if they made it to a city like New York or L.A. Did law enforcement have markets too? How big a deal was it to be an FBI agent in Miami?

"Well Miss Billings," Graham said. He sat down in the chair next to her rather than behind his desk. An interesting move, Jazz thought. "I've heard of you, Miss Billings. I've even read some of your pieces. You don't normally pursue criminal cases. So what can I do for you?"

He leaned towards her. She pushed her chair back, away from him. "I'm working on an article on the disappearances of several people. One of them is Chris Whitman. I understand you are handling that case."

"Yes."

If we're dealing in monosyllables, Jazz thought, it could take 24 hours to get four sentences. "Could you tell me what you have?" she asked.

"In relation to what?"

"Mr. Graham, I know she is missing. I have spoken to her family, her friends. I need to know what the FBI's take is on it. Could you please help me out? Tell me your formal position, if you want to start with that."

"It will also have to end with that, Miss Billings. We can't discuss ongoing cases. Chris Whitman was reported missing by her family. They have since received a note from her saying she is all right and not to worry. But they still do. So we're looking into it. When a Congressman asks you to, you make sure you do. "

"Doesn't it seem strange that there would be no more contact from her? Not with family, or friends?"

"Strange? Maybe. Criminal? We don't have any evidence of that."

"What about her being seen getting on Guyera's plane, and looking as if she had been drugged?"

"How did you know about that? Congressman Whitman told me he hadn't said anything to you about Guyera."

"I have my sources. Did you check out Guyera?"

"Yes. He was nowhere near West Palm on the day she supposedly got on his plane."

"What did airport officials say?"

"Miss Billings, I'm not going to tell you what airport officials said or didn't say. I've been around a long time. I know how reporters are. You think you can solve crimes by deadline. Well, it takes a lot more than that. I've told you what our policy is. We don't discuss individual cases."

"What if they are linked to other cases?"

For a moment emotion showed in Graham's eyes. He stared at Jazz, almost sadly, she thought. Odd. "What other cases are you referring to?"

"I know of the disappearances of other young socialites and what some call the beautiful people and I'm going to write about them. Now I can do that with or without your cooperation. I would think it would be to the advantage of the FBI to show they are working on these cases. "

"What number of missing people do you have?"

BINGO. Jazz smiled. "What number do you have?"

CHAPTER 15

There were ten actually —nine Americans and one European. All were alive although the weaker ones often wished they weren't. The newest arrival was Eva Long. She awoke in a bed, a large bed with designer satin sheets. The room the bed was in contained no windows and was claustrophobic in size. It was more a cell than a room. But it did have a mural painted on the wall facing the bed—a scene of palm trees and a white sandy beach. When Eva opened her eyes, that was the first thing she saw. For a moment she thought she was in a hotel. Then she realized how close the mural was, how close the walls were.

She attempted to sit up and a wave of nausea overcame her. What happened? The last thing she remembered was Guyera's party. She was waiting for A.J. Billings by the front door. She wanted to tell her about what she just heard, that the last time Chris was seen, she was leaving a restaurant drunk or on something, and a man got into the car with her. The person who saw her leave whispered to Eva that she had a good description of the man. She hadn't told the police because, well she had been with someone she shouldn't have been with, and besides she didn't want to get involved. But maybe it was time to tell someone.

Eva suggested the reporter, A.J. Billings. She assured her that A.J. would hide her identity. The friend agreed to talk to her.

Eva was waiting by the front door when a waiter handed her a note. It read "I'll meet you back at your house—A.J." She followed Donald Trump out the door. As they waited for their cars, he joked about something. She remembered hugging him after the valet brought his car. Then she got into hers. Had she made it home? She couldn't remember. Where was she? She thought she recalled the hum of a plane. Was she on a plane? She willed herself to sit up. The room wasn't moving. No, she wasn't flying.

She attempted to stand. Her head pounded. She realized she was in the dress she wore to the party. Her shoes were gone. Her wrists had marks on them, as if from rope indentations. Had she been tied up? How much time had passed since the party?

On the wall to the right of the mural was a closet door. She opened it. Neatly hung up were many of her dresses, blouses and shorts. Even her shoes were there. She didn't remember packing. To the right of the closet was a bathroom. It had a toilet, sink and shower. She splashed some cold water on her face and went back into the bedroom. Next to the mural was a large door. She hesitated. She wasn't certain she wanted to know what was on the other side. But not knowing was even worse. She turned the handle. The door wouldn't open. It was locked from the other side. The first sense of panic rose in her chest. Who had locked her in? Why? All those clothes. How long would she be here?

She sat down on the bed, and waited. After an hour, she lay down. After two hours, she got up and paced. After three hours, she lay back down on the bed. After four hours, Eva Long did something she hadn't done in many years. She put her face in her hands and cried.

Next door Paine Hayes was being raped. Although she had long ago stopped calling it rape. They had programmed that into her. It was the end of a date, they told her. Like many dates in her life had ended. Only she no longer had control over whom she slept with, or how often.

The beginning had been the hardest. She too had awakened in a small room. Her wall was painted with a mural of the New York City skyline. A nice touch, she thought as the man on top of her humped away. Giving each room a scene from the kidnapped person's hometown. Was it suppose to make you feel less lonely? Less violated?

She remembered what Chris Whitman told her the other night at the party, the mandatory weekend party, where they were subjected to the most degrading of acts. They had only a few minutes to speak before the abducted women and two men, Jeff Worthington, an actor and Sam Blake, a photographer, were ordered to entertain the hosts. Chris whispered "Don't let them defeat you. We will survive this, and after we do, we'll take pleasure in chopping off their dicks!" Paine had actually smiled. If Chris could maintain her sanity, so could she.

She wasn't sure about some of the others. Jessica Lawrence, 25, who won an Oscar at 14, was a beautiful but fragile young actress. As a prisoner, she was almost catatonic. Paine remembered reading about her disappearance in a plane crash. After appearing at a big wine festival in Naples, she had charted a small plane to take her to The Bahamas. The world thought she died in the crash, since the plane disappeared over water and no bodies were ever recovered. Rumor had it that Jessica was made to watch her funeral on satellite television. Now she spent most of her time staring into space. The male hosts called her the "living ghost." They used her, but were growing tired of her. Something would be done soon with Jessica, Paine thought.

Jeff Worthington wasn't a homosexual, but that didn't seem to matter to the male host who was gay. He appeared to take extra pleasure in "dating" Jeff. Another liked to watch him perform with the women captives. Jeff was always gentle with her. A nice person, she decided. Not the type she had been interested in before, but if she ever got out of this ——.

The other male hostage, Sam Blake, was gay. Paine remembered applauding for him at a banquet when he won several awards for his photo layouts in *Vanity Fair* and *Vogue*. Now she pitied him. Only one man abused him, but it seemed nonstop. Since Sam arrived, she hadn't been able to speak to him. Nor the woman from Europe who kept to herself.

Were they now in a foreign country? She couldn't be sure. Once, one of the hosts took her back to his bedroom upstairs instead of her own. Before he pulled the drapes she had seen the dark outline of palm trees and thought she heard the distant crashing of waves. She knew the climate was tropical. Each day they were sent separately into a courtyard where they could see blue sky above the high walls, and feel the hot sun. Dressed in the skimpiest of bathing suits, they were made to sunbathe. The hosts liked tan dates.

How long could all this go on, Paine wondered. Were they all to die? There was no way they could be released. They had seen their captors' faces. They had seen every inch of their captors. She focused on the painted Manhattan skyline as the man above her grabbed her buttocks tighter and reached his climax. Would anyone ever find them and free them?

CHAPTER 16

T he nighttime skyline of New York was only partially visible from the roof of Jazz's apartment building in Brooklyn. Across the street a giant billboard promoting Verizon obscured all but the Empire State building and a few other tall buildings.

With the temperature hovering at 40, Jazz pulled her jacket tighter. She often went to the roof to escape the telephone. A few tenants had set up chairs. There was even a little table for eating pizza while gazing at the moon. The full moon on this Saturday night in November glowed so bright Jazz could make out the lines of the old man's face. The stars shone like glitter around him. What a sight. What a month it had been.

After the article was published, other media pounced on it. Her scoop became the lead story on every network. "According to the *New York Tribune* and reporter A.J. Billings, five renowned young Americans have disappeared in the last year." The tabloids were going crazy. "The Vanishing A-list" one headline screamed. People Magazine did a cover story. The FBI had come through with the number five. And that was before she brought up Eva. Instinct told her Eva had been kidnapped or murdered as well. Nobody had heard from her since the party. Graham wouldn't confirm any investigation of her disappearance. But he wouldn't deny it either. Paine, Chris, and Jeff she knew about. But there were also: Sam Blake, a celebrity photographer from Aspen, Colorado, and Kensington Washington, a young socialite who was a direct descendent of George Washington. Graham predicted the number would go higher. It did the day after the article appeared. Eva's father officially reported his daughter missing to the press. The next day, another prominent family, the Bellinghams, owners of a chain of department stores in the Northeast, contacted Jazz to tell her their daughter, Spring, had disappeared off a cruise ship in the Caribbean two months earlier. No body had ever been found. Could there be a link? Jazz did a short piece about it.

A few days after that ran, the brother of Tracey Wise, a New York cabaret singer, called to say his sister too had disappeared while cruising. There had been several incidents of people vanishing on cruise ships. People thought they were accidents or maybe individual incidents of foul play. But like Spring, Tracey's body was never found and she did party with some of those missing. Her brother wanted her to be included in all future articles about A-list disappearances.

A week after the first article, Jazz wrote a lengthy follow-up. The number was now eight. The FBI had started a task force. Ron Graham was in charge.

Jazz still couldn't believe it. How could so many rich and prominent people be missing and she be the first to put it together? "It's so implausible," Joe said. Yet it was true. With the exception of the cruise ship happenings, there had been no media coverage of the other disappearances. Because of an aversion to public scrutiny, the wealthy relatives of the missing had avoided the press. As had the law enforcement officials investigating the individual cases. They weren't anxious to publicize their ineffectiveness, or announce that a serial killer or kidnapper was on the loose.

And what about an FBI agent opening up to her? Graham

called her after the article and told her about the task force. He said if she needed anything to contact him directly. Perhaps the agency had decided it was time to tell the world.

The world certainly knew now. What people didn't know was whether or not the eight were dead. No bodies had been found. But that might not mean anything. The tabloids were calling the missing socialites and celebrities the "A-list eight." Although it was a long shot, Jazz prayed they were alive, and that the articles hadn't jeopardized their lives.

At the paper, editors were talking Pulitzer. Congratulatory calls flowed in from friends, colleagues, and relatives. Then there was the call from Delilah, her melodious southern tones recorded for posterity on the answering machine.

"Agatha Jasmine, this is your mother. I'm calling about the article." Pause. Long pause. "I just wanted you to know—" another pause—"your father would have been so proud of you. This is your finest hour." It was the nicest thing Delilah had said to her daughter in years. Jazz choked up when she heard it.

Of course, there was the rest. "I didn't think it was necessary, however, to discuss the sexual proclivities of some of the missing people. As I have told you before, delicate matters like that should be left to the privacy of the boudoir. But all in all, you did a wonderful job. I will see you Thanksgiving. Please bring some appropriate clothes. And have your hair styled. It looks so much nicer when it's off your face. I have invited the neighbors over for Thanksgiving dinner. Bye, bye, love."

"Bye, bye, happiness," Jazz said as she did each time Delilah called. Her mother always ended phone conversations with bye, bye, love. Jazz always thought of the Everly Brothers' song. As she sat on the roof, the words kept running through her brain. "Hello loneliness —I think I'm a-going to die."

"Where do we go from here?" she asked Willie who lay snoring at her feet.

The A-list story had become her life. How she wanted to share the excitement of it with someone. "All this hoopla about living for yourself," she said to the sleeping dog. "I need love. I want to be loved. Carrie has it. But she thinks I have a better life because of my career. Why does everyone else's life seem better?"

Willie snorted in his sleep and began twitching. She touched his side to stop the bad dream. After a few more nudges, his breathing returned to a normal rhythm. Her mind went back to work. Where to go from here? Eva was going to tell her something. Now there was no Eva. She could try to interview everybody who attended the party, but would someone know what Eva wanted to say. Was the party the cause of Eva's disappearance? Paine disappeared after a party. But many of the rest had not.

Delving into the backgrounds of the new people missing, she found similar lives to the ones she already had written about. All had been awarded celebrity status because of their careers or their wealthy backgrounds. All were attractive, and in their 20s or early 30s. They attended the same parties in Manhattan, the Hamptons, L.A. and South Beach. They probably all knew each other by name, or face. Their disappearances had to do with their social circle, she was sure of that. Whoever was responsible must travel in the same circle.

She had begun investigating service businesses that catered to the rich. The photographer, Jay Warrens had access to many parties. She had Roger researching him, as well as a publicist, Judith Weigold who set up movie premieres and who frequented the same clubs that Paine did. Whoever was responsible for the disappearances could travel around the country at will.

She ruled out Judith after speaking to those who knew her and worked for her. Judith was bright and absolutely committed to her public relations company. The clients she represented were worth more to her alive and out there on the red carpet, than vanishing from the scene. There was no motive. No it wasn't Judith, Jazz felt certain. And with so many beautiful young women disappearing, she was sure it was a he who was responsible.

The more she reflected on it, the more Jazz felt the killer or kidnapper was someone rich, maybe even famous. When she mentioned her theory to Joe, he warned her not to go there. He already found the story pretty incredible. "What are you saying?" he asked. "That Donald Trump is going to kidnap Rosie O'Donnell?"

Still she couldn't stop thinking of people like Guyera. Armando seemed so possessive of Eva the night of the party. Did he know the others? And how was Wit connected?

She thought of calling him after her meeting with Graham. He had asked her to. But he wanted to hear something about Chris's disappearance. She had nothing new on that.

She decided to call him anyway. That meant talking to Miss Personality—Betty Norris. Jazz named the press secretary that after the cold way she handled all of Jazz's questions. What was her problem? Did she lust for Wit? Did she think Jazz was competition?

Betty was out to lunch when she called. Instead of leaving a message, she asked the receptionist if the congressman was in. "If he is," she said in her sweetest voice, "would you please tell him A.J. Billings is on the line?"

"Just a minute." A few minutes went by.

Then she heard that voice. "Hi. I was going to call you. I wanted to tell you that I thought your articles were fair to Chris and our family. Even my mother didn't have that many negative things to say."

"I'm glad." Maybe this would be easier than she thought. "I was wondering if we could talk. There could be something you have, or I have, that could help each other." There was silence. Then he said, "Maybe we should talk—in person. I've got a meeting in New York on Wednesday afternoon. Would you be available, say after four?"

Wednesday was a Willie stud day. Well, she really didn't have to be with Willie every time he mated. He certainly wasn't with her every time. Not that there were that many times.

Larry could pick him up and take him to his rendezvous. "Wednesday is fine," she said.

"Good. I'll be staying at the St. Regis. Could you meet me in the lobby at say four-thirty?"

"Fine. See you then."

Interesting. But she wasn't sure in which way—career-wise or personal. She couldn't forget the way his voice sounded when he said, "dance with me."

"Dance with me," she said out loud. The black blob at her feet started wagging his tail.

"I want to do more than dance with him," she whispered, stroking Willie's ears. "And that could be a big problem."

CHAPTER 17

Pink message slips overflowed the "In" basket when Jazz arrived at the paper the next morning.

"Jazz, I didn't know you were coming in," Roger said as she stopped at his desk. " I think I've got something really hot for you. It's about one of the missing guys—Sam Blake. I just found out about it. But your phone has been ringing off the hook."

"It's okay, Rog. I have time."

The phone rang again and Roger answered it. She took the first 10 messages out of the wire basket. Many were from friends offering more congratulations. Two were from Ben Luvana from Miami. "Urgent," one said. Well, now he knew she was a reporter.

The next stack contained a message to call Barbara Worthington. In her last call, she told Jazz she and her husband had hired a private investigator. Maybe the investigator had something. She put that one aside, along with the Luvana messages.

As she looked through the pink slips, the phone kept ringing. Roger was too busy answering to talk to her. She walked over to Joe's desk. He was on the phone but motioned for her to sit in an empty chair.

"Yes she's working on it," he said into the phone. "I'll let you know as soon as I meet with her." He hung up.

"That was about you. It was Mancox. He wants to know what your next piece on the A-list people is going to focus on, and when it will be ready. You are working on another article, aren't you?"

"Yes," Jazz said. "I'm waiting for some new leads. But I thought I would also do a piece on why so many prominent people could be missing without everybody knowing about it. I want to write about how the rich value their privacy so. Remember Julius Irving, the former basketball star. He took two weeks to tell the press his son was missing. They're all afraid that the media will start digging into their lives. Plus with the A-list eight, several relatives told me they were concerned that if they did get coverage and there was a ransom attempt, the kidnappers would be turned off by the publicity."

"That's fine, anything Jazz. You've created a tidal wave here. Keep the water coming."

It was an interesting analogy. She smiled at Joe and headed back to her assistant. "Talk to me Roger," she said. "I'm thinking of going home to work."

"Well, I found out that Sam Blake, the guy from Colorado is gay. Now he's the only one of the eight who is. So I think it puts a new light on the sex angle. Of course the other guy, Jeff put a new light on it too. With all women, you think it's gotta be about sex. But with two men, it can't be just that. Whoever is kidnapping them or murdering them is doing it because they're good-looking and they all hang out together at the same parties. So I started researching what parties they've attended in the last year, you know the big ones. I called the friends you have listed for each. Then I hit the bonanza. Sam Blake's current lover told me Sam kept a party diary. He listed every party he attended, who he met there, and if anything special happened. The lover—his name is Fred Polk—said you would find it very interesting. He wanted to know if you would pay for it. I said you didn't operate that way. But that this could help Sam. That seemed to help. He said he would show it to you, or me. But we would have to go to Aspen to see it."

"Good work Roger. I tell you what. You go to Aspen and bring it back, or if this Fred won't let it leave his sight, make a copy of it."

Roger beamed. "Do you think I can go? The regionals have deadlines tomorrow."

"I'll speak to Joe. I'm sure he can get you off that work."

"Thank you Jazz—for your confidence in me. I'll call Fred and the travel desk right away."

"Good, I'm going to return some of these calls." She walked into her office and dialed Mrs. Worthington's number.

"A.J. how are you?" the mother said. "Your latest article was wonderful, but I want some clarification about Jeff's letter. Moira is accepting that it came from him and that he is breaking off the engagement. It suits her purpose, to go on with her life. But I want you to know my husband and I do not believe that letter was drafted freely. Jeff would have written or called us directly if he could. He is still missing as far as we are concerned and we want to make sure you include him in all your articles."

"I will, Mrs. Worthington. I promise."

"Thank you. Please call if you learn anything else."

"I will. Good-bye."

She decided to call Ben next. He answered on the first ring.

"Jazz, oh, I am so delighted to hear from you. I have not stopped thinking of you. I need to talk to you about the articles you've written. Can we have dinner tomorrow?"

"In Miami?"

"No, I will be in New York. You name the restaurant and I will meet you there, unless you want me to pick you up."

"No I live in Brooklyn, it's not the place to be picked up. Well actually it depends on what type of pick up you're talking about."

"You are so funny. Name a restaurant. What type of food do you like?"

"Plain. I'm not the gourmet type. How about O'Malley's in Midtown?"

"What time?"

"7:00 p.m.?"

"I will be there. I can't wait to be there. You are a woman of so many talents."

"I'll see you tomorrow night, Ben."

"I will be counting the hours."

The dance card was getting full. Ben tomorrow night, Wit the next. Wait until she told Carrie. She was becoming a femme fatale.

"It's all set, Jazz." Roger had rushed in. "I spoke to Fred. He said I could make a copy of it. I've got a ticket for a flight at 8:00 tomorrow morning. With the time difference, I'll see Fred and be on a plane back to you tomorrow night."

"Roger, you can take time to sleep and breathe the fresh Rockies air."

"No that's okay. I know how important this is to you."

Jazz smiled. "You're great Rog. I'm going to treat you to lunch."

"Now?" he asked. "With the phone ringing like this?"

"That's what voice mail is for. Let's go."

At the elevator, Jazz was surrounded by reporters offering more congratulations. By the time they reached the street, Roger was telling her how exciting all this was. Jazz tucked her arm into his and headed him towards Broadway. Neither noticed two men get out of a black van and start following them.

CHAPTER 18

A light snow fell as Roger's plane touched down in Denver. He hoped it wouldn't delay his leaving later. Anxious to prove to Jazz how valuable he was, he booked a return flight for 8:00 p.m. that evening. That meant driving to Aspen at once, getting the diary, then driving right back to the airport. If all went well, he could return to Denver by 6:00 p.m. But he hadn't counted on snow.

Dumb. It was November and he was in Colorado. Of course it might snow. At the car rental counter, he decided to pay extra for a 4-wheel drive sports utility vehicle, rather than the compact car he reserved.

The road to Aspen started as a major highway and the dusting of snow was no problem for the seasoned Colorado drivers. But for Roger it was as if he was on ice skates for the first time. Although his parents now lived in a suburb of Detroit, he grew up in New York City. His car-driving experience consisted of weekend trips to the Hamptons. And that was in the summer. This white stuff was petrifying. As he drove, he gripped the steering wheel tighter and tighter until his knuckles turned the color of the landscape.

Sam and Fred lived in a condominium complex on the side of

a mountain. Driving up to it put Roger almost in a catatonic state. At each turn he felt fainter and fainter. But he kept going. He had a schedule to keep. When he arrived at the condo community, he parked in a guest parking space as Fred had directed and headed for number 286, an upstairs unit on the end. It looked as if it had a nice view of the valley below. Since it was snowing, Roger could only guess. When he knocked on the door, a voice from the other side shouted "Who is it?"

Roger identified himself and Fred opened the door a crack, the chain still attached. "What's going on?" Roger asked. He was getting nervous because Fred looked so nervous. "Show me some identification," Fred said.

"Are you kidding?" Roger asked, taking out his wallet. He found his driver's license and held it up. Fred opened the door and pulled him in, quickly locking the door behind him.

"What *is* going on?" Roger asked again.

"Somebody's been following me, ever since I talked to you yesterday. I went to work, and a blue car followed me. I went to lunch I saw the same blue car. A half-an-hour ago I saw it parked in one of the guest spots. It's not there now, but I think it has something to do with Sam's disappearance and maybe this diary. So here —." He reached into a draw and took out a blue folder. "I made you a copy. Take it and go. I'm going to put the original in a safe deposit box tomorrow, and then I'm going to take a vacation somewhere, just to get out of here."

"I think you're worrying too much," Roger said.

"Did anybody follow you here?"

"I don't think so. But I wasn't looking for anyone. I'm on a flight out tonight. I'm anxious to get this to Jazz. She really appreciates you giving this to us. Where can we reach you if we need you for anything?"

"I'll call you in a few days, when I figure out where I'm going. But you should watch your back."

The statement sent a shiver through Roger. He never thought that this might be a dangerous assignment. But Fred was so upset, he began to worry. He thanked Fred again and rushed back to his car. As he drove out of the parking lot, a blue car pulled in. Roger didn't see it. He was too intent on having to drive back down the mountain.

A tall thin man got out of the blue car and strode over to Fred's door. He knocked hard.

"Who is it?" At the same time Fred shouted, he was walking over to the window to look out. He saw the blue car. "WHAT DO YOU WANT?" he screamed at the door.

"Mr. Polk, I'm with the FBI."

"Oh Thank God," Fred said.

It was the last words he would ever say.

As he opened the door, the man rushed in and pinned him against the wall. Without hesitating, he took a gun from his pocket, put it to Fred's head and shot him. Fred crashed to the floor, the look of surprise frozen on his face. After checking the pulse of his victim to make sure he was dead, the killer ransacked the apartment, stopping only when he found the diary—buried in a pile of dirty laundry. Smiling, he headed back to his car. A thin layer of snow covered the windows. He pushed it off using the diary as a scraper. After getting into the car, he dialed a number on his cell phone.

"It's done," he said.

"They're both dead and you've got the diary?" asked the person who hired him.

"I've got the diary and I killed the guy with it. The other guy hasn't shown up yet." He didn't tell his new employer that he left his stakeout for 10 minutes to get something to eat. With the snow, how could anybody have come and gone that quickly?

"Roger Barron landed at Denver Airport four hours ago," he was told. "That means he should be arriving any minute. He's driving a beige Ford Explorer. He is scheduled to fly out tonight at 8:00 on United. He is not to get on that plane. Is that understood?"

"If he shows up I'll get him," the killer said, hanging up. A beige Ford Explorer? He felt a sense of concern. An Explorer had pulled out of the parking lot as he returned. Could that have been Roger's? It had to be. He started the engine and quickly headed down the mountain.

CHAPTER 19

It took Roger longer to return to Denver. But he didn't care. Happiness kept him going. He had a copy of the diary. He had succeeded! He was anxious to read what was in the folder, but he wanted to be out of that car and in the airport when he did. He arrived at the airport entrance at 7:00 p.m.. It had stopped snowing and the evening aviation commute was well underway. Men and women in blue business suits hopped out of taxis, heading for their flights.

After returning the car, he placed the copy of the diary in his one carry-on bag and headed for the United terminal. As he walked he took the shoulder strap of the bag and put it over his head and across his chest. No thief was going to steal this treasure. The departure board said his flight would be leaving from gate B-27. He headed towards it, going through the x-ray machine. His watch read 7:15.

The Killer arrived at the airport at 7:20. He parked his car in short-term parking then ran for the United terminal. The departure board said the flight to New York would leave from gate B-27. He ran towards it.

At the gate, Roger had checked in and was told boarding would start in ten minutes. He sat down to wait. Now was the time to look at the diary. He took the folder out of the bag, and quickly scanned the copied pages. A party in New York, one in Miami, another in L.A. Then he saw the notation for the last party. This is it, he thought. He put the pages back in the folder and the folder back in his bag. Then he took it out again. He had to see one more time what he had just read. Jazz would be so excited. On the folder he wrote "To Jazz, from Roger, your Perrie Masin." Then he carefully put the document back in his bag. "Oh Jazz you are going to love this," he said out loud. He had to call her. He took out his cell phone and dialed her home number. The machine answered. Probably out walking Willie, he thought.

"Jazz," he said to the machine. "I have it and it's got something really big. But I'm not going to tell you on the machine. My plane lands at 5:00 a.m. I'll go home and change and I should be in the office by 8:30. I'll call you then. You are going to be so happy with me!" He was so excited, he realized he had to go to the bathroom.

"In just a few minutes the New York flight will be boarding all rows," the gate attendant announced. "First we would like to board all those needing special assistance."

"I've got time," he thought. He put the strap of the bag across his chest and ran to the men's room. It was two gates down. A tall thin man followed him in.

A few minutes later two businessmen having just arrived from Newark walked into the men's room. "LET GO OF THE GOD-DAMN BAG," they heard a man shout from the stall nearest the door. Then the stall door flung open as a man who seemed to be struggling with something, came out backwards.

"Hey what's going on here?" one of the businessmen asked.

The man in the stall turned, revealing a body slumped over the toilet.

"I'M GOING TO GET SECURITY!" the other businessman shouted.

Having shot Roger, the killer was trying to take the bag strapped to his victim's chest. But Roger's hand still tightly clenched the shoulder strap. Hearing the shouts, the killer realized he didn't have any more time. With head down he barreled past the startled onlooker and raced out into the terminal.

The businessman started running after him, shouting "STOP HIM! I THINK HE JUST MURDERED SOMEBODY!" But the killer was swallowed up in a crowd of disembarking passengers from Chicago. By the time a security guard arrived, he had fled the terminal. In the restroom, Roger lay in a pool of blood, the bag still attached to his now dead body.

CHAPTER 20

"Tell me about this Ben guy," Carrie said as Jazz sipped a Fresca. "Is Ben gay? Bengay, get it?"

"You've been working with diapers too long," Jazz told her. "Ben is not gay, at least I don't think he is. He has the most incredible smile." Jazz had run up to Carrie's to get Willie before the dinner with Ben.

"But what about Wit? I thought he was the one who got your juices flowing?"

"My relationship with Wit is complicated. Ben doesn't seem that complicated. He likes to flirt and he is very good at it. I figure I'm entitled to a night out with no deep meaning." She looked at her watch. "I've got to get going. I said I would meet him at 7:00."

"Then why take Willie? I'll feed him. You want to stay with your Aunt Carrie, don't you Willie boy?"

Willie wagged his tail. He loved all females. Especially these two. Now that he was a seasoned stud, he loved everything feminine. His first offspring were due in three weeks. Wilhemina by Riverside had proven a good teacher.

"We will soon be grandmothers," Jazz said to Carrie. Willie

headed under the kitchen table to lay down. "All right stud-dog," Jazz said. "Don't miss your mother. Stay with Carrie, see if I care. I should be back by eleven."

"If you're not, don't worry, he'll just stay overnight. George can walk him. He should be home by ten—I hope. He seems to be getting home later and later. "

"Is everything all right Carrie?" Carrie had told her the pregnancy scare was just that. She was not pregnant again. So things should be fine. Were they? "You sure everything is okay?"

"George is just getting a lot of overtime."

"Well you know you can tell me anything. Maybe I spend too much time talking about me."

"I love hearing about your life, Jazz. And nothing is wrong with mine. George is just working too hard. So get going."

"Well I don't want Willie to be a bother. So please bring him down when I get home. It shouldn't be too late. Having a dog is almost as complicated as having a child. You know I was thinking today that I would like a child. What do you think? PMS?"

"Go enjoy your date."

✯ ✯ ✯ ✯ ✯

Why couldn't she have children and a career, Jazz wondered as she rode the subway back to Manhattan. She just needed a man who would share the responsibilities. Someone who wouldn't have a problem staying home with a toddler when she needed to go out on a story. Or maybe she'd stay home. Give up her job and become a homemaker. She would make pot roast. Pot roast? She didn't even like pot roast. Definitely PMS.

Ben was waiting outside the restaurant. He didn't have a coat on. "Aren't you cold?" she asked as they walked in.

"Your smile will keep me warm." He nodded to the maitre d'. They were quickly seated in a desirable booth in the far back corner. "Come here often?" Jazz asked.

"No, I just came here early. I had some calls to make."

The waiter arrived. "What would you like to drink?" Ben asked.

"I'd like a Harvey's Bristol cream sherry."

Ben smiled. "I'll have a Stoli on the rocks with a twist." The waiter headed for the bar and Ben moved closer in the booth. "A lot of excitement in your life," he said.

"In what way?"

"The articles. It's quite amazing, all the work you must have done on them. I'm sure you are hearing from many people. Will you do more?"

"Yes, but now it gets harder finding new information. We may have something, though. Stay tuned."

"We? Who is we?"

"I have a desk assistant, Roger. He's just terrific. He's out West right now working on an angle. He's like the cub reporter in *Superman*. Do you know Superman? Where were you raised Ben? What do you do? I really don't know much about you."

"My life is very boring compared to yours. I sell business equipment. My father is from Puerto Rico. He is a doctor."

"A P.R.—D.R."

Ben laughed. "My mother is from Curacao. I was raised in San Juan, but went to college in the States. So yes, I know of Superman. And maybe you need a superman in your life. What you are working on, Jazz, it could be dangerous."

"I can take care of myself, Ben. The FBI is involved in this, you know."

"Yes, I do know. But the person who is responsible for all these kidnappings, or murders, may not want you to keep digging. Perhaps you should move on to another subject."

The waiter arrived with their drinks. Seeing that they were still talking, he didn't ask if they would like to order. Instead he stood off to one side and waited.

"I'm not going to quit. I see things through, Ben."

"Well I am worried for you. Promise you will call me if you need any protection. I have a black belt in karate."

"Do you? You don't seem the type."

"And what type is that?"

"You seem more the lover than the fighter."

"Is that an invitation, Jazz?"

"I don't know."

"Is there someone else?"

"I don't know."

"Well you are a mystery. I told you I like mysteries." He lifted his glass, "To Jazz the big challenge in my life." They clicked glasses and took sips.

Two hours later they had finished dinner and were walking toward the subway stop. The dinner had been enjoyable. They talked of their childhoods and their successes and failures. Jazz quizzed him about A-list parties. In the past year, he attended many through his connection with Sebastian Guyera. As for Sebastian, and Armando, he said little about them.

They had stopped in front of a luggage shop, when suddenly Ben grabbed Jazz and pulled her to him. People passed by without looking. "You excite me, Jazz Billings," he said, brushing his lips against her hair. She didn't move. She wasn't sure whether she wanted to move. He lifted her face up so their eyes met. He smiled. Really a great smile, Jazz thought. Then he kissed her—an all-consuming kiss. Too much of a kiss, Jazz realized as his tongue began probing, almost to the back of her throat. She started to pull away. His hand fondled her breast. What was going on? Jazz struggled. But Ben held her in a vise grip as he whispered in her ear—"Don't fight me, they are watching. I'm with the FBI and you are in danger. So God damn it kiss me back."

CHAPTER 21

The subway ride back to Brooklyn passed in total silence. Ben said he would see her home. He whispered he would explain everything but not until they were alone. The swaying of the cars rocked them together, than apart. As Ben put his arm around her shoulder, Jazz pretended to sleep. She couldn't believe what she had just learned. Ben an FBI agent? And who were the "they" he was talking about. And why were they watching her?

It wasn't until they were walking down the street near her apartment that he spoke. "You are probably very confused," he said. "I work for the FBI in Miami. I know you met with Ron Graham. I also knew you were going to Guyera's party. I've been working undercover on the Guyera import case for the last year. There is a lot going on there that the government is concerned about. We didn't want a reporter getting involved. When you asked questions about Guyera at the Whitman press conference, an agent was assigned to make sure you didn't interfere with our operation. You were followed to Naples and Palm Beach and I intercepted you at Guyera's party. But Jazz, I want you to know I do find you very attractive." He went to touch her face. She pushed his hand away.

They had reached her door. Emotions churned inside her. She

wasn't sure which she felt more—anger for being used, or humiliation in thinking he cared for her.

"What about the disappearances?" she asked.

"My bosses don't think Guyera has anything to do with that. But I keep an open mind." She didn't want to invite him in. She never wanted to see him again. It was silly, however, to be standing outside talking. And what if "they" were looking? She unlocked her door and walked in. He followed.

She turned on the living room light. "What about the people following me? Why am I in danger?"

"I'm not sure if anyone in Armando's operation is on to me, but I overheard him talking about you the other day. He was concerned that a reporter had accompanied Eva to his party. He wanted you checked out. I saw one of his men in the restaurant while we were eating. Then I saw him on the street. It's important for both of us, that Guyera think we're having an affair."

"It's not important to me."

"I know you are trying to link him to the disappearances. So is Whitman. He's been trying to play super cop. Both of you are foolish. Guyera is a dangerous man, Jazz. And there are other more dangerous people out there as well. I don't want to see you hurt. I'm sure you are very mad at me now—." He reached for her. As she pulled away, her hand hit the answering machine on the table. The light was blinking.

"I think you should leave," she said.

"It would be better if I stayed awhile. So they think—."

"I don't care what they think."

There was a knock at the door. Both were startled. Jazz looked through the security peephole. It was Carrie with Willie.

"Hi, I hope I'm not disturbing you." Willie rushed past Jazz into the hallway. The dog realized someone new was there. He sniffed Ben's trousers as Carrie whispered, "Sorry, bad timing."

"No good timing," Jazz whispered back. "This is my neighbor

Carrie," she told Ben.

"Ah the dog sitter."

"A bit more than that."

Carrie looked at both of them and made a quick exit. Jazz kept the door open for Ben.

He started to walk out then turned, "I will call you tomorrow," he said. "Please don't be upset with me. I just want to keep you safe. And I can help you in your work. You can talk to me about what you find. But please, you can't tell anybody what I told you tonight. It would mean my death." He took her hand and kissed it. She closed the door and walked back to the living room. Then she noticed the blinking light on the answering machine. She pushed the button.

"Jazz," Roger said. "I have it and it's got something really big. But I'm not going to tell you on the machine. My plane lands at 5:00 a.m. I'll go home and change and I should be in the office by 8:30. I'll call you then. You are going to be so happy with me!"

CHAPTER 22

With identification on the body, Roger's death was reported quickly. By midnight the Denver police had notified his parents in Bloomfield Hills. Their shock was twofold. First they had to face the murder of their son. Second, they had to figure out why his life had ended in Colorado. He was supposed to be at work in New York at *The Tribune*, Stephen Barron told the detective. Mary Barron was too distraught to speak. Roger was the couple's only child. Roger was their life.

The detective, Bill Willis, gently prodded Mr. Barron for more information about Roger. He was a research assistant, the father said. He worked for the Pulitzer Prize winning reporter, A.J. Billings. Perhaps the detective should call Jazz. That was her nickname.

That was also the name on the folder found in Roger's carry-on bag. At 9:00 a.m. Eastern Time, Willis dialed *The Tribune* and asked for A.J. Billings.

She was seated at her desk waiting for Roger's return. She had just hung up with Carrie. Carrie wanted to know about Ben and what happened the night before. Jazz told her she would talk about it later. Thinking about Ben made her feel sick. She tried to focus on Roger and what his big news could be. Still her mind wondered back—the phone ring jarred her.

"Miss Billings," a male voice said. "This is Detective Willis in Denver, Colorado. Do you know a Roger Barron?"

"Yes, he works for me. Is he all right?"

"I'm sorry. There's no easy way to say this. Roger Barron is dead. He was killed last night. Can you tell me what he was doing in Colorado?"

"Oh, God, how did he die? Oh Roger." Tears welled in Jazz's eyes.

"He was murdered Miss Billings, at the airport. Do you know why he was in Colorado?"

"He was there on a project for me. Do his parents know? They are such a close family."

"I told them last night. They're on their way here. Among his possessions was a folder with Xerox pages in it. It has your name on it. The folder says 'To Jazz from Roger, your Perrie Masin'. He spelled Perry Mason wrong."

Jazz began to cry.

"Can you tell me what that's all about?"

The diary. Could Roger have the diary?

"I'd have to see it first," Jazz said. "Could you send me a copy? Or could I come there and see it?"

"It's evidence and it can't be released. But if you come here, I suppose I could show it to you."

"I'll be on the next plane out. Please give me your phone number and I'll call you when I arrive."

She quickly told Joe what happened and that she had to go to Colorado. The news about Roger hit Joe hard. He had been instrumental in getting Roger hired.

They agreed that no one should know about the diary except the two of them. Joe wanted to hire a bodyguard for Jazz. She told him that was ridiculous. She was going to a police station. After that she would find Roger's parents and help them anyway she could.

In less than an hour, she traveled to Brooklyn, packed, told Carrie about Roger and asked her to take care of Willie, and then was on her way to Kennedy Airport. The paper's travel agent had booked her on the first flight out. It wasn't until she was seated on the plane that the reality of what happened hit her. Roger was dead. "He's dead because I sent him to Colorado," she thought. "I killed Roger."

CHAPTER 23

D etective Willis was on the phone when Jazz entered his office. He motioned for her to sit down. She figured his age at about 50. The paunchy stomach showed a less than athletic bent. Seeing the young attractive woman, Willis instinctively pushed back his hair and straightened up in his seat.

"Let me know as soon as you have the autopsy report," he said into the phone, never taking his eyes off Jazz. "Yeah right, well call me, okay?" He hung up and smiled at her.

"Are you Miss Billings?"

"Yes."

"Well I'm sorry about your friend. I was just with his parents. They had to identify him at the morgue. His mother collapsed. It's never a pretty scene. They're making arrangements to ship the body back to Michigan. I told them you were on your way here. They want to see you when you're through."

"It must be so hard for them."

"I'd like to ask you a few questions, if I could."

Jazz nodded.

"Tell me what Roger was doing here. You said a project. What project?"

"He was going to meet with a roommate of one of the people who disappeared from the A-list. I've been reporting on that."

"Yes I know. I've read the articles. Samuel Blake is from Aspen."

"That's where Roger was going, to speak to Sam's roommate, Fred Polk. Fred had information he wanted to give me. Roger was to bring it to me."

"I guess that's what is in the folder we have. Do you think that's why he was killed?"

"I don't know."

"If it was, why did he still have the folder?"

"I don't know. Maybe the killer didn't know about it. Fred had the original."

"Well I guess we should speak to Fred." He picked up the phone. "Find out where a Fred Polk lives in Aspen. Ask one of the locals to go out and make sure he's all right. Then have them call me from there."

He picked up a blue folder and smiled at Jazz. "Well this could be what the fuss is all about."

Fuss? Roger's death a fuss? She did not return the smile.

"I'd like to see it," she said.

"I'm sure you would. But I'm not supposed to show it to you. If I do, you have to make me a promise."

"What's that?"

"Tell me what you think is important in it. You probably know as much about Blake's case as the FBI. I'd like to tell my chief that we've got some new information on it. We'll be going over the contents anyway and we'll probably have to turn the folder over to the FBI eventually. But this could give us a little head-start."

"If you let me see it, and I find something, I'll tell you."

"Good. Now I have an errand to run. Don't you go looking at anything on my desk while I'm away." He winked as he pushed the folder towards her. "Wave to the desk clerk over there when you're finished. She'll find me." He left and Jazz looked at the front of the folder. Written in a neat slanted handwriting were the words "To Jazz, from Roger, your Perrie Masin."

"Oh Roger," she said, tears welling in her eyes. "There wasn't even time to tell you how to spell Perry Mason's name." Her hands shook as she opened the folder. "Thank you my Perry," she said.

CHAPTER 24

"Sometimes you act like such an ass."

As Betty Norris chastised her boss, he stared out the window at the Capitol building across the street. Betty yelled at Wit. Wit yelled at Betty. She was his first hire, straight out of law school. Starting as his secretary, she quickly advanced to office manager, and confidante. When he left Naples for Washington, he asked her to come along.

She stuck with him through marriage and divorce—his. Betty never married and seemed happier when he wasn't either. He knew why. Years ago he realized she was in love with him. Once when they were delayed at an airport for several hours, she started drinking at the airport bar. After two martinis, she rested her hand on his leg, telling him what a good team they made. He ignored it, as he had all the innuendoes.

In Betty's mind, her only competition had been Wit's wife, Deirdre. After the divorce, he didn't seem serious about anyone. Until A.J. Billings.

"How can you be so blind?" Betty asked. "The only thing that reporter is interested in is the story. Why are you going to see her tonight? And why for dinner? That sends the wrong message."

She had no idea that Wit and Jazz had been lovers. This obses-sion with a reporter made no sense, unless he was interested in her romantically. And that worried Betty. Wit now read the *N.Y. Tribune* every day. He talked about Billings constantly. And tonight they were having dinner in New York.

"I don't want to talk about it, Betty. I told you. I think it's wise for us to work together. She has sources I don't."

The intercom buzzed. "Mike Slayton is on the phone," his receptionist said.

"Put him through." Mike was the friend in Palm Beach who saw Chris board Guyera's plane.

"Congressman, how is our Nation's capital?"

"Still standing Mike. How are you?"

" I'm fine. But Jenny and I are getting worried that we never see you. We're going to be in Washington next week to spend Thanksgiving with my brother. Are you going to be around? I thought maybe your mother was coming up."

"No, darn it, I'm going to Palm Beach to be with her. This will be our first major holiday without Chris."

"I know, I'm so sorry. I'm sorry too that the plane thing didn't pan out. I received the message you left that the FBI said Guyera was somewhere else that day. I swear, Wit. It was him. Sebastian and I were at Penn State at the same time. I used to see him on campus. I know that little loser."

"Sebastian? Mike, you never said it was Sebastian. You said it was Armando."

"I never said Armando. Wit, I've never met Sebastian's father. I told you it was Sebastian Guyera. Okay, maybe I just said Guyera, but I've told you stories about Guyera—about Sebastian. I assumed you knew who I was talking about."

"This changes things, Mike. I've got to make some calls. I'll speak to you soon, okay?"

"Sure, sorry. Let me know what you find. And let's get

together soon."

"What?" Betty asked as he hung up the phone. "What?"

"The Guyera who Mike saw help Chris on the plane? It was Sebastian, not Armando. I can't believe I got that wrong. I don't know if Armando's involved. But we need to start looking into Sebastian's life, too. I think we—the Whitmans, not the Congressman, understand?—will hire a private investigator to keep track of Sebastian Guyera. I want to know where he goes and what he does. Call that guy my mother used when Chris first disappeared. He seemed competent."

Wit looked at his watch. It was 1:10 p.m. and he had to take the 2:00 shuttle to make the meeting in New York and then his dinner date. "I've got to go. Have the investigator call me at the St. Regis."

Grabbing the overnight bag he kept in his office closet, he hurried out the door. Betty watched him leave. When he gets excited, she thought, he opens up to people. And he was going to see Billings. This was not good. This was not good at all.

CHAPTER 25

S itting in the detective's office in Denver Colorado, Jazz had forgotten her date with Wit. With the three hour time difference,
it was fast approaching. But she didn't realize it. Her entire focus
was on the document in front of her.

Sam titled his diary "THE PARTY BOOK." The first entry was
in late January, after a party in South Beach. A photographer for
trendy magazines, Sam was invited to parties all over the country.
He had been working on a photo shoot, he wrote, when two of the
models suggested he go with them to a party at a record producer's
house. He talked about who was there, who came on to him, and
the man he eventually went home with, a well-known sportscaster
whom Jazz did not know was gay. In graphic detail, he wrote about
what they did to each other.

The diary was hotter reading than a best seller. But Jazz had to
find what Roger considered so important, what he died for. Sam
disappeared after a party in L.A. So she flipped through the pages,
parties in Naples, Florida, Aspen and Malibu. She went to the last
entry. Nothing seemed out of the ordinary except for "Big Ears is
starting to give me the creeps. He was at this party too. Is it a coincidence that I'm seeing so much of him?"

Who was Big Ears? The diary didn't say. She turned back to the previous entry about another party in L.A. "I met the most gorgeous man," Sam wrote. "I have to admit my heart fluttered. Fred would be upset. He doesn't understand flirtations. Anyway, this gorgeous creature was dancing with someone and he turned and our eyes met and it was a bit of magic. But before I could find out who he was, he left. I asked Jay Warrens who he was. He was busy taking pictures. Does the guy ever take time off?

"Anyway, Jay didn't know. Earlier in the night I saw the hunk talking to Sebastian Guyera, the guy I told you about from the party two nights ago. Unfortunately Big Ears, Sebastian's friend, was at this party too. He tried to pull me outside into the garden. I had to tell him 'You are not my type, you will never be my type. Get out of my face!' I later asked Sebastian who the handsome man was. He said 'You won't meet him until you are nicer to my friend.' He was talking about Big Ears. Please—are they crazy? I told Sebastian he was nuts if he thought I could ever be interested in someone whose ears were as large as Dumbo's. Well maybe they're not that big. But they are huge. Sebastian glared at me and said, 'I think that you will have to be taught some manners.' That little nothing. He's no prize either. I walked away."

A few pages back was the other reference to Sebastian and Big Ears. It was the first time Sam met them at a party in Malibu. Big Ears tried to get Sam to dance with him. He never danced with men at mixed parties, he wrote. It just wasn't done. Sebastian had come over and said "Maybe I'll buy you for him."

"I told him I was involved," Sam wrote," and to please not talk about me like that. I don't like this Guyera guy. I hope I never see him again."

Jazz closed the folder. Jay Warrens had been at one of the parties—interesting, but more importantly, so had Sebastian Guyera. Here was a link between a Guyera and one of those missing. Were there more? Roger was right. This was exciting. But what was she going to tell the detective? Maybe she could tell him that he should check out all the names mentioned in the diary. Especially find out who this Big Ears was. She waved to the desk assistant. In a few minutes Willis appeared. Walking beside him was a man with the largest ears Jazz had ever seen.

CHAPTER 26

W it waited almost an hour for Jazz in the lobby. By that time at least twenty employees had asked him if there was something they could do, something he needed. Her absence caused him to alternate between resentment and concern. Resentment finally won out. She was sandbagging him again.

Disgusted, he returned to his room. After taking off his jacket and tie, he plopped on the bed and turned on CNN. Then he noticed the telephone message light blinking. Tom Underly, the investigator had called. Wit immediately dialed his number.

"Congressman, good to hear from you," Tom said. "I understand you have some work for me regarding your sister's disappearance."

Wit told him about the possible link with Sebastian Guyera. He wanted Sebastian followed. He didn't care how many people it took. He wanted to know all about Guyera, who his friends were, where he lived. He had a list of questions he wanted answered. He had jotted them down on the plane. He was reading from the list when he heard a familiar voice on the television. He looked up.

"I have nothing to say. His parents have nothing to say. Please give them some privacy." It was Jazz! Surrounded by a sea of cameras and reporters, she and an older couple were attempting to push their way to a waiting police car.

"Hold it Tom. I've got to watch something on television."

"There are many questions to be answered in the murder of Roger Barron, A.J. Billings' assistant," the television reporter said as the camera showed Jazz and the couple get into the car and speed away. "But nobody was talking as the reporter and Mr. Barron's parents left the Denver police station today. If Roger Barron was killed because of his work on the A-list story, does this mean A.J. Billings will continue to write on the subject? She wouldn't answer that question or any others. Sources tell us she is headed to Detroit for the funeral. There is no new information on the A-list eight. This is Bob Vander reporting from Denver, Colorado."

For a few seconds, Wit said nothing. Then he heard Tom's voice. "Congressman are you there? What's up?"

"Tom, there's another person I want you to put a tail on. Her name is Jazz Billings, or A.J. Billings. She's a reporter for the *New York Tribune*. She's on her way to Detroit, I think, for the funeral of her assistant. It looks like he was murdered in Denver. Find out all you can about that, and keep an eye on her. I think she's got some information on this case, but I think she's way over her head. Keep her safe, Tom."

"Sounds like she means more to you than a reporter."

"No, it's strictly business. I need her alive."

"Well. I'll make sure she stays that way. I'll have a man in Detroit tomorrow."

CHAPTER 27

Jazz didn't remember the date with Wit until 7:00 p.m. which was 10:00 p.m. New York time. She called his Washington office and left a short message on the voice mail. Someday she might tell him all that happened today.

The biggest excitement occurred when she met the man with large ears. "This is Louis Morrow," Willis told her as she entered his office. "He says he's a friend of Sam and Fred's. He also says he has some information about Sam's disappearance."

Jazz couldn't stop staring. She had to tell Willis about the man with big ears whom Sam wrote about. This could be him. If it was, he was no friend. "Can I see you outside for a moment?" she asked Willis.

They excused themselves and Jazz pulled him around the corner. "You haven't read Sam's diary, have you?"

"No. Haven't had a chance. But you can tell me the good parts."

"The best part is how creepy he thought a guy with big ears was. That could be somebody involved in his disappearance. Have you noticed this Morrow's ears? He could be the guy Sam wrote about. He could be Sam's kidnapper or killer."

"Well then we'll have an interesting talk with Mr. Morrow,

won't we?"

They started back when a detective shouted to Willis that the Aspen police were on the phone. If Morrow was involved, Willis didn't want him hearing this call. He decided to take it at the nearest desk, away from his office. The call was brief. Fred had been found shot to death.

"And most likely with the same gun," Willis told Jazz after hanging up. "His place was ransacked."

"Which probably means the original diary is gone," Jazz said. "Thank goodness for the copy." They looked at each other, then raced back to Willis's office. Sitting in it was Ron Graham, the FBI agent. Morrow was gone and so was the folder. "Geez," Willis said. "Who are you? And where is the other guy?"

"I'm with the FBI and there was no other guy here when I arrived."

"Geez," Willis said again. "Jan, Jan!" He yelled to the desk assistant. "Where did that guy with the big ears go?"

"I don't know. I never saw him leave."

"Notify the front desk—we've got to stop him."

But they didn't. Morrow had disappeared and so had the copy of the diary. "How desperate is this man that he would walk into a police station to steal the copy?" Jazz asked.

"Copy of what?" Graham asked.

"There was a diary," Willis answered. "A diary of Sam Blake's. Roger Barron had a copy. Is that why you're here?"

"I'm here because Miss Billings' assistant was murdered, and I'm in charge of a task force regarding the disappearances of the people who Miss Billings and her media friends refer to as the A-list eight."

"Maybe he just lucked into the diary, "Jazz said, ignoring Graham. "What do you think he would have said if I hadn't pulled you out of the room?"

"We'll never know."

"But we all had a good look at him. We can have a sketch made."

Graham stood up. "And what if this person was in disguise, Miss Billings? It's amazing what they can do with latex."

"Well those ears couldn't be fake. Why would anyone have ears like that if they didn't have to?"

"Like what?" Graham said.

"They're big, jumbo size," Willis said shoving a yellow pad and a pen in front of Jazz. "I want you to write down everything you remember from the diary. And fast."

"As if my life depends on it?"

"Since you're the only one who read the diary, it very well might."

CHAPTER 28

After Jazz wrote down everything she could remember, she went to find Willis. He and Graham were across the hall talking. She started towards them when she saw Roger's parents seated by the elevator. They noticed Jazz and ran to her. Hugging and crying, the three clung to each other. "I'm so sorry," Jazz whispered over and over.

"I know," Mrs. Barron said. "I know. We had to go the morgue. It was horrible."

"They've finished the autopsy," Mr. Barron said. "We're taking Roger back to Michigan."

"I'd like to go with you and help with whatever I could," Jazz said.

"We would like that," Mrs. Barron said. "Roger just thought the world of you."

When told of her plans to accompany the Barrons, Willis urged Jazz to stay under Denver police protection. There was no way of knowing what the murderer thought she knew. Graham agreed. He said he had to talk to her. But Jazz insisted she was leaving now with the Barrons. There was no legal way to detain her. Frustrated, Willis ordered a car for the three and they headed downstairs to meet it.

With the murder now linked to the A-list disappearances, the media was waiting when they left the station. That was the scene Wit saw on television.

A few hours later, the three landed in Detroit. Jazz had yet to unpack from New York. After making arrangements for the body to be brought to a funeral home, the Barrons headed home. They insisted Jazz stay with them. As their taxi turned onto a long driveway, more like a private road, Jazz's mouth dropped open. The estate in Bloomfield Hills consisted of a mansion on a dozen landscaped acres. Never had Roger said anything about being wealthy. He just wanted to be a reporter. Given this house he could have bought a newspaper.

The next two days were spent making funeral arrangements. Jazz helped as best she could by calling people from a list Mrs. Barron gave her. The morning of the funeral, it snowed. Big gentle flakes fell as Roger's casket was lowered into the ground. The sound of sobbing echoed through the white world.

"I caused this," Jazz thought as Mrs. Barron clung to her husband. "If I hadn't pushed Roger. If I hadn't made this all seem so important."

The service at the gravesite was brief. A few minutes later a caravan of black limousines headed back to the Barron estate. Jazz rode alone in the last car. As the funeral cortege passed a small row of stores, she remembered she needed to buy something. Female products, her mother called them. She hadn't asked Mrs. Barron for any. She didn't know if Roger's mother still used them. Menopause was not a topic she wanted to discuss with a grieving mother.

"Can you pull over?" she asked the driver. "I need to buy something in the store."

He parked across the street from a small supermarket and Jazz ran over. Because of the snow, no other customers were in the store. She was out in two minutes. The street seemed deserted as she stepped off the curb. Then she heard a sound. A car engine was revving loudly. "It's snowing," she thought. "Why is anybody revving their engine like the Daytona 500?" She looked down the street. A black sports utility vehicle with dark windows was stopped in front of a gas station. The driver kept revving his engine. Stupid kid, she thought.

She started to cross the street. Her eyes picked up movement to the right. The SUV was moving. It started to move fast. Too fast. She froze. It was coming right at her. "GET OUT OF THE STREET!" her driver warned as he opened his car door. The SUV kept coming. Jazz stood immobile in the street. "MOVE!" her driver yelled. But she didn't know which way to go. It was like dodge ball. She was never very good at dodge ball. She couldn't get her feet to move. The car kept coming. Her driver started running towards her. She put her hands out as if to fend off the car. Her driver screamed again, "MOVE NOW!" And finally she did, falling back on the curb as the car swiped a parking meter, missing her by inches.

"Are you all right?" Her driver said, helping her up.

"Why was he going so fast?" Jazz asked. "He—he was coming right at me." She dusted off snow as they walked back to the car. Her body was shaking.

"Are you sure you're all right?" the driver asked, as she got into the backseat.

"Yes," she said, not too convincingly. Driving down the back roads in Bloomfield Hills, her driver kept watching her in his rearview mirror. Was she in shock?

Jazz said nothing. Her mind, however was a blur of thoughts. Was it intentional? Was someone trying to kill her too? What should she do? Who should she tell? The local police? No, probably the FBI. But who in the FBI? Graham? She didn't trust him. Why did he appear as the diary disappeared? Ben? She wasn't sure she trusted him either. But he said he could help. She had to tell someone. Who?

After dropping her off at the Barrons' estate, the driver immediately made a call on his cell phone. "Hey Tom," he said. "Your client was right. A few minutes ago somebody tried a hit and run on A.J. Billings. You better tell him to warn her. Otherwise I bet she doesn't live out the week."

CHAPTER 29

Foolish, foolish he thought after the botched attempt on Billing's life. It had been too hurried, not planned out. He prided himself on how he researched every detail. That was stupid, stupid. It would not happen again.

He had laughed when her articles had come out about the A-list eight. She and the rest of them had no idea how many people were missing or what they were being used for.

It was amazing what you could do when you had power and money behind you.

God bless America.

Kensington Washington was waiting. Tonight "Washington slept here" would take on new meaning.

CHAPTER 30

It was 6:00 p.m. the next day when Jazz arrived back in Brooklyn. She had hoped to get a half a day of work in, but her plane had been delayed, and then canceled. She had to wait in the Detroit airport for four hours. She was uncomfortable in the crowded terminal, looking this way and that for anyone watching her. It was definitely time to tell someone about the car incident. It might as well be Carrie, she decided, as she knocked on her neighbor's door. Willie would be waiting for her. She missed her dog. He might be a little standoff-ish after her days away.

He was not only standoff-ish, he was asleep under Carrie's kitchen table. But it wasn't Willie who surprised her. Seated at the tiny table was Wit. He and Carrie were sharing a pot of coffee. Jamie was cooing in his highchair. It looked like the perfect family scene.

"Hi," Carrie said. "Guess who's here?"

"I can see," Jazz said. "What are you doing here?"

Wit stood up to give Jazz his seat. She waved the gesture away.

"I came to talk to you," he said. "Your office said you were on a flight landing at 1:00. I got here at 3:00. Carrie took pity on me and invited me in. We found out your plane was delayed."

"We've gotten to know each other," Carrie said. "I found out that I grew up a town away from Wit in Massachusetts. Isn't that something?" Carrie was beaming. Jazz felt the urge to shake her.

"Let's go downstairs to my place," she said to Wit. Willie had begun to stir. Hearing his mistress's voice, his tail started wagging and he inched out from under the table. Jazz perfunctorily patted his head, then grabbed his collar and hustled him towards the door. He looked back at Carrie as if to say "Did I do something?"

Wit hugged Carrie good-bye. He's hugging Carrie, Jazz thought. Please.

In her apartment, she couldn't sit. She turned on one light, then another. She took her coat put it on a chair, then picked it up and hung it in the closet. She checked her phone messages, got water for Willie. She was perpetual motion until Wit finally yelled, "Stop!"

"Please," he said. "I need to talk to you. Please sit down." She plopped on the sofa. He sat down next to her. "I know you've been through a lot with the murder of your assistant. But are you mad that I'm here? Or that I was with Carrie?"

"Just tell me why you came."

He didn't want to start right off with "I know someone tried to kill you." Instead he said, "I want to share something I learned about Chris's disappearance. A friend of mine told me he had seen her getting onto Armando Guyera's plane and she appeared to be drunk, or on drugs. That's why I got involved with Guyera.

"But he claimed he never met her. I didn't believe him. So I kept meeting with him, hoping he'd slip up. But then my friend called again the other day. We were talking about the plane and I said something about Armando and he said, "I never said it was Armando." He must have mentioned Guyera and I just assumed it was Armando. He now tells me it was Sebastian who Chris was with."

Jazz stared at him. "Then I've got some news for you too." She told him about the diary and Sebastian's connection to the man with the big ears. She told him about the man being in the police station and the copy of the diary disappearing. She didn't stop until she told him about Graham showing up, and Fred being murdered. She described everything to him including the fact that a car had almost run over her in Michigan. He took her hand when she told him that. She didn't pull it away. When she finished, she took a deep breath and smiled at him. He smiled back. They were still holding hands.

"I have to go back to the City to fax something in my hotel," he said. "Come with me and we'll go out to dinner."

She agreed and they headed for the subway. After changing trains they arrived at a stop near The St. Regis Hotel where he was staying. He suggested she come up to his room. She said it would be better if she waited in the lobby. When he returned, he asked if she'd like to go into the bar and have something quick to eat. She liked that. They drank wine and shared oysters and shrimp cocktails. They laughed at a couple singing doo wop at the table next to them. It was like a date, and Jazz didn't want the night to end.

"Want to walk down Fifth Avenue and see the Christmas decorations?" she asked. Thanksgiving wasn't until the following weekend, but the Christmas decorations were already up.

"I would love that," he answered.

The night was beautiful—clear and crisp. The lights sparkled. The crowds seemed mellow. He took her hand and tucked it into the crook of his arm. By the time they took the subway back to her apartment, Jazz was tingling.

Willie rushed to greet them as Jazz turned on the hall light. His tail wagged so hard he knocked the mail off the entry table. "He probably needs water," Jazz said, walking into the kitchen to find his bowl. As she suspected, the water dish was empty. She picked it up and filled it at the sink. Wit came up behind her. Turning to put the bowl down, she bumped into him. Water splashed all over his jacket. She couldn't help but laugh. He did too. Then he grabbed her and pulled her towards him. His mouth was on hers before she could utter a sound. The first kiss was urgent, the second soft and probing. As she started to put her arms around him, water cascaded onto the floor. Willie started licking the tile. Jazz put down the water dish and led Wit into her bedroom.

Their mouths stayed together as they flung off clothes. They fell onto the bed. He kissed her in places she didn't know could quiver like that. She wanted to touch him and kiss him everywhere. And she did.

As their naked bodies rolled on the bed, Willie watched from the doorway. He had brought his squeaky toy for everybody to play with. With the action on the bed showing no signs of stopping, he dropped the toy and lay down, his head resting on his paws.

It was as good as she remembered. No, better, Jazz decided the next morning. Now emotion fueled their lust. She awoke first, at 6:00 a.m., too early for Willie who was sleeping between them. How did that happen? Willie's head lay under Wit's chin, and Wit had his arm around the lab. It was like seeing father and son. What would he be like as a father? Jazz wondered. She already knew he was a great lover.

This is one sexy man, she thought, staring at him. Wit stirred. Seeing Jazz sitting up, he attempted to pull her down. Until he realized a 90-pound dog lay between them. He patted Willie and kissed her. They both laughed.

"I want to tell you what happened that night I met you," he said.

"I'm not sure I want to hear," she said.

"No, You have to hear. I felt so good about what happened and I wanted to make sure you knew that. You were still sleeping and

I got a call from my mother." Jazz's phone rang at that moment.

"Is that her again?" she laughed answering the phone. It was Betty Norris. "I need to speak to the congressman," she said. "Right away."

Jazz looked at Wit. "It's for you. How did your office know you were here?"

He took the phone. "Yes?—Yes, All right I'll be there. I'll catch the first shuttle." He looked at his watch. "Tell him I can be there by 9:00."

"I have to go to Washington," he told Jazz, hanging up the phone. "We've got a crisis brewing in Central America. I'm on the House Intelligence Committee. And they've called a special session. But first I have to talk to you about that car in Michigan and the danger you could be in."

"How did your press secretary know you were here?"

"A good guess? I told her I was meeting you."

"No, that wasn't a guess. She didn't ask "Is the congressman there?" She said, "I need to speak to the congressman." Tell me how she knew. Are you wired?"

"Jazz, that's not it." He paused. She waited. "When I heard about your assistant getting murdered I started to worry about you. So I hired a private investigator, just to make sure you're safe."

"You are having me followed?"

"It's for your own good. Jazz in Michigan —."

"Don't you think I can decide about my own good? How dare you. And this?" she pulled the sheets around her. "Did you tell the private eye 'I know I'll be able to stay the night, so just tell my office to call me there in the morning.' You have one hell of a nerve."

Willie jumped off the bed. He didn't like it when Jazz raised her voice. Usually it was on the telephone with her mother. He headed for his green rug. Jazz got out of bed, whipping the sheets aside as she did.

"Why can't you let someone care about you?" Wit asked.

"I'd like to be the one who decides who cares."

"You always have to be in control, don't you?"

"Why don't you just get out of here and go back to Betty and your life in Washington. I liked you better when—when you were just a good lay."

This time it was Wit who whipped off the sheets. In silence he dressed. In silence he left. Willie followed him to the door, then flinched when the door slammed. He flinched again when he heard something crash behind him. Jazz had thrown the phone on the floor.

CHAPTER 31

T wo days later, she was still fuming. Carrie called several times wanting to talk about Wit. Jazz didn't want to discuss him. She didn't want to discuss anything with Carrie. That had never happened before.

She threw herself into her work. Without Roger there were calls to return, mail to answer. Without Roger. It was so hard to accept what happened. She called the Barrons every day. It was like penance. Although they told her again and again they didn't blame her, they seemed to understand her need to be forgiven. Even with their suffering, they made sure they reassured her. As did Joe. He tried to make her focus on her work. He asked if she wanted another assistant. Absolutely not, she said.

Ben called three times. She looked at the pink slips with his messages. "Please call," one said. "Urgent" said another. "I will keep calling until you call me," said the last. Finally she dialed his number. A machine with a computer-generated voice answered. She quickly left her name, relieved that she didn't have to talk. She wasn't sure about Ben. She wasn't sure about any male.

A few minutes later, he called back.

"We haven't talked since you lost your friend," he said. "I'm sorry. I know this must be very hard for you. But I think I have something that will help with your story. The Guyeras own an island in the Florida Keys. Did you know that?"

"Yes."

"Well Armando recently deeded it to Sebastian. I've been trying to get an invitation there. I think maybe it's a stopping off point for the smuggling. But what if it was used for something else? What if it had something to do with the disappearances?"

"What are you saying? That bodies are buried there?"

"I'm just saying the island needs to be researched. I'm doing it on my end. Maybe you want to start digging on yours."

"Thanks Ben, I will."

"Both Armando and Sebastian asked the other day if I was still seeing you. I think we need to get together for dinner or something. I promise not to attack you."

"Maybe after the holiday."

"All right. I'll call you next week. Take care Jazz. This person who killed Roger, I don't have to tell you how dangerous he is. If he thinks you have any information—."

"Well I don't. The police have everything I know about the diary."

"Good. If there is more, let me know."

Everybody wanted to know what she knew, where she went. Was Wit still having her followed? If there was someone trailing her, she hoped they liked southern cooking. She was leaving for Decatur, Georgia that night. It was time for Thanksgiving with mother.

CHAPTER 32

D elilah was always glad to see her successful daughter, even if she didn't show it. She had been raised in a home where affection was dosed out only on rare occasions. She continued that practice with her only child.

Jazz read somewhere that having a less-than-loving mother caused a person to achieve more in life. You needed to prove you were worthy of love. Barbra Streisand was cited as an example. Maybe it was also true for her. Right now she would take affection over accomplishments.

When Jazz's father died, Delilah moved back to Georgia. She used the insurance money to purchase a rambling three-story home on the edge of town. Built like an old plantation house with columns and a large front porch, Delilah decided to modernize the house by adding bright yellow aluminum siding. Tara gone Tulsa, Jazz secretly called it. Neighbors referred to it as The Canary House. Although it included six bedrooms, Delilah lived there alone. "You never know who might drop by," she said.

The first day at her mother's house, Jazz spent alone in a guest room, alternating between sleeping and crying. Roger's death weighed heavily. Delilah let her be. She knew her daughter would eventually open up. She never could keep anything inside.

On Thanksgiving Day, the next-door neighbors, the Randolphs, arrived for turkey dinner. They brought the turkey. It had grown up on their small farm. Jazz felt a bit squeamish eating what was almost a family pet. But when in Georgia, do as the Georgians do. The other guest was Delilah's pastor, Gene Weylings. He regaled the group with stories of his evangelical wanderings. The Randolphs also kept the conversation lively talking about their rooster. (Probably next Easter's dinner, Jazz thought.)

It was a nice respite, she decided later. She needed this time away from the uncertainty of what lay ahead.

The only argument between mother and child took place on the last day of the three-day visit. Delilah started pumping her daughter about the men in her life. Jazz wanted to tell her she slept with a congressman. But since she hadn't known he was a congressman when she first slept with him, she wasn't sure it counted. As she now wasn't speaking to him, it didn't seem appropriate to bring him up.

When her mother wouldn't stop asking questions, she left the room. She hadn't brought up Roger or the A-list disappearances. It all seemed too depressing.

Delilah finally had enough. This mopey woman was not her Agatha Jasmine. A few hours before returning to New York, Jazz was summoned into the sunroom. Delilah said the room was where she did her greatest thinking. It was where she once asked Jazz "What if the hokey pokey is all that it's about?"

"I think it is time for you to talk," mother said to daughter.

"About what?"

"Don't be coy with me Agatha Jasmine. I haven't seen you like this since your father died. You are upset about Roger's death. I understand that. But where is the fire in you? Who killed Roger? You are a reporter, a good one. You know how to research these things. You should be working on finding Roger's killer, not moping around like some lily-livered possum. Now tell me all about it. Tell me why you think he was killed, and how we can find out who did it."

Delilah always envisioned herself a southern Sherlock Holmes. "I would have made a great detective," she once told a younger Jazz after discovering who stole $50 from the cash box at a PTA fashion show.

When Jazz started in the newspaper business, she often used her mother as a sounding board. But the more successful she became, the quieter her mother got. "Oh you don't need me," Delilah would say. "I'm just a simple Southern housewife." Jazz grew tired of hearing it and stopped talking about her work.

This was like old times, and Jazz felt herself opening up. She desperately needed someone to talk to. She spoke about Roger and the diary, of the man with the big ears, the FBI and her concerns about Ben and Graham. She talked about her research about who could be behind the disappearances, and how uneasy she felt around Graham. She told her mother about Armando and Sebastian Guyera, and the son's connection with the diary, and Chris Whitman's connection with Guyera's plane. She told her mother everything, except about her involvement with Wit. She also omitted the fact that somebody tried to kill her. Delilah, however, was no dummy.

"This could be dangerous, Agatha Jasmine. Perhaps you should get a bodyguard."

"Why is everyone saying that? I took a self-defense course."

"Yes, to defend yourself against purse snatchers. But you are writing about women and men disappearing, probably being murdered. Your assistant was killed. Would it be so horrible to have someone follow you around?"

"You sound like Wit."

"Who is Wit?"

Jazz sighed. "I've had a few conversations with Chris Whitman's brother, James Whitman. People call him Wit. He's been investigating all this too."

"And what has he found out?"

"I don't know. We haven't spoken recently. He hired a private investigator to find out more about Sebastian Guyera. He was already tracking Armando."

"Tell me about these GEE-AIR-AHS. What nationality is that?"

"Argentinean. But Sebastian grew up here in the States, in Miami. I've read everything that's been written about him. There isn't much. His father receives most of the publicity. Armando seems to know everyone in power. The man is very handsome and worth billions. Why would he be involved in something like this? And yet —."

"What?"

"He has no close relationships. There is definitely something lacking in his life. Does he need the thrill of killing or kidnapping people?"

"And his son?"

"Sebastian is a playboy. He's in his 30s but has no job. He likes the party life. His father buys him everything. He even bought him an island in the Florida Keys. Sebastian has never been married. He's short and mousy-looking. And his personality leaves much to be desired from what people tell me, and what Sam wrote in his diary."

"He sounds like somebody who would have a problem with women. What about his mother?"

"She died when he was fourteen."

"What is his current relationship with women? You need to find that out. Do you think he is capable of murdering the missing women—and Roger? And what about the father? He sounds like a ladykiller. Lady killer. Why I do believe I've made a joke."

Jazz had to laugh. "I don't know if either is involved, Mother. But what about the men who are missing? This can't be just about sex."

"How do you know one of the Guyeras isn't bisexual?"

Delilah rarely discussed sex. It was not something Southern ladies did. Jazz found out about periods in the junior high girls' room. It wasn't until David, the doctor, asked her to move in with him that her mother asked, "Do you have any questions about sexual relations?" She responded "Mother, I'm 30. I could teach a course in it." It was said to shock her mother. And it did. The word sex had not passed between them since. Now her mother was talking about bisexuality. Delilah and Decatur had come a long way.

"I don't know if either is bisexual," Jazz said. "You're right. I need to find out more about them, and Graham too. I need to research their relationships. But where do I start?"

"You mean where do we start?" her mother asked. Jazz smiled. This renewed interest from her mother could be a good thing. Or not.

CHAPTER 33

He knew she now considered him one of her prime suspects. He knew he should do something about it, something about her. And yet, he loved the attention. It was making up for all those years when no one paid attention. He would let her continue for a while, just a while.

She and the others still had no clue of what he had done with his little playmates or who, beside himself, was playing with them. Oh this was all such fun. It was time to party again. Whom should he choose tonight? The rich bitch Paine or the holier-than thou Chris? Why not both?

CHAPTER 34

Jazz was getting nowhere in her research on Graham. She found out he was in the service before joining the FBI and he had been married once. But that was all. She hadn't much more luck with Sebastian Guyera. Little mention of him appeared in any of the clippings she went through. Besides the work Joanne Meltzin had done, she couldn't find out much about where he spent his time, or who he spent it with.

Armando was different. The father appeared to live his life through the media. At all the big charity galas, all the movie premieres—there was Armando, smiling at the camera. And the photo credits were almost all Jay Warrens. What was their connection? And did it have anything to do with the A-list disappearances?

She tried to interview Armando. His office turned her down, saying he didn't need any publicity. Then why all the photos in the tabloids? It was obvious he was avoiding her. She decided to interview Jay Warrens. A meeting was arranged in his loft down in Soho. She had to take a freight elevator to get to the apartment. He was waiting at the landing. "Miss Billings, what a pleasure," he said, taking her hand. "Come in and see where I work."

The loft was immense. Half of it had been turned into a studio with lights, cameras and a selection of backdrops. The other half was living space. But there were no partitions. So the bed was but a few feet from the sofa. And the sofa was but a few feet away from the refrigerator.

"Do you like it?" Warrens asked, watching Jazz survey the space.

"It's very, ah— unusual," she replied.

"I take that as a compliment," he said, sitting down on the sofa.

She took a seat in a folding chair nearby. "I'd like to talk to you about celebrities."

"So you said on the phone. I have taken pictures of hundreds of famous people. Are you interested in anybody in particular?"

"Well you seem to take an incredible amount of photos of Armando Guyera."

"I find him a fascinating subject."

"How so?"

"He has such an aura of power around him. It makes for wonderful photos."

"But can you make a living from taking pictures of mostly just one person?"

"Armando treats me very well."

"He pays you to take his pictures?"

"Miss Billings, just what is your article about?"

"Well I am curious about Armando Guyera and your relationship."

"And this would be of interest to your readers?"

"It's of interest to me."

"There is no mystery here. I've known Armando for 35 years. He was married to my sister Sylvia. You look stunned. You didn't know that, did you? I changed my last name. It was originally Weisenberg. Too Jewish sounding for business. Sylvia of course became known as Sylvia Guyera. She died about twenty years ago in a skiing accident. Armando has been good to me. My father disowned me after the name change and some other things which I won't go into. Armando gave me money to start my business and to this day makes sure I have work. I love what I do, and I owe much of that to Armando. Others may find him arrogant or ruthless. I find him compassionate. I owe him my gratitude."

So that's the connection, Jazz thought. That is why Warrens hovers around Armando—and Sebastian?

"What about Sebastian?" she asked. "What—." Her question was interrupted by the front door opening. "Hi baby." A gorgeous redhead, about forty, entered the room, carrying packages. Warrens jumped up and embraced her. "This is Kristie, the love of my life," he said. "Kristie, this is the reporter A.J. Billings." They shook hands.

"I'm interrupting," Kristie said. "I'll just go put some things away." As there were no partitions, she never left the room, but simply went over to the bed and began opening her packages.

"We have been together three years," Warrens said. "She is my jewel. Now what can I tell you about Sebastian? We really are not that close. He is nothing like his mother. She was so full of life. Armando worshiped her. You know he never remarried. Sebastian is a brooder, and spoiled. I wish I cared for him more. But I don't. I take pictures of him and his friends because Armando wants me to."

A few more questions, and Jazz left. She had found out what she needed to know. The connection with Armando was not sinister. It was family. And Warrens, in love and happy in his career, was probably not a serial kidnapper or killer.

That left only the Guyeras and Graham, or, of course someone she knew absolutely nothing about.

✶ ✶ ✶ ✶ ✶

To research the Guyeras in Argentina, she asked the paper's South American bureau to hire someone to do leg work. So far the bureau had only come up with real estate holdings. She wondered if Wit was having better luck with his private investigator. She thought of calling him, of setting ground rules. Their relationship would be strictly professional. She was about to dial his Washington number when the phone rang.

It was Charles Hayes, Paine's father. "We are having a meeting tomorrow night," he said. "A very special meeting. The others have agreed that you should attend."

"What others?" She asked.

"You will find out tomorrow at the Plaza Athenee Hotel. You will not be disappointed." He gave her the suite number and told her to be there at 8:00.

★ ★ ★ ★ ★

As usual, she arrived late. Willie's after dinner walk took a long time to accomplish what needed to be done. The subways were running slow. None of that could she tell Charles Hayes as he opened the door, a scowl on his face. "You're late," he said. "We are anxious to begin."

In the spacious suite trimmed in dark mahogany, Jazz saw just about every parent she had interviewed for the profiles of the missing A-list eight. The Worthingtons were talking to Sam Blake's parents and Eva Long's father. Two Washingtons chatted with two Bellinghams. In a corner sat a white-haired woman who dripped of elegance. Jazz had seen pictures. This was Chris's mother. And Wit's mother. Thank God she didn't see him in the room as well.

"Miss Billings has finally arrived so let's get down to business," Hayes said.

The relatives took seats at a long table in an adjacent dining room. Jazz waited at the door. "You can sit too," Hayes said to her. As she did all eyes focused on her.

"I hope you brought your reporter's notebook," Hayes said. "We have something to tell you. Then the rest of the conversation will be off the record."

Jazz took out a pad and pen. They didn't have to tell her any-thing. The meeting alone was a story.

"A.J., I told you a few weeks ago that we would do anything to find Jeffrey," Mr. Worthington began. "The other parents and rel-atives feel the same. After the disappearances of our loved ones we immediately hired private investigators. We had no idea if any of this was linked. Even today, we can't absolutely be certain it is. But we have been meeting and sharing information for some time. I'm sorry I wanted to tell you. But we—."

"As the FBI has done absolutely nothing," Mrs. Whitman interrupted, "we decided to spur someone on. So we're offering a reward. Charles, tell her about it."

Hayes stood up as if making a presentation to his board of directors. "We would like you to inform the public that we are offering a reward of five million dollars for information leading to the whereabouts of all our children.

"Now I know what you're going to say. That this will bring out all the nut cases who will try to fleece us. Well it is our opinion a nut case is responsible for the disappearances of our loved ones. So we are ready to pursue all leads. We have hired an agency—the Kiedall Group. They deal in private investigative matters. They have set up a toll-free number, 1-800-555-6688 and anyone who knows something can call that. They will send investigators to pur-sue every lead."

Jazz knew about the Kiedall Group. They worked for the big corporations and the government. "But what about the FBI?" she asked. "How will they react to this?"

"We don't really give a damn," Hayes said. "Chris Whitman has been gone for almost nine months. What have they found out? Nothing. And I learned a few days ago that a European model is missing as well. How big is this? And what have this person or per-sons done with our children? We need answers. Money buys answers. Now unless you have any further questions, we'll take a break for a few minutes so that you can leave. The rest of our meeting is off-limits to you. Oh, and you should know, the Barrons of Michigan, your assistant Roger's parents, are now part of this group too. As they are still in mourning, they didn't want to come tonight. They urged us to give you this information."

Finished, he nodded to her, then walked to a credenza that held hors d'oeuvres and liquor. The others followed. With nothing else to do, Jazz stood up. She wanted to find out about this European woman. As she started to follow Hayes, she felt a hand on her sleeve. "My son for some reason seems to trust you," Mrs. Whitman said. "I want you to know I do not. I will never rely on a reporter after what happened to my husband. But if you serve a purpose, so be it."

Jazz didn't know what to say. So she said nothing. Turning back towards Hayes, she felt her beeper vibrating against her hip. She looked at the message "Urgent, call national desk, 555-8901."

"Could I use the phone?" she asked Hayes. "I have an urgent message."

"Do it in the bedroom over there," he said, pointing to a door. She went in and closed the door behind her.

"National Desk," a voice answered.

"It's Jazz Billings. I'm returning a page."

"Hold on. I'll find out who paged you."

A brief pause, then a man's voice. "Jazz, it's Bob Feger. Some news just came in from my source in Jersey. I knew you'd be interested."

"What is it?"

"You know that Sam Blake, one of the A-list members who is missing? They just found his body. Looks like he killed himself in a car parked near Newark Airport. My friend says there's a suicide note. It's dynamite. Explains why he's been in hiding and get this, it says Blake killed his lover Fred, and your assistant Roger, and explains why. None of this is official yet because they haven't found his parents to notify them. But my friend knows it's Blake because he's got some distinctive tattoo and the FBI had put out a missing person bulletin about Blake and the tattoo. What do you think?"

"I think this is incredible. And you are terrific, Bob. I'm still in the city. I'll come down to the paper. See what else you can find."

She hung up and sat for a moment. Then she slowly opened the door. Hayes was waiting for her. "It's time for you to leave Miss Billings, unless you have something else to say." She looked across the room at Sam's parents. "I'm afraid," she said, "there is definitely more to say."

CHAPTER 35

I t was ironic that Sam was the first to die. He was the most accepting of the captives. Perhaps because only one "host" abused him, Sam rarely complained and always tried to cheer up the others. He made funny faces as he took their pictures.

The photos were the idea of the leader of the "partnership" as the hostages were told to call their abusers. Besides videotapes, the leader wanted candid shots of his A-list parties. So why not have them taken by one of the world's leading photographers? On certain evenings, Sam would be given a camera and told what to shoot. He would develop the film in a small dark room. The pictures and negatives stayed in the leader's possession.

Because of the photography, Sam eventually had contact with all the captives. He formed a special bond with Paine, Chris and Jeff. In the brief moments they could talk, he joined in their longing to escape, if only they could figure out where they were.

Paine thought maybe it was the coast of Mexico, or Central or South America. Chris guessed the Caribbean. They tried figuring it out by the birds they saw. But no one was a proficient bird-watcher. The only type they could agree on was the pelican.

All tried to do some reconnoitering. By now they knew the

layout of the dark house as it was called. Besides their nights in the party room, each had been upstairs in the larger bedrooms where members of the partnership stayed. They also had access to the courtyards on both sides of the house. As the months went by, security was lessened. They now were allowed to use the larger courtyard to sunbathe. It had an outside gate leading to a garden. What lay beyond the garden, one could only guess.

They found out they were on an island through Sam. He had traveled past the gate. It happened only once. The leader strictly forbade the captives from leaving the house or the courtyard. He also mandated no parties or dates except at night. That kept the captives from viewing any of the landscape. But one day when the leader was away, the gay host visited the house. He wanted a day date. And of course he wanted it with Sam. He considered the photographer his property. He was the only one to have sex with Sam. And he was beginning to have deep feelings for him.

With a silent dare for anyone to try and stop him, the host found the key to Sam's room and ordered him to follow. Sam later told the other captives he had thought of overpowering him and trying to escape, but where to? And could he have overpowered him? He didn't know. So, instead of fleeing, he carried the picnic basket, and allowed the host to lead him through dense vegetation to a beach. He could see blue sea and off in the distance a boat. Upon reaching the beach, they walked along the shore for quite a while. The water was so shallow that if they wanted to go swimming, the host told him, they would have to go almost around the "island." Sam was so excited to learn it was an island. But depressed too. How would they ever get off of it?

When the two walked about half a mile, they stopped and set up the picnic. After munching on sandwiches and sipping wine, they undressed, had sex, then went swimming. It had been a beautiful day, Sam recalled. The host was so relaxed, Sam asked if they could walk even further along the shore. The host said fine.

Holding hands they traveled another quarter of a mile to where the water was even deeper. And that is when Sam saw it—the other house.

"There is another house about a mile away," he whispered to Jeff, who told Chris, who told Paine. "There could be help there."

"Or there could be more danger there," Chris said to Paine. The leader later found out that a host had disobeyed his orders. Although the abductors were called a partnership, the island was ruled by dictatorship. The leader changed the locks on Sam's door and kept him away from the gay host for two weeks. The host was furious.

The leader knew Sam's death would make him even madder. But it was necessary. He decided on Sam's murder-to-be-considered-suicide after learning of the diary. Infuriated that there might be a link to him or anyone in the partnership, he decided to destroy the connection. All the captives would have to die eventually. Sam just would be first.

If a note was left with Sam's body offering an explanation of why he disappeared and stating that he killed Fred and Roger, suspicion about any of the partnership would cease.

Getting Sam to write the suicide note was not easy. The leader, however, could be extremely persuasive. He gave Sam a choice. Write the note, or his parents and younger sister, Molly, would die. Sam valiantly chose to end his life so his family members could continue theirs.

He sobbed when he learned Fred was dead. He sobbed harder when he had to write that he killed him. As the leader dictated, and an employee named Venta held a gun to his head, Sam wrote that he disappeared so Fred would miss him. When he didn't, and even took on a new lover, Sam killed him. He believed Roger was that new lover. Now that Fred was dead, Sam wrote, he had nothing to live for.

Satisfied, the leader ordered Venta to take Sam to Newark on a private jet. The day before, another employee named Ralph traveled to the New Jersey city where he found a homeless man about the same height as Sam. He offered the man $100, and said there would be $500 more if he would do an errand. The man readily agreed.

After cleaning him up, Ralph bought him a winter coat, blue jeans, a western shirt, sunglasses and a Broncos' baseball cap, then sent him into a less than reputable car rental agency. Using Sam's credit card and license, the homeless man rented a black Chevrolet Malibu. He turned the keys over and received five $100 bills. Still homeless, but now fashionably attired, the man vanished back into the world of street living.

Sam knew he was going to die. He just didn't know when. Every minute living became agony. When the plane landed in Newark, he felt the time was near. His body shook as the men, now wearing gloves, dressed him in a winter coat and Broncos' hat and walked him to a car parked in the last row of a nearly deserted parking lot. They directed him to get in on the driver's side. Venta got in next to him and took out a gun.

"May I pray first?" Sam asked.

"Make it fast," Venta said.

"Oh Lord," his voice broke, "please forgive me for all my sins. And please forgive this man for what he is about to do." For a moment Venta couldn't move. He had killed before. The leader even ordered him to kill a pregnant girl once. But he didn't know her. He knew Sam. He sort of liked him. And now this prayer. But there was no stopping. He put the gun to his victim's right temple. Tears ran down Sam's face. Venta felt a wetness in his own eyes. He pulled the trigger. Blood spurted on his overcoat. He quickly put the gun in Sam's hand and took out the note, leaving it on the front seat.

In ten minutes he and Ralph were back on the jet, heading south.

It rained all the next day. It wasn't until evening that a passenger about to board a private jet discovered Sam's body. The passenger wanted to park his new Jaguar away from other cars. Seeing a black Chevrolet all by itself in the far end of the parking lot, he pulled in two spots away. As he got out, he noticed dark splotches on the front window of the other car. For some reason he wasn't sure why, he told the police later, he walked over to it. The blood-soaked head of Sam caused him to scream. Then he rushed back to his car phone. One of the first officers on the scene was the brother of Bob Feger from the national desk. Less than an hour after the body and note had been discovered, the cop took a break, went to a pay phone and called *The Trib*.

CHAPTER 36

Jazz knew about Sam's death before the medical examiner. But she wasn't sure what she was going to say to his parents. Nothing was official. It could be a mistake. Hayes was waiting for her to speak. "I need to talk to the Blakes," she said. The look on her face stopped him from saying anything more. He simply moved out of her way.

"Could I talk to you in private?" she asked the couple. They both looked at Mrs. Whitman who stood next to them. "Whatever you have to say," Mr. Blake said, "it can be said in front of all of us. We share a common bond."

"Mr. Blake, really, I need to talk to you alone."

"What is it, A.J.?" Mrs. Blake asked.

"It's about Sam."

"Oh, please tell me. Look we'll go into the bathroom right here. Won't we Richard?" She pulled her husband towards the small powder room adjacent to the front door of the suite.

After the three were inside, Jazz closed the door. "I just got a phone call that there may be some news about Sam. Do you have a law enforcement agent you are in contact with?"

"Ron Graham of the FBI has met with all of us," Mrs. Blake

said. "I have his phone number. And we've dealt with a detective in Denver, a Willis. Richard, do you have his number?"

"Forget the phone numbers, Bonnie. Miss Billings, tell us what you know."

"I know that the police may be trying to reach you, Mr. Blake. I would suggest you call them."

Mrs. Blake grabbed Jazz's arm. "Have they found him, A.J.? Is he alive?"

"I don't know what's happened. I just know we got a tip about something that's going on in Newark and your son may be involved."

"I have Graham's number right here," Mr. Blake said, taking a card out of his wallet. Too bad, Jazz thought. She would have preferred he contact Willis.

They left the bathroom and headed for the bedroom. "We've got to use the telephone," Mr. Blake said. Everyone stared.

"Operator, how do I get an outside line?" Mr. Blake asked the woman who answered the hotel's switchboard. She told him how to dial Graham's number.

"I need to find Ron Graham," he said to the person who answered. "It's an emergency —. What? Oh, this is Richard Blake, the father of Sam Blake —. Yes I'll hold."

"They're patching me through to him," he told his wife. "He's in transit somewhere."

"Yes, Mr. Graham, this is Richard Blake. I've been told there may be some news about my son —Where am I? My wife and I are in New York City. What is the news? – I'm at the Plaza Athenee hotel – Yes, I can meet one of your men in the lobby. When?—We'll be there. Can't you tell me anything?—I see. We'll wait—What? Who told me? The reporter, A.J. Billings. She is with me now. Yes I'll tell her—yes—we'll be downstairs in 15 minutes. Good-bye."

He took his wife's hand. "He's sending someone to pick us up.

Graham says he'll meet us in about an hour. He didn't say where, or why. Miss Billings, he said he wants you to come too."

I bet he does, Jazz thought. He's probably dying to know how I found out. Her mind raced trying to figure out how to get a photographer to the scene. She turned to the Blakes. "I'll meet you in the lobby in ten minutes."

She hastily said good-bye to the others and sprinted to the elevator. Here is where it gets hard, she thought, balancing compassion for the Blakes and doing her job as a reporter. But this was her story. And tonight she had two exclusives with little time to write either. Graham might keep her busy the whole night. She needed a photographer and her own car. She had ten minutes to get them.

In the elevator she took out her cell phone and called Feger. It was 8:30. The paper's deadline was midnight. She quickly told him the problem. He said he would get a car there in fifteen minutes with a photographer. He would also try to hold a slot in the front page. She said she would delay the FBI until the photographer arrived.

The only way to file the story about the parents' meeting was to dictate to the desk while she drove to Newark. So she had to be in the photographer's car, not the FBI's. She felt confident the tip about Sam's death was right. But a suicide? And Sam, the killer of Roger? She didn't know what to believe. She only knew that this was the story of her career and she was not going to let it go.

CHAPTER 37

Sitting in the lobby, Jazz was going over her notes, when two men in dark blue suits arrived. So obvious. Couldn't FBI agents dress like they weren't going to a funeral? As one of the agents headed towards her, the elevator door opened. Sam's parents were getting off. "Miss Billings, I'm Agent Stevens. You need to come with us as soon as we find the Blakes." The couple had already seen Jazz and was rushing over.

"I have to use the ladies' room," Jazz said. "It will just be a minute." The two agents looked at each other. "Make it quick," one said. Jazz walked to the front desk and asked where the restrooms were. The desk clerk pointed past the elevators. Good. A nice long walk. She looked at her watch. Eight minutes had gone by since her phone call to Feger. She waved to the Blakes and walked down the corridor into the restroom. Entering a stall, she took out her notebook and pen. Five minutes later, the lead was written as an agitated Bonnie Blake rushed in. "A.J. are you in here? We really have to go. Are you all right?"

"I'm sorry Mrs. Blake. I'm having a little problem. I'll be right out."

"Well hurry. Oh, and there's some man with cameras in the

lobby looking for you."

Bingo! Jazz quickly washed her hands and followed Mrs. Blake back to the lobby. Eddie Francis, a veteran photographer was waiting. "I'm sorry," Jazz said to the now hostile agents. "I'm not feeling well. Since my photographer's here, I'm going to ride with him. We'll follow you."

"We were told to bring you with us," Agent Stevens said.

"We will be right behind you. If I need to stop for a bathroom again, we won't delay you. We're going to Newark Airport, right?"

"Yes. All right, follow us then. We're going to the parking lot on the south side of General Aviation."

As the group headed out the door, Eddie winked at Jazz. "Want to tell me what this is all about?" he asked.

"Can't Eddie, just listen as I dictate." His car, with N.Y. Press plates, was parked right in front of the entrance to the hotel. She hopped in and dialed Feger. He answered immediately.

"All right," she said as they headed for the West Side, "I think we should do this in two parts. First get me a rewrite man. I'll give him my lead and my notes about the meeting and the five million dollars the parents of the missing A-list eight are offering. The death of Sam Blake we can't do until we get to Newark. And there may be a problem there. This FBI agent, Graham, he wants to see me. I'm sure he'll keep me isolated somewhere for questioning on how I found out. Legally he can't do it. But of course he will anyway. You better send another reporter to work with me and at least get the story out for deadline. We're going to the south parking lot by General Aviation. Does that agree with your source?"

It did. Feger yelled to a desk assistant to find a national reporter and get him, or her, down to General Aviation at Newark Airport right away. Then he quickly found a rewrite man. Jazz gave him what she had. Eddie's eyes grew wide as he listened. They had just turned off the Jersey Turnpike when she finished. She checked with Feger one more time. He had found Ozzie Yumiz, a metro reporter who lived in Newark. Ozzie was already at the parking lot. He had called in on his cell phone. The police wouldn't let him near the car, he said, but the good news was there wasn't another reporter in sight. Jazz liked Ozzie. He took no prisoners. Nobody was going to push Ozzie around.

Feger spoke to Eddie and told him to start shooting pictures the minute he arrived. Get the Blakes crying, get whatever he could of the car. Jazz didn't hear the conversation. If she had, she would have protested. It was enough that she had the story. Pictures of the scene would be fine. Pictures of the Blakes would be too intrusive.

As they pulled in to the parking lot next to the FBI car, Eddie jumped out. Jazz was as shocked as the Blakes when the strobes started flashing as soon as the parents got out of the car.

"Eddie, what are you doing?" Jazz screamed as the parents tried to shield their faces. An FBI agent rushed over to grab the camera. But Eddie was a veteran. "Touch me, or this camera, and you become the story," he said. "I'm in a public place. I have every right to take pictures." The agent froze, then turned toward Jazz. "Don't think your photographer is getting any nearer to anything," he said. He called over a Newark police officer. "Make sure this photographer stays behind the police line. And if you want to make the line extend back to the Turnpike, that's okay with me." The officer, one Harold Feger, nodded and escorted Eddie away.

"Billings follow me," the agent said. He grabbed Jazz's arm and steered her towards a group of men clustered about 100 feet away. As Jazz protested, Ozzie rushed over. "I'm here Jazz," he said. "I'll get what I can."

Jazz tried to tell the Blakes that she was sorry, but they refused to acknowledge her. A few minutes later, they were escorted to a car near where she was being taken. They complained, asking why they had been brought to the airport only to be taken somewhere else. But the agent was adamant. As they took their seats in the back of a car, Graham approached them. "I'm sorry you had to come here first. But I needed to talk to you and I can't leave for awhile."

Jazz was standing near enough to hear him say, "Mr. And Mrs. Blake I'm sorry to have to tell you this, but I believe your son is dead. We need you to identify the body as soon as you feel able. I wanted to tell you this before the media contacted you." He stared over at Jazz.

Mrs. Blake began sobbing. Mr. Blake asked, "How did it happen? Is that Sam in the car over there? Do you know who killed him?"

"It looks as if it may be a suicide," Graham said. "There was a note. But it's too early for all of that. I'm sorry for your loss. One of our agents will take you to the local police station or to a hotel, wherever you want to go for a while. The body should be at the morgue in a few hours. I just thought we should get you somewhere where you can have some privacy."

"Thank you," Mr. Blake said. "If you could arrange for us to get a room in a hotel here by the airport that would be helpful. My daughter Molly doesn't—I have to make some calls."

"Of course," Graham said. He gave instructions to the driver. A few minutes later the car headed out of the lot, passing but a hundred feet from the black Chevrolet.

"I think we have some serious talking to do," Graham said turning to Jazz.

"First I have a job to do," she replied. "This story will be on all the radio and television stations tomorrow morning. But I have it tonight. You have to let me file at least part of the story. As it is, I will only tie my competitors, even though I was way ahead of them."

"I don't have to let you do anything Miss Billings. You ought to be disgusted with yourself, taking pictures of that distraught couple at a time like this." Jazz was about to protest, when he continued. "I have to admit I admire you. You don't give up. But a little compassion might be a nice addition." She knew better than to argue. Instead her eyes implored him. "Please," she said. "I found the Blakes for you. Let me file my story."

She was amazed at the answer. "All right, I'll let you, with no attributions of course. You're right. It's going to come out anyway in a few hours." He opened the back door of a nearby FBI car, sat down and motioned for her to get in and sit next to him. "Now what would you like to know?"

What was going on with this man? This was the second time he gave her a story. It was all so odd. "Tell me what you found," she said. And he did. He told her about Sam slumped over in the car. It looked like a self-inflicted gunshot wound.

How did he know it was Sam?

Sam had a tattoo of crossed skis on his right arm. So did the corpse. The parents' identification would make it official. Then there was the suicide note signed by one Sam Blake. The note stated Sam had killed Fred and Roger.

She asked if he would go on record as to what this meant for the rest of the missing. He said it would be better if he didn't comment, especially if she had no one else going on record. It would be too obvious where the information came from.

He said he was impressed that she had gotten the story before speaking to him, and would have to question her about that in the near future. But he knew deadline was near and shouldn't she be writing?

She didn't ask to see the body. She knew he would have refused. At least she thought he would refuse. There was no telling how far he would let her go. But she had enough and it was getting late. She rushed back to Ozzie who was talking to a police officer. She pulled him aside.

"What have you got?" she asked.

"Just that there's a dead body, blonde guy, looks like he shot himself. There's a note. I don't know what's in it."

"I do," she said. "I've got enough to call this in. Where's Eddie?"

"Getting pictures of the car."

"You've got to be kidding."

"About Eddie? Never. If he says he's going to get the car. He's getting the car."

"Well where is your car? I need to sit in it, and call the desk." He led her to a beat-up Dodge with four different hubcaps. She pushed aside the used coffee cups and Dunkin Donuts bags on the passenger seat, sat down and pulled out her phone. She gave the rewrite man all she had. It didn't take long. There wasn't much. But what she had was explosive. After she finished, she asked to speak to Feger. She explained who her source was. He, too, was amazed. "Why is this guy talking to you?" he asked.

"I wish I knew. We can't quote him of course. But it all agrees with what you had. Will we make deadline?"

"You are the lead story. I just hope Eddie's photos make it too. He's racing back here. He says he's got fantastic shots."

"Oh God," Jazz said.

CHAPTER 38

Once again A.J. Billings was the talk of the New York media. How she obtained two exclusives in one night became the topic of conversation in newsrooms all over the City.

Fortunately for Jazz, her editors decided not to use Eddie's close-ups of the blood-soaked body slumped over the steering wheel. They chose a more genteel shot, the silhouette of the car that Sam died in. On the jump page, however, they ran the picture of the shocked Blakes. Jazz asked Feger not to use the picture, but he was adamant. "This is a newspaper," he told her. "It is made up of words and pictures. And you asked for the photographer." She argued that a photo of the Blakes would hurt her relationship with the other relatives. But he refused to omit it. When Charles Hayes called, she expected the worse. She was not disappointed.

"How dare you run a picture of the Blakes!" he shouted at her. "Have you no decency?"

"It was not my decision," she said. "I am terribly sorry about it. If you could convey to them—."

"I will convey nothing. I don't understand you Miss Billings. They are just destroyed by what the police are saying. We give you a story, an exclusive story about the reward, and you pay us back by this?"

"Mr. Hayes, the story of Sam's death is being broadcast on every radio and television station in America. It will be in every newspaper tomorrow. It is a legitimate story and I make no apologies for reporting it. My only regret is that my paper ran a picture of the Blakes in their moment of agony."

"I will speak to Campbell Mancox, your boss, about the photo. I hope you realize that you will probably have no more access to the relatives. Many feel you have betrayed a trust."

Jazz took a deep breath. "It's always been hard for me to separate journalism and my sympathy for people, Mr. Hayes. With this story, especially. But I am a journalist and I have an obligation to my readers as well as those I write about. Now I hope you will keep in contact with me. And so will the other relatives. I won't stop with this story until we have an answer to what happened to everyone. And I plan on doing more investigating of Sam's death. I hope the relatives know that."

There was silence on the other end of the line. Finally Charles Hayes said "this has been very difficult for all us, Miss Billings. It's been four months since Paine disappeared. And now this with Sam, whom we all assumed was taken by the same person or group. I just don't know what to think."

"Well, let's wait to learn more about Sam's death."

"You think it might not be a suicide?"

"I'm not sure what I think. Don't forget he confessed in his suicide note to killing Roger, my assistant. I have a major investment in the truth here."

"Let me know if you find out anything."

"Are the lines of communication still open between us?"

"Perhaps with us. I can't speak for anybody else. Especially Doris Whitman. She is absolutely hostile towards you. Do you know why?"

Wit's face floated in front of hers. It had been two weeks, three nights and several hours since their night together in her apartment. "I have a hunch."

"Well, you might try to smooth things over there."

"Perhaps I will. I'll keep in touch Mr. Hayes."

"Good day, Miss Billings."

A half-an-hour later, Jazz was summoned to the publisher's office. Already seated there were the photo editor and the national editor. Mancox wanted a review of what happened the night before. The executive editor had interviewed Eddie and Feger. It became apparent to Mancox that the decision to use the photo had nothing to do with Jazz. As for the story, Mancox said nothing until everyone was walking out the door. "A.J.," he said as she passed, "Charlie Hayes is a friend. But he is not stupid. He knows what a great job you did as a journalist last night. So do I. Congratulations."

What a 24 hours, Jazz thought as she headed back to her desk. Ups and downs, ups and downs. Pink message slips papered her desk. Ben called—was that an up or a down? Roger's mother called. What she must be going through. Betty Norris had called. What did Wit's press secretary want? And her mother called. The message said "Urgent." Delilah would have to be first.

"Agatha Jasmine. I called over an hour ago. Didn't you get the message it was urgent?"

"Yes mother, but I was in a meeting—with the publisher of the paper."

"Well I'm sure he's congratulating you. But I have a problem down here that I need to talk to you about. Now since it's taken so long for you to call, I can't talk to you about it. I'm already late for my bridge club's championship. My partner is Harriet Overbright, the banker's wife. We may win today. Well I have to go. I'll call you at home tonight. Bye bye love."

Delilah was gone. The urgent problem would have to wait until after no-trump.

Roger's mother and father both got on the line when Jazz returned the call. "Jazz, can it be true?" Mr. Barron asked. "Have we found Roger's murderer?"

"I don't know. The FBI is leaning that way. But there's a lot to be looked into."

"Roger was never gay," his mother said. "CNN makes you think that was a possibility. I'm going to call them."

"No, you are not," her husband said. "Do you want to be interviewed? Aren't you sick of reporters? Oh, sorry, Jazz."

"That's okay. I know how tough this is for you. I'll let you know as soon as I hear anything."

Ben was in New York. He wanted to have dinner that night, to celebrate her scoop. She decided why not? She wanted more information on Graham. Maybe Ben could help. Maybe some male attention would help.

She put off calling Betty Norris until the end of the day. The woman always made her feel uneasy, like she was invading an animal's territory. And if Wit wanted to talk to her—well that would make her more uneasy.

"Betty, It's A. J. Billings."

"Oh yes, thanks for getting back to me. You must be very busy today, what with your story."

"Yes, it's been a busy day."

"Well I won't keep you. The Congressman doesn't know I'm calling you. He doesn't even mention you anymore. His mother specifically asked me not to tell him that I was calling you. That puts me in a very awkward position."

Get to the point, Jazz said to herself.

"Anyway, Mrs. Whitman asked me to contact you."

"Is there a reason she couldn't contact me, herself?"

"Doris Whitman is used to having people do things for her. She wants to meet with you. She wants me to make the arrangements."

Jazz sighed. The last thing she needed was to have someone yell at her.

"Do you know what it's about, Betty?"

"No, just that Mrs. Whitman said 'Arrange it.' She wants to meet with you before this weekend. In New York."

"I can see her tomorrow night."

"Fine. I'll check with her. Would her hotel be all right? She always stays at the St. Regis."

So does her son, Jazz thought. Do you know he makes this little snoring whistle? And his thumb plays with your naked breast, even when he's asleep? She' wanted to say that to Betty. But of course she didn't.

"The St. Regis will be fine."

"I'll call you back to confirm. Good night."

Jazz looked at her watch. It was 6:00. She told Ben she would meet him at seven at the restaurant. If she went back to Brooklyn to feed Willie and change, she would barely make it. She called Carrie, who as usual said no problem. She would take care of Willie.

In the taxi on the way to the restaurant Jazz tried to figure out what Mrs. Whitman wanted. Perhaps it would be a "stay away from my son" lecture. Or was it about Chris? Hayes said it had been four months since he last saw Paine. Chris disappeared five months before that. Nine months. Could she still be alive? If so, where? And having to do what? The odds were strong she was dead. As were Paine, Eva, all of them. Would their bodies start popping up around the country, perhaps as suicides, too?

And what about Armando or Sebastian Guyera? Instinct told her one, or both of them was involved in this. "I'm going to get you," she said out loud, making the cab driver look in his rearview mirror. She didn't notice. "One of you is the key," she muttered, "even if Sam killed himself—and Fred and Roger—you are still involved, and I'm going to find out how. Somebody must know. Somebody is going to talk about the real you and what you are capable of. And I'm going to find them."

CHAPTER 39

S he could have started with Binky Brandon, he thought, after hearing from the cab driver, one of several employees he had following Jazz. Binky was the first female he sexually abused. She was 12. So was he. Binky made the mistake of laughing when he asked her to a Halloween dance at their private school. She was the prettiest and most popular girl in the class. He was considered the "dorkiest."

"Why would I go anywhere with you?" she asked, then laughed. He grabbed her budding breast and pinched the nipple until she screamed. "Because I am a Guyera," he told her. "And I am all-powerful." Binky ran to the principal who called his father. A mild reprimand, and it was forgotten. But not the thrill he felt overpowering a female.

After many lectures on treating women with wealth a certain way, he spent his teenage years avoiding his female peers. Instead he visited the poorer sections of Miami where he would pick up girls delighted to sit in a Ferrari, and be seduced in a Ferrari. The few that weren't, he forced himself upon. They never reported him. After all he was a Guyera. He was all-powerful.

In college, money bought friendships and female favors, as it did later in his 30s. He never wanted for companionship, but women in his social circle never accepted him. Socialites thought him creepy and arrogant. Publicists just thought of him as rich, which was why he received so many invitations to celebrity parties. He would attend with the two or three friends he groomed to do his bidding. Some rich and beautiful young women would dance with him. A few even attended a gala or two, with him. But no one wanted a serious relationship with the homely son of the all-perfect so handsome Armando Guyera. Frustrated, he became meaner, and thus more repulsive.

Sebastian Guyera became a pariah on the A-list. Then his father bought him Reef Key, a small island southwest of Key West.

The Florida Keys don't end with Key West. They straggle on to the Dry Tortugas. Reef Island or Key, as islands are known in Florida, came with two homes—one on the beach, the other hidden in the tropical foliage. The bright house and the dark house, he called them. For the good and the bad Sebastian. The bad Sebastian usually won out. After being mocked by several inebriated models at a party in Manhattan, he devised a plan to never again be an outcast. Snobby rich bitches who thought they were too good for him would pay, and pay.

He spent a year planning it. When he felt satisfied that he had thought of every obstacle, he hired two men to carry out the plan, Venta Morex and Ralph Sejun. Both had sworn loyalty to his family. Venta's family home in Argentina had been saved from foreclosure by Sebastian's grandfather. Ralph's family worked for the Guyeras for generations. Although Venta and Ralph had been criminals since childhood, they understood allegiance. When Sebastian asked them to work for him and ask no questions, they quickly agreed.

He sent Venta to kidnap the first woman. She was French. Sebastian had attended a party in Paris where a model named Fanee caught his eye. She ignored his flirtation. She ignored him.

For a month he had Venta follow her and learn all about her. Fanee's parents were dead and she had few close friends. Few realized when she disappeared. Venta kidnapped her as she arrived home from a dinner party. He made her pack her own bags and write a note to one friend saying she was taking a trip to India with someone she just met. After, he made her drink a drugged glass of juice. When she passed out, he put her in a shipping crate that Sebastian had specially built in Mexico. It contained breathing holes and a contoured outline for a body to lie in. The man who built it assumed Sebastian wanted to smuggle someone into a country. He never thought it would be used to take a person out.

On the exterior of the crate were painted the words "ART-WORK—special handling." Inside, Fanee lay unconscious, unaware that she was being shipped to Miami on the Guyera private jet.

After delivering an envelope filled with cash to a Miami customs agent on the Guyeras' payroll, Venta watched as the crate was transferred to a smaller plane, which immediately took off for Reef Key. A narrow runway had been carved out of the hardwood hammock that grew in the middle of the key. When not in use, the runway was covered with palm leaves and brush.

Still asleep, Fanee arrived at the dark house.

In the last months of his planning, Sebastian brought workers from Guatemala to renovate the lower floor of the dark house. A dozen small rooms, each with its own toilet and shower, were constructed. None of the workers asked what the rooms would be used for. They had families to feed. They were paid well.

Fanee was placed in one of those rooms. For the first two days, she saw no one. But Sebastian saw her. He had video cameras installed in each of the rooms. The monitors were in his large master suite on the main floor. Lying in bed he could watch his guest dress and shower, and cry.

On the third day, he told Venta to instruct her to dress for dinner. She was going on a date, and she was to act as if it was the most exciting date of her life.

Fanee was escorted upstairs to the main section of the house where a candlelit table was set for two. She was told to sit and wait.

Sebastian watched for a while. He had a camera set up in the dining room as well as his bedroom. But he would not seduce her yet. He wanted the relationship to evolve. They would date for a while. He wanted all that he had missed. He would have preferred an American, one of those snotty bitches from Palm Beach or New York. But if this worked out, well that might come later.

With fear in her eyes, Fanee waited. Who was her abductor? What did he want from her? Sebastian entered the room. He smiled. She did not. "SMILE WHEN YOU SEE ME!" he shouted, then lowered his voice. "You will always smile when you see me. Do you understand?"

"Yes," Fanee said. And smiled.

CHAPTER 40

Fanee amused him for months. The first week they only dined together. The thought that he could have her at any time and yet didn't, kept him in a constant state of arousal. For a man not used to wooing, he took pride in how considerate he became. He asked if the food was satisfactory. He held her hand at the table. After dinner, he led her over to the couch and offered her brandy. The first night she declined. The second night she gulped it down. He put his arm around her, leaving his hand hovering a few inches over her breast. He was a teenager in the balcony waiting for that first sexual contact.

In the beginning Fanee acted like a robot. He asked her to talk about herself. She couldn't. So he did all the talking. After three days of one-sided conversations, he decided to give her more wine at dinner, and more brandy after. In her halting English, she began to speak of her life growing up in a suburb of Paris. He talked of his life and the people who mistreated him and how they would pay.

"This is a relationship," he thought.

"Am I going to die?" she thought.

After the first week, he allowed her outside for a few hours each day, in a courtyard open only to the sky. A chaise lounge was the only piece of furniture. She acquired a companion, a wild parakeet that flew in each day to see if she had food. Breakfast and lunch were served in her small room. She smuggled out crumbs for the bird.

By the end of the second week Sebastian realized he could not keep his hands off her. She realized she would have to do something to gain more freedom. After dinner when he pulled her to him on the couch, she did not resist. Through the material of her gown, his fingers traced the outline of her breast. He had never been this gentle, this slow in his lovemaking. He wanted this moment of anticipation to last forever. He took her hand and put it on the bulge in his pants. Again she did not pull away.

He planned just heavy petting for weeks. But the moment he unzipped her evening gown and saw the white lace bra with the overflowing breasts, he couldn't stop himself. He asked her to undress completely before him. She did, taking each item of clothing and placing it neatly on a nearby chair. She was gorgeously proportioned, slim but not emaciated like some models. And the breasts. He touched them. He licked them. He had her take off his pants. He buried her face between his legs and told her to satisfy him. She did. She would do anything he asked.

Later he tried to wait, to prolong this sense of power. But he couldn't. He pushed her down on the carpet, and took her.

The next day he decided to have sex with her in the courtyard. He brought a blanket. Naked, they made love in the sun. She pointed out the parakeet. A mistake. She never saw it again. Sebastian did not want to share her affection. The morning after the session in the courtyard, he went to her room before she awoke. She rolled over, and there he was, ready for more. After several mornings of finding him in her bed, she asked if they could go to his room. But he didn't want her to know too much about the layout of the house, not until he could trust her.

They became a couple, the abductor and his captive. He would go to Miami or New York and attend parties, knowing that waiting on the island was his girl, his Fanee.

After several more months, Fanee began to bore him. There was no challenge. The power came too easily. Sebastian decided there had to be another woman, perhaps several. He could simulate A-list parties in his dark house. "Venta," he said, "we need to get another one. And this time she will be an American. We will take one from Palm Beach, the rich bitch capital of the world."

CHAPTER 41

Although she had been born into money, Chris Whitman never flaunted it. She drove a Volvo. Her apartment contained basic furnishings and clothes. No Picassos adorned the walls. No Versaces lined the closet. She preferred the understated looks of designers like Calvin Klein and Ralph Lauren.

The female characters in her novels were just the opposite. They bought the most ornate things, partied hard and discarded men like junk mail. Chris's life was subdued in comparison. She dated one man at a time. Her affair with Gary Dire lasted a year. At one point she considered marrying him. He was always so attentive. But there was a dark side, something she sensed but couldn't quite unveil. When he asked her to marry him, she hesitated. A week later, when he asked again, he grabbed her in his excitement. Instinct made her say "No. It's not going to work out." And the dark side erupted. He slapped her, called her a bitch and walked out of the apartment. Thank God, I didn't marry him, she thought.

Approaching 30, her life took a turn. Gary had introduced her to cocaine. She began to party like her characters. She loved to dance, often jumping on a table as the night turned into a music frenzy. It was at one of those parties that Sebastian decided Chris Whitman would be his next girlfriend. She had this vulnerable waif-like look, yet there seemed such fire in her. And her parents were from old money, and her brother was a Republican congressman. The perfect American rich bitch.

Ralph was assigned to follow her and learn her habits. Abducting her turned out to be easy. While waiting for the crate to be delivered to Palm Beach, Ralph watched Chris get drunk at a restaurant party and barely make it back to her car parked on a side street. Seeing her slumped over the steering wheel, he decided to seize the moment. He simply pushed her aside, started the car and took her back to her apartment. He packed the bag. But in her state she couldn't leave a note. That would have to wait. As he drove to the airport, she started coming around. He pulled over and gave her a shot of muscle relaxant.

At the airport, Sebastian was asleep in a company jet, having just completed an overnight trip from Europe. The family jet was with his father in New York. But his favorite pilot—the one who never questioned anything—was with him.

He hadn't expected Ralph to take Chris for two more days. But after being awakened and told she was in the car, he wasn't upset. He told Ralph to take a blanket from the plane, wrap it around her and carry her up the jet's stairway. It was 6:00 in the morning. Nobody was around. But as Ralph tried to get Chris out of the car, she awoke once more. She stumbled and fell. Sebastian hurried out of the jet and helped her up the stairs. That was the scene Wit's friend happened upon as he prepared for an early departure on his company's jet.

Chris didn't realize she had been kidnapped until that night, when she awoke with a horrible headache. She didn't know where she was, and at that moment didn't care. By the next morning the effects of the liquor and the muscle relaxant had worn off. Groggy, she got up and tried the door of the small room. It was locked.

Where was she? She couldn't remember. She lay back on the bed. Hours went by. Where was she? Why was nobody around? Hunger pains started. She started banging on the door.

At the end of the second day, the door opened and Venta walked in with a tray of food.

"Who are you? What am I doing here?"

"You will find out everything when it is time," he said. "Now I suggest you eat, then take a shower. Your clothes are in the closet." He left the room.

Sebastian watched as she devoured the food. Not even a tear. "She is strong," he thought. "She will be much more interesting than Fanee."

CHAPTER 42

After a while, he grew bored with Chris as well. She never fawned liked Fanee. She never showed any emotion. After the initial isolation, then dating time, she allowed him to make love to her, but she never seemed involved in the physical action. He tried being rough. The detachment didn't change. She was enduring it, saving a part of herself for someone. It was not him.

To add spice to his secret life, he tried a threesome with Fanee and Chris. By this time Fanee would do anything. She knew he had someone else. The few times he spent with her, he talked of his other girlfriend, and he made Fanee, who had gone to art school, paint a beach scene on the wall of Chris's room.

Fanee was afraid she was going to die. Of course eventually she would. He had done nothing to hide his identity. These women would die, as would any who followed. But before they did, he hit upon another idea for his project. The ice princess attitude of Chris gave it to him. You couldn't have an A-list party without more people. He would invite a few select men to share his dark house; men who like himself hated these bitches.

His first choice came easily. One night while having sex with Chris, he slapped her because she was staring off into space.

"You're just like Gary," she said.

What about inviting Gary to the island? Gary could have Chris as much as he wanted and Sebastian could watch on the monitors. Could Gary keep a secret? They worked together on stolen art deals. Gary was deeply involved in illegal importing. Sebastian knew he was unscrupulous. Was he also willing to hide this dark secret?

A few days later he flew to Miami and called Gary. At lunch, Sebastian mentioned Chris. A torrent of expletives followed. Gary had definitely not gotten over her. They talked of the rich bitches who think they have it all. "What if Chris was a prisoner?" Sebastian played with him. Gary took the bait. If he had Chris tied up somewhere, he would make her his sex slave. The "what ifs" continued, until Sebastian knew he had found his first ally.

The next weekend he invited Gary to the bright house on the far side of the island. They got drunk and Sebastian told him the secret. He had Chris, and Gary could make love to her the whole weekend if he wanted. They would get more women and have parties. But if Gary ever told anyone about the island, his death would be immediate and the most painful imaginable. Gary's lust for Chris made the decision easy. That night a double date took place in the dark house on Reef Key.

CHAPTER 43

In the beginning Sebastian worried about the FBI, Interpol, or some private investigator stumbling on his paradise prison. But when he had taken care of one agency and saw the others making no progress, he became bolder. He planned his greatest triumph—the abduction of Jessica Lawrence, the movie star. He had fantasized about her when he was in school. Now those fantasies would become reality. Fearing that her absence would be too well publicized, he faked her death. She was scheduled to fly on a small private plane from Naples to Nassau, in the Bahamas. He bought off her pilot, then arranged for their plane to land on a dirt runway on a unpopulated Bahamian island. The pilot told Jessica there was an emergency. Venta was there to greet them. He took Jessica and told the pilot the rest of his money would be waiting for him in Nassau. But he didn't tell the pilot that on the trip back to Nassau, his instruments would be jammed. He was simply told to fly low over the water. It was a stroke of luck that the pilot's body was never found after the crash. Sharks probably destroyed all the evidence.

As months went by and nobody put the disappearances of Chris, Fanee and Jessica together, more women were abducted and brought to the dark house. The abusers grew to five. They called themselves The Partnership. Gary had a friend Ted Steinman, a wealthy owner of a chain of shoe stores. He had always been kept off the A-list. Now he was creating his own. Sebastian decided to include Clorio Tinto, another Argentinean who grew up in Miami. In school, they had formed an alliance with their cruelty. Clorio was gay. He asked if the parties could include some men so that he could be satisfied. Sebastian found the idea intriguing, and Sam was abducted. The fifth man, whose real name and occupation were known only to Sebastian, enjoyed Chris and Paine and their superior attitudes. But the man, known as Arthur when he was on the island, also wanted to watch another man—a straight male captive—have sex with the women.

If another male hostage was brought in, Clorio said he wanted to have sex with him, too. They argued over who would have the rights to the new captive. Sebastian always deferred to Arthur. That made the others wonder who he really was. Clorio vowed he would find out.

Arthur picked Jeff from photos taken at a party in Aspen. It was Arthur who decided what woman Jeff made love to. Clorio could have Jeff whenever Arthur was busy elsewhere.

Sebastian especially liked the kidnappings at sea. Everybody on the cruise ships thought the rich bitches had fallen overboard. Instead each was stowed in the cargo hold in his false-bottom crate. He had actually reached the point where he thought there were enough captives, when Eva insulted him at the party. Watching his father fondle her, he decided to add her to the parties. He wondered if he should find Binky Brandon, too. No, she was probably a cow by now. He had the pick of the most beautiful women in the world. He had little fear of being caught. He was after all a Guyera. He was all-powerful.

CHAPTER 44

Jazz's date with Ben had gone well. He kept his tongue in his mouth, not hers. He was a perfect gentleman, except for sitting alongside her at the restaurant instead of across from her. That meant a lot of rubbing thighs. But she could deal with that. While they waited for the entrees, she asked about Graham.

"I'm not going to talk about another agent," he said. "Except to warn you he is not to be trusted."

"Why?"

"I'm not sure what his agenda is. He certainly is not working this A-list case the way he should."

"What do you mean?"

"How much progress have you seen?"

"Well, I don't want to defend him. But this is a complex case. And now with Sam's death, we may all have to go back to the drawing board."

"Maybe Graham doesn't want anybody at the drawing board."

"What are you saying?"

"I don't want to scare you, but it's possible Graham is involved. Didn't you tell me he showed up in Colorado and the diary disappeared, not to mention all the killings?"

"Are you saying he murdered all these people?"

"I'm not saying anything except that he is not to be trusted. I'm doing some investigating on my own."

"My money is still on Sebastian. Maybe he is a serial killer. And this island he has, Reef Key in Florida, tell me about it."

"I don't know much more about it then you do. Why the island now?"

"Well, you first suggested it. What if the island is somehow involved? He takes them there, kills them there."

"That's a bit macabre, isn't it?" Ben put his hand on her thigh.

"This is macabre case." She took his hand off her thigh.

"All right, I'll ask him to let me see the island."

"I would love to go, too."

"It's only by invitation Jazz. This is not a tourist stop."

"I know. But maybe you could take me."

"Eat your fish."

When he escorted her home, he kissed her gently on the lips, patted Willie and said goodnight. She didn't know what to make of it.

★ ★ ★ ★ ★

Dressing to meet Mrs. Whitman the next night, Jazz felt like a schoolgirl on the first day of classes. She changed her outfit three times, finally deciding on a conservative blue suit. She pulled her hair back into a pony tail. When that looked too casual, she put it up in a modified French twist.

What was wrong with her? She hadn't spoken to Wit since he walked out of her apartment. He probably had forgotten her by now. Still, she was curious about what he might have found out about Guyera. She also wanted to tell him what Ben said about Graham. If the meeting with Mrs. Whitman went well, she would call him.

Riding the elevator to the floor where Wit's mother was staying, Jazz remembered the icicles when they first met. Maybe this encounter would go better.

"Miss Billings, you're on time, a plus for you." Doris Whitman motioned for Jazz to enter the massive hotel room. There was no sign that anybody was staying there. Not an article of clothing was in view. Not a glass or towel looked used. Could anybody be that neat?

"Please sit down," Wit's mother said, pointing to the couch. She sat in a chair by the window. "You probably wonder why I have asked to see you." Jazz offered a small smile. "My son speaks of you often, too often for my taste. I must be blunt, Miss Billings. I have an aversion to newspaper people. I think you feed off of the ills of others.

"Two years ago a reporter called and told me my husband had been killed in a car crash. I had to be sedated. It turned out he wasn't dead. But I didn't know that the reporter was wrong. I found out several hours later that my husband was still alive and in the hospital. I rushed there and a few days later he did die. So I mourned his passing twice. How dare a reporter invade my privacy like that? And the way you handled the Blakes' tragedy only reinforces how callous you all are. I think your interest in the disappearance of my daughter and the others is for your own self-aggrandizement. You want to win another Pulitzer."

Jazz had to speak. "I assure you Mrs. Whitman—."

"I'm not interested in your assurances. I thought we should have this little chat, because I want to make it clear. You are not going to win any Pulitzer off my family's suffering. Christine means too much to me. My son may be blinded by your whatever, but I am not. I think what you are doing, what you are writing, is dangerous for the safety of my child. I told James that. He thinks your articles help. I think he is foolish. I told him that too. So please, no more calling my home asking to speak to me. Because I will never speak to you on this subject, or probably any other." She glared at Jazz. Her mouth was so pursed she looked as if she had sucked on a lemon.

"I'm sorry that you think I have ulterior motives," Jazz said. "I am a reporter. It is my job to investigate and to write about what I find. As I told Mr. Hayes, I am committed to this story. I want to know what happened to your daughter and the others. I have some ideas how to do that. It would be helpful if you would work with me. That's why I've called you several times. But please understand, I will continue on this story, regardless of what you decide to do."

"Well, you are a cheeky thing, aren't you? Nothing like James's other women. I wonder if that's what attracts him. Yes, Miss Billings, I know my son had some type of relationship with you, although it was probably just a one night stand." Jazz cringed. Mrs. Whitman didn't notice as she went on. "He prefers to date women of his social class. I don't mean to be unkind. I'm sure you have admirable qualities. But my son is destined for greatness. We haven't ruled out President of the United States. The woman by his side should be like Eleanor Roosevelt. A Barbara Walters will simply not do. You're throwing yourself at him is really in vain."

Jazz was furious, so furious she simply could not think of a thing to say that wasn't a curse word. She wondered what this woman would do if she just gave her the finger.

"Well I'm glad we had this little chat," Mrs. Whitman said, standing up. "I do not wish you ill, Miss Billings. But I hope you realize it would be best if you stayed out of the lives of my son and myself. I hope we understand each other."

"I think I understand you perfectly," Jazz finally said. "I'm not sure you care to understand anything about me. You don't have to worry about a relationship between your son and me. I have not thrown myself at him. Did you know he hired a private investigator to follow me? Does he get that paranoia from you?"

"Miss Billings, you have—."

"Please, no more. I'm going to leave now. You know the sad thing. Of all the victims I've written about, I liked your daughter the best. From what I found, she seemed the most natural, the most unassuming. I don't know where she got that from."

Now it was Mrs. Whitman's turn to be silent. Before she could think of anything to say, Jazz left, slamming the door behind her.

CHAPTER 45

"Could it have been any worse?" Jazz asked Carrie. She called Carrie the minute she got back to the office. She had to talk about the meeting. The conversation would forever be frozen in her memory banks. What an obnoxious woman Wit's mother was.

"Maybe she's like a lioness defending her cub," Carrie said. "She feels threatened by you—from two fronts. First the loss of her daughter and her inability to do anything while you keep getting scoop after scoop. Then there is her son. She can sense how strong his feelings for you are."

"Right, so strong I haven't heard from him in three weeks."

"Well who was the one who started the fight?"

"Carrie, who was the one who put a private eye on me?"

"To protect you."

"To spy on me and find out what I've got on the case."

"You could be wrong, Jazz."

"Why are you defending him? You are supposed to be my friend."

"I am. That is why I defend him. Because I know how much you care for him. You just won't admit it."

"Let's change the subject. My mother is arriving tomorrow. Christmas Eve dinner is my treat, right? We'll go to a restaurant down by the water. And you're having Christmas Day dinner."

"Yes, It will be a houseful. My brother Bob and his wife Suzanne are coming from Ohio. They'll stay with Suzanne's parents who live on the Island. And my cousin Steve from New Jersey is coming. Am I crazy to have so many?"

"No. It will be good. This way my mother can't spend the whole time pumping me about my love life."

"I can't wait to meet your mother."

"My mother? My mother makes Doris Whitman look like a pussycat."

☆ ☆ ☆ ☆ ☆

The morning of Christmas Eve, it rained, a hard cold rain. A few hours before her mother's plane was scheduled to land, Jazz went to the office. It was supposed to be her day off, but she decided to do some research. Because of the holiday, it would be days before the world of work was right again. Nobody would be around to answer calls until after New Year's.

For New Year's Eve, Jazz hadn't made any plans. She was invited to two parties but didn't want to go alone. She wondered what Wit was doing for New Year's. Probably some black tie gala in Naples or Palm Beach. She would probably spend the night with the one devoted male left in her life—Willie.

As she got off the elevator on the fourth floor, she was surprised to see Joe standing there. He was supposed to be in Fort Lauderdale spending the holidays with his sister Helen.

"Don't ask," he said. "Helen's sick with the flu. The whole family has the flu. Since I didn't want the flu, I'm staying here."

"What are you going to do tomorrow?"

"For Christmas? Have a turkey TV dinner, I guess."

"Well you'll have to come to Carrie's. My mother and I are

going, along with about twelve of Carrie's relatives. She's not going to mind another person."

"I couldn't Jazz, that would be an imposition. I've only met Carrie once."

"That's more than my mother has. I'm sure it would be all right. I'll call her. Please say you'll come. You can't spend Christmas alone. We'll meet at my apartment at 2:00 p.m." They walked together towards Jazz's desk.

"Okay," Joe said. "Call Carrie, see what she says." He was about to walk on, when Jazz stopped him.

"Joe, Do you have a minute? I want to talk out this so-called suicide of Sam Blake's."

"Sure let's go to my office." They headed down another corridor past a maze of empty desks. A skeleton crew worked the day before Christmas.

"All right, "'Joe said taking a seat behind his desk. "Why are you calling it a so-called suicide when even the FBI seems satisfied?"

"Well, for one thing, I have a real problem with the FBI agents who are involved in this case. Let's talk about Ron Graham. First he gives me the A-list eight. Why did he do that? You know we both thought that was strange. Then he shows up in Colorado and the copy of the diary disappears. Coincidence? Then he commands me to be at the crime scene where Sam's suicide note is discovered, and gives me the contents. Is this my guardian angel, or is he using me for some ulterior purpose?"

"What purpose could that be?"

"I don't know. I'm paranoid. Ben thinks he could be involved. Then there is Ben, who says he's an undercover FBI agent. But I can't check that out because he tells me it could get him killed. He says I shouldn't trust Graham. But he has some ax to grind with Graham. He says they had a falling out when he was assigned to cover the Guyera family and the import case. Graham tried to get him transferred off the case. At least that's what he tells me. And since he isn't supposed to mention to anybody he works for the FBI, I'm not supposed to say anything either. So how do I check him out? Something is not kosher about the FBI's handling of these cases. Why are they turning up nothing? I'd ask our Washington bureau for a good reliable source in the FBI, but I'd have to deal with Ed Towstin, and you know how he feels about me."

"Well, I can certainly make some calls. But maybe you are getting a bit paranoid. Unless —. You'd tell me Jazz, wouldn't you, if you were in danger? Nobody's tried to hurt you since that automobile thing in Michigan?"

"No, although there are times I feel I'm being watched and followed. But then I think it could be Wit's stupid private eye."

"I don't know what that means. What private eye?"

"It's a long story. Congressman Whitman and I know each from another life. Anyway, he hired a private eye to follow me. He put one on Sebastian Guyera as well. He says mine was to protect me. I say it was to find out what I knew. We had quite a fight about it. I think he called off the investigator following me. But I really don't know that. Anyway I'm fine. Let's talk about Sam Blake's death. If he did kill himself and Fred and Roger, why would the diary disappear?"

"Maybe it's not related to his death."

"But it is related to Roger's death. A witness heard whoever killed him, say 'Let go of the God-damn bag.' Now does that sound like a revengeful lover?"

"It could, if he was trying to make it look like a robbery."

"Then take his wallet and his watch, which was not done. And Sam Blake was a fairly well known photographer. Wouldn't he be recognized in his hometown airport, or anywhere else he was in the last six months?"

"Not if he was in disguise."

"For six months? And why wouldn't he have contacted his

parents, his sister? This was a close family. And Roger talked to Fred before he got the diary. He was deeply in love with Sam. It just doesn't wash that Sam disappeared on his own, killed his devoted Fred, then Roger, then himself. But look at it this way. If somebody else was responsible for Sam's and the others' disappearances, and he thought his name was in Sam's diary, he would have to get the diary and kill the two people who had access to it. And if that someone is Guyera, he now knows his name was in the diary and so he had to break the link between himself and Sam.

"If all that is true, then we have a major problem."

"What's that?"

"It wasn't two, but three people who had access to the diary. You also saw it. If your premise is right, he's going to have to kill you too."

CHAPTER 46

In the warm Florida sun, Sebastian's thoughts were on A.J. Billings. After Sam's suicide note, most of the media began questioning whether any of the A-list disappearances were connected. One tabloid reported a sighting of Paine Hayes in South Africa. That was good. That was what he wanted. But his sources said A.J. was still digging, still researching information about him.

He knew she had seen the copy of the diary and passed on what she read to the Denver police. None of that would stand up in court. She had no proof he was involved.

But now there was a reward. Would someone talk? It wouldn't be any of the partnership. He made sure of their allegiances with the tapes and pictures of their partying—in several cases, their brutal partying. The four men knew he had the videos and photos. And they didn't know where he kept them. Besides, they enjoyed their secret lives as much as he did.

Venta and Ralph? No. Family honor was involved. Not only family honor but family survival. They knew he would kill their family members if he was betrayed. The problem was A.J. Billings. Something would have to be done about her. Ralph had tried a quick hit and run in Michigan. That was stupid. The next attempt would be more clever, and successful. And it would have to be soon. She was taking time away from his party plans for Christmas and New Year's. He couldn't believe how excited he was about both holidays. This would be his first Christmas with his new family. He had begun to think of his captives in that light. He was going to allow them to sit down together for a Christmas Eve dinner. Christmas Day, he had promised to spend with his father in Palm Beach. But tonight he would receive the presents his captives were giving him.

As shopping was impossible, he told them he wanted gifts of writing. He ordered each to write down what they would have liked to give him, and how much he meant to them.

He expected glowing remarks. Although he shared the female captives with the rest of the partnership, the women knew they lived or died at his pleasure. The male captives were different. Sebastian kept them only for the pleasure of his associates. Clorio had been furious when Sam was killed. He immediately asked for another gay man to satisfy his needs. In the meantime he used Jeff Worthington, making Jeff's life even more loathsome.

Worthington was getting to be a problem. The women were turning to him as a kind of protector. Kidnapping heterosexual men was not what he originally planned. He considered getting rid of Worthington and abducting another gay man for Clorio. But Worthington was a favorite of Arthur's who enjoyed his voyeurism. He delighted in watching Jeff with Paine or Chris. As Arthur was important to him, Sebastian reluctantly allowed Worthington to live. But he would tell Venta to watch him more closely.

A.J. was the immediate problem. How to deal with her? How? And then it came to him. A perfect solution. It would make the holidays even more exciting. He would set it all in motion tomorrow. Tonight a party awaited.

CHAPTER 47

In her small room, Paine dressed for the party. She didn't know who would choose her tonight. She didn't care. Paine was a survivor. While some of the others had been broken, not Paine Hayes. Her body might be theirs, but she would never surrender her mind. These emasculated males who had to pretend women found them fascinating. They were scum. And Paine treated them as such. Her disdain fascinated the partnership.

Each man tried to conquer her, yet each knew he failed. To them, Paine Hayes epitomized the rich bitch. By being so bitchy, she unwittingly kept their obsession with her alive.

Kensington Washington and Spring Bellingham had been easy to conquer. They were so fearful of displeasing their captors they became almost slaves, doing whatever was asked of them and being grateful for any kind word or gesture. Kensington had been taken because she was related to George Washington and pretty. But she didn't have a strong personality and as a captive she simply did whatever she was told.

It was Spring's uncanny resemblance to a young Michelle Pfeiffer that made Sebastian choose her. As a boy he had fantasies about the actress. Now here she was still young. But Spring did not act like a star. In captivity, she was timid and the most submissive of the group.

As the months went by, the captives gained more freedom to talk and socialize during the parties. Except for the new arrival, Eva Long. For some reason she was kept apart from the others. Paine knew she was there. She saw her briefly one night. Eva was being let out of her room at the far end of the hall to be "escorted" to one of the host's rooms. She tried to talk but Ralph quickly pushed her away. Paine wasn't sure who she was but when she described her to Chris and the others, Chris said it could be her friend Eva. Then Paine remembered the interior designer she had seen at several parties. Yes, that's who it was. Chris was beside herself. She needed to talk to Eva. But she never got the chance.

As the only black woman, Eva was subjected to the most degrading uses by the partnership. When she realized that Chris and the others had been victimized like this for months, the hopelessness of the situation overwhelmed her. Where was A.J? Where was the FBI? Hadn't they figured it out by now? Each person has their breaking point. After another night of being passed from one partner to the other and Sebastian "branding" her by taking white paint and painting his initials on her dark buttocks, Eva took a scarf from one of her dresses, tied it to the ceiling fan in her room, and hung herself.

When her body was discovered the next morning, Sebastian's only response was "One less to kill." The captives found out what happened a few days later, when in a drunken rage, Sebastian yelled at Kensington Washington "You can either do what I say, or go hang yourself like Eva Long."

Learning that her best friend had committed suicide before she could talk to her, devastated Chris. She thought of ending her life as well. But something inside willed her to go on. She was the one who had encouraged the others not to give up. She had handled her humiliation in a different manner, by becoming almost friendly with the partnership. She appeared to enjoy herself dancing with the men. She led the group in "YMCA." She was the life of the party. "It's my way of surviving," she whispered to Paine. "Believe me, I will be first in line with the machete when the times comes."

Tracey Wise, the singer, was as defiant as Paine. One night they had joined together in a rendition of *RESPECT*, the Aretha Franklin hit. The irony was not lost on the group. When the two finished singing, there was silence. Then Jeff applauded. Chris and Sam joined in. The rest were too afraid to respond, fearful of what the partnership might do. But Arthur began clapping, and so did Clorio, forcing Sebastian to smile.

An alliance was formed that night of those who still possessed their souls. When Sam disappeared, the group mourned. They knew he had to be dead. They also knew if they weren't rescued, they would be killed too. And rescue seemed such a distant hope. They still didn't know where they were. How could anyone else?

Chris and Paine talked often of what Sam had seen. After he died, they made a decision. They would not wait for death to come to them. They would devise some plan of escape. Paine was in favor of finding the other house. Perhaps there was a computer or a phone there. Chris was skeptical. She wanted to find a boat and get off the island. "But how far would we have to go?" Paine asked. "And in what direction?"

The escape talk usually ended there. "We will find a way," Chris always said. "We will get out of here."

"I just hope we're breathing when we do," Paine said.

CHAPTER 48

Carrie had no reason to worry about Christmas. Families merging and making merry made for a joyful holiday.

As they had for decades, Jazz and her mother exchanged gifts at 8:00 a.m. on Christmas morning. Jazz never knew what to get her mother. Nothing seemed to make Delilah happy. "Buy me clothes," she often said. But if the size was right, the color was wrong. If the color worked, the length didn't. Delilah's mouth would tighten into this little smile and she would say "How thoughtful of you, Agatha Jasmine." Jazz immediately knew she hated the gift.

This year she stayed away from clothes and bought her mother a hand-painted music box with a delicate little carousel horse on top. It played her mother's favorite song *Somewhere My Love*. Delilah appeared genuinely touched.

"Now open your present," she instructed her daughter. Her gifts were usually homemade. Jazz had a closet full of crocheted shawls and strangely shaped ceramic bowls. But this year Delilah gave her a book—an autographed copy of *To Kill a Mockingbird* by Harper Lee.

"I found it in a bookstore in Atlanta," she said.

Jazz hugged her mother. "I love it. I will treasure it." The two looked at each other and smiled—an open loving smile. It was a moment Jazz would always treasure.

At Carrie's party, Joe hit it off with Marcia, an ex-wife of Carrie's cousin Steve. Steve brought both his ex-wives. He was closer to them now then when he was married to them. The two women had developed a friendship as well. Both were named Marcia, which made for an interesting dinner conversation. "Marcia, please pass the potatoes" resulted in both women reaching for the dish.

A good time was had by all, Jazz thought as she lay in bed that night. Even Willie loved his gifts—a new squeaky toy, and a bag of beef jerky treats. Jazz considered buying him a new green rug. The old one was so tattered. But he didn't seem as attached to it anymore, now that he was a proven stud. He had made several female Labradors happy, and pregnant. Stud-dog was his nickname.

Draped over her feet at the end of the bed, he snored loudly. They both were asleep when the phone rang. Groggy, Jazz looked at the clock. It read 11:30 p.m.

She reached for the phone. "Hi," she heard on the other end. The voice sent its customary electric charge through her body. "I'm sorry it's so late," Wit said. "Were you asleep?"

"No," she lied. There was a pause. The tingling continued. What technically was a tingle? She could be making medical history.

"I wanted to wish you a Merry Christmas," he said. "I've been thinking about you, and then my mother announced at dinner that she met with you. I'm interested in knowing what that was about. She refused to tell me."

"It was not pleasant."

"My mother can be that way. Was it about Chris?"

"It was about several subjects. I prefer not to go into them. Let's just say that my career choice and me are not her two favorite things."

Another pause. "Did you have a nice Christmas?"

She could feel herself softening. "Yes, it was really wonderful. My mother is here and we went to Carrie's for dinner. She had her whole family, and Joe came from the office. We had the turkey and all the trimmings." She paused. "Wit, why are you calling?"

"I miss talking to you about Chris. I have some information that I thought you might find interesting. I also wondered how you were dealing with the news that Sam killed Roger."

"I don't think Sam killed Roger. I don't think Sam killed himself. But as they say, especially in my business, that's another story. What new information do you have?"

"Could we get together and talk about it?"

"Every time we get together something happens. And then we wind up regretting it."

"I don't regret it Jazz." She didn't say anything. Her heart was pounding so hard she thought he could hear it.

"I was thinking," he continued. "I know this is probably too late. But do you have plans New Year's Eve? I thought maybe you could come down here. There's this dinner dance at the Ritz-Carlton. If that's too much we could just have a quiet dinner somewhere. I have plenty of room at my place. You could stay there."

"I'm surprised you don't have plans."

"I do, I did, I—" he knew he said the wrong thing. "No, listen to me. My mother organized a dinner in Palm Beach for New Year's. She invited the chairman of Teem Oil. She figures he will finance my senate bid—that's her idea—the senate bid, not mine. At least not right now. Anyway, he has a divorced daughter. My mother made sure the daughter was available and invited her as well. I didn't find out about all this until today. I told my mother to forget it. That's when she mentioned you, and that maybe I would rather spend New Year's dictating to a reporter. It didn't seem like a bad idea. That's when she said she met with you in

New York. The only thing she would tell me about the meeting was that you are after my money. Are you, after my money?"

"How much do you have?"

"Enough to splurge on New Year's Eve. Will you come down here?"

"Wit, I need to think about this. I was going to call you. But I was going to suggest that we keep our relationship strictly professional."

"I want more, Jazz. I can't stop thinking of you—of your mouth, your body. I love your breasts. Have I told you that?"

Was this a dream? Was this phone sex? "Wit. I—." A knock on her bedroom door was immediately followed by its opening. Dressed in a pink peignoir, Delilah barged into the room. "Agatha Jasmine," her mother said, "Are you asleep? Oh, I'm sorry you're on the phone. I need a Tylenol. I have a splitting headache." Jazz knew her mother would continue talking. And she did. "Who are you talking to so late at night? Is it someone I know?"

"I'll have to get back to you," Jazz told Wit.

"Tonight? I'll give you my phone number here in Palm Beach."

"Tomorrow. Where will you be?"

"Naples, but I'd prefer tonight."

"Good-night Wit."

"Good-night Jazz."

"Who is Wit?" her mother called from the bathroom. "Do you keep the Tylenol in here?" She was opening the medicine cabinet. Jazz realized if she changed the subject her mother would forget the phone call.

"I know where it is. Here." She had found a bottle in her night-stand and brought it to her mother. "Wasn't that a fascinating party with the two Marcias?"

"Yes, it was. You know we had two Evelyns once in Decatur. They were sisters. Both their parents had mothers named Evelyn, so they decided to name their two daughters after them. They said

190

if they had named only one child Evelyn, the other Evelyn would have been upset." Jazz laughed. Her mother continued on about the two Evelyns and forgot about Wit's call. Jazz didn't. She knew it would be a long night.

The next day after Carrie told her she was crazy if she didn't go, and Joe, now dating Marcia The First, urged her to find something to care about besides work, Jazz decided to spend New Year's with Wit. She called the congressional office about 4:00. He wasn't there. So she left a message. "Please tell him Miss Billings called and she can make the appointment on the 31rst. She will call later in the week to arrange the time and place."

Two days later, they spoke briefly and decided to have a quiet New Year's at Wit's condo overlooking the gulf in the Park Shore area of Naples. He said they could walk the beach, eat at a waterfront restaurant, and then watch television as the ball dropped in Times Square. It sounded perfect. Jazz ordered the plane ticket. Because of the short notice it cost a fortune. She didn't care.

The next few days were spent researching Sebastian's island. She had found out that the FBI had a file on a wealthy Columbian woman who planned to kidnap John F. Kennedy, Jr. before he died and keep him as a sex slave on a secluded island she owned. What if Sebastian was actually doing that on his island?

Although it was considered part of Florida, Reef Key was miles west of Key West. Located between the Marquesas Islands and the Dry Tortugas, Reef Key had been a favorite haunt of pirates in the 1800s. A large coral reef surrounded much of the island. Thus its name. Armando bought it from a Texas businessman who built two homes there but rarely used it. The reef made the island inaccessible by boat except through one treacherous channel. Visitors usually arrived and departed by small planes, which landed on a narrow runway carved through the middle of the island.

Few outside Sebastian's inner circle had seen the place. Few could reach it. An isolated island owned by the man she felt certain was linked to the disappearances? It had to mean something.

Somehow she had to visit Reef Key. But it was too far from Miami to take a casual boat ride. How was she going to get there?

As if by psychic intervention, Ben called on December 29th. "You told me you wanted to see Reef Key," he said. "Well here's your chance. Sebastian has decided to host a small party on the island for New Year's Eve. I'm allowed to bring a guest. How would you like to be that guest?"

"Oh Ben, that would be great! But I've made plans for New Year's."

"You've got to be kidding. With who?"

"Congressman Whitman."

"Really? Well cancel him. This will be your only opportunity, and probably mine too. I thought we could do some investigating while everybody's sleeping it off on New Year's Day. If anything is there, we'll find it. Sebastian is supplying planes to caravan us all back and forth from Miami. He's also offered the jet for anybody who has to go farther distances. It's in New York now. If you can get to LaGuardia in an hour, you can take it down here with some of his friends. That will give you a chance to talk to them. I could meet you in Miami, and we could head for the island tomorrow. Jazz, this is an amazing opportunity for you. And I need to bring a date who knows the real reason I'm going there."

Riding on Guyera's jet? Visiting his island? She couldn't turn this down. She owed it to the families she was writing about. She would have to tell Wit. Hopefully he would understand.

"I need time to pack and make arrangements for Willie," she said.

"You've got your overnight bag there at the office. You told me you always have it ready. Just get to General Aviation at the airport. You can call Carrie from there. You know she'll take care of things. And you can buy an outfit for New Year's down here. They dress differently in Florida you know."

Yes, she did know. Why not go on a little shopping spree? Live a little.

"All right, I'll do it. I'll just tell Joe and head off to the airport."

"That's my girl. I'll see you in Miami tonight."

She rushed to Joe's office. He wasn't there. Then Jazz remembered. He was meeting Marcia for lunch. She wrote a note telling him where she was going and left it taped to his phone. Then she headed for the elevator. A taxi was dropping someone off as she reached the street. "My lucky day," she said to the driver. "LaGuardia."

As the cab darted in and out of New York traffic, she reached into her purse and pulled out her cell phone. She tried dialing but the battery was dead.

The cab arrived at the General Aviation building 35 minutes later, just about the time Joe returned from lunch, and just a few minutes after a man with large ears left Joe's office after removing Jazz's note from the phone. In its place he put a typed message. It read: "Have decided to take some R and R in Florida. I even have a New Year's date. I may be gone for a week or so. Will contact you in the New Year.—Jazz."

CHAPTER 49

Jazz had no trouble finding the Guyera jet. "It's over there, the one with the large red G& G painted on the side," an airport employee told her. She walked over to a man standing at the bottom of the plane's stairs. "Excuse me," she said. "A friend of Sebastian Guyera's—Ben Luvana—asked me to come here and possibly get a ride to Miami."

"You must be A.J. Billings," the man said. "Ben called me. I'm Ted Steinman. I'm a friend of Sebastian's, hitching a ride too. Come aboard, I think the pilot is anxious to take off."

Jazz thought of Wit and Willie. "I was hoping I'd be able to make some phone calls."

"There will be plenty of time in Miami. I have to call my office later too."

As soon as they boarded, the jet door closed and the pilot started the engines.

The interior of the jet was plusher than Jazz imagined. Beige leather couches and chairs formed several conversation groupings. A large desk with a marble top and a bright red leather chair were anchored in the back of the cabin next to a door that opened into another compartment. "The bedroom," Ted said, following Jazz's eyes. She ignored his suggestive look and took a seat in a swivel chair that allowed her to face the window.

Ted plopped down in the chair facing hers. He couldn't stop smiling as his eyes traveled down her body to the shapely crossed legs and the edge of her skirt. She quickly uncrossed her legs and pulled down the skirt. Is he leering at me? she wondered. What could she expect from a friend of Sebastian's?

With little traffic on the runways, the jet was airborne in less than ten minutes. "A record for taking off at LaGuardia, don't you think?" Ted asked.

"Could be," Jazz said. "Do you use this jet often?"

"Only on special occasions. Sebastian's New Year's Eve party will be that. Now tell me all about yourself, Miss Billings."

"I'm a reporter, Mr. Steinman. That means I'm used to asking the questions. May I?"

He nodded.

"How long have you known Sebastian. Where did you meet him? Is he as mysterious as some suggest?"

"Questions about Sebastian. I was hoping your questions would be about me."

Jazz said nothing, so he answered. "Sebastian and I met through a friend. It turns out we have mutual interests."

"Such as?"

"Well, we both love beautiful women. That is why it is such a pleasure to be alone with you."

"Are you married, Mr. Steinman?"

"Ted, please. No, I'm having too much fun. And how about you A.J.? May I call you that? Any special male in your life? Besides your dog?"

"How did you know about my dog?"

Ted's face changed, as if he had said something he shouldn't. Then the smile returned. "Because you've written about him. He is a champion Labrador, isn't he?"

"Yes." She had written about Willie, and talked about him on television shows. Still Ted's knowledge of her personal life was unnerving. It also reminded her to call Carrie about Willie. He couldn't stay inside alone, indefinitely.

But Jazz needn't worry. Willie was no longer in her apartment. A man with large ears had taken him. It was so easy. Willie was never a watchdog. Add to his already docile nature a dangling piece of raw steak, and Willie would follow anyone anywhere. His tail wagged as he happily pranced out the door with the stranger.

After stowing the Labrador in a cage in the back of a white minivan, the man headed back to the Farley apartment. Carrie and Jamie were out, as they were every afternoon between 1:00 and 3:00. The two attended a play session called Mom and Me run by the local Y. That left the Farley apartment vacant. It took no time for the man with big ears to slip in and alter the family's answering machine. Carrie's message remained, but incoming calls would no longer be recorded.

As he left, the man taped a typed note to the front door. It read: "Had a chance to leave for Florida and see Wit early. He's supplying a private jet and Willie is invited. We'll be gone until after New Year's. Maybe longer. I'll tell all when I return.—J."

★ ★ ★ ★ ★

As the Guyera jet cruised 30,000 feet over Virginia, Ted unpacked a special cell phone from his briefcase. It was 2:00 p.m. "My battery is low but I think it's good for one call. You could make that call." He handed the phone to Jazz. "Who will it be?"

Jazz decided on Carrie. Wit could wait until Miami.

The Farley answering machine picked up. "You've reached Carrie, George, and Jamie. We can't come to the phone. Please leave your message at the beep."

"Hi Carrie, It's Jazz. You won't believe this but I'm in the Guyera jet on my way to Miami. Ben and I are going to the

Guyera island in the Florida Keys for New Year's. I'll explain everything to Wit. Can you take care of Willie? Thanks, I'll call you again later."

Jazz felt better. Willie would be in good hands.

"Is the dog taken care of?" Sebastian asked his associate, now in Kennedy Airport, and waiting to board a jet to Miami.

"Yes, I stashed him in the Bronx. I told the owner of this ware-house that I'd be traveling. I might not be back for a couple of weeks. I gave the guy a couple of hundred. He seemed happy. I figured you'd decide later whether you needed the dog anymore."

"Good, now you better get back here. We have a special guest arriving."

CHAPTER 50

When the jet landed at 3:30, Jazz was relieved the flight was over. She had gotten nothing from Ted, other than leers. This did not bode well for the weekend. But Ben would be there. And she could see how Sebastian interacted with women. Which women would be especially interesting.

A black limousine waited as the jet door opened. "Ben asked me to take you to the hotel," Ted said. "I guess he booked you a room."

Jazz was anxious to make calls—to Wit, Joe, and Carrie again. She probably should phone her mother too, and tell her where she would be on New Year's. They always spoke on the first day of the year.

It would be best to make calls in the privacy of her hotel room. But it took an hour and a half to reach it. Ted stopped at one of his stores. She waited in the back seat for a half-an-hour. "I should have taken a cab," she told him when he finally returned.

The hotel turned out to be a small inn off a side street in South Beach. There were only four rooms. Ben, Ted, and Jazz were booked in three of them.

The desk clerk handed her a note from Ben. It said he would

pick her up at 5:15. He had something interesting to show her. She looked at her watch. It was already 5:00.

In her room she tried dialing Wit's office number, but she kept getting a busy signal. The same for Carrie's number. She called the front desk.

"We've been having a problem with the cable and the phones," the desk clerk told her. "They're fixing something across the street." Jazz looked out the window and saw a construction crew working on the road. Who knew when they would be done. Behind them was a small cafe. It could have a public phone.

She hurriedly changed clothes and raced out the door as the desk assistant shouted something. The pay phone was in the back of the cafe. A man in a brown UPS uniform was using it.

"Honey, I can't get home until after 9:00. They have me working overtime—Well, you'll just have to take care of it. He'll have to listen to you." Jazz looked at her watch. It was 5:10. "All right, put him on." The man turned, looked at Jazz and rolled his eyes as if to say, "This is not something I want to be doing." She looked at her watch as if to say, "I'm in a hurry. Get off the phone!"

He turned his back to her. "Hi Howie. Your mother says you are talking about going out and not studying for the history test tonight. Now you know what the teacher said. One more failing grade and— Howie, I don't want to hear that. You're not going out. Do you understand me—Put your mother back on." Jazz tried tapping her foot. "All right, look, someone here wants to use the phone. I told Howie he's not going out. I'll see you after 9:00—Yes I know —I know – all right, I'll see you later." He finally hung up. Jazz practically grabbed the phone out of his hand. She dialed Wit's office number in Naples. A receptionist answered. The congressman was in Washington for the day. "It's important he get this message," Jazz said. "Tell him A.J. Billings called and—"

"The reporter?" the receptionist interrupted.

"Yes, tell him I can't make New Year's Eve. I'm with Ben

Luvaṇa. We're going to Guyera's Island in the Keys. Do you have that?"

"I think so." Jazz heard footsteps. Ben was rushing towards her. "Make sure he gets the message, okay?"

"Right, Miss Billings."

She hung up as Ben reached her. "I've been looking for you," he said. "Who were you talking to?"

"I was trying to reach someone," Jazz said. "But I wasn't able to."

"Well, are you ready to go? We've got a busy night." He escorted her out of the restaurant and into a gold Lexus.

Meanwhile Wit's district receptionist was calling Washington. When she told the congressman's personal secretary that the reporter A.J. Billings was trying to reach him, she was connected to Betty Norris. Betty took the message. The New Year's comment really got to her. "This is getting serious," she said to herself. She had to stop this relationship with Billings. When the congressman phoned later she told him A.J. Billings had called. "Where is she?" he asked. She didn't like his excited tone.

"She didn't say," Betty lied. "She just wanted you to know she couldn't make New Year's Eve. She was spending it with Ben Luvana."

There was silence on the other end. She could feel the hurt through the phone. She almost told him about Guyera's island. But it was time to practice tough love. "Wit?" she said. The silence was agonizing. Still she said nothing.

"Thanks, Betty," he finally said. "I'm heading back to Naples."

"Why don't you stay here for New Year's?" she asked.

"It's best I get back," he said. "I'll talk to you in a day or two."

CHAPTER 51

B en kept Jazz busy until past midnight. First, they took a boat
ride around Biscayne Bay. The boat, a 40-foot Sea Ray, was
owned by a friend of Ben's.

It was a wonderful trip, seeing all the luxurious homes including one of the Guyeras. But Jazz didn't know what it had to do
with the story. When she questioned Ben, he looked sheepish.
"I just thought you might have a good time and forget about your
work for a while. You won't stop thinking about it once we get to
the Island."

She certainly couldn't stop thinking about it then. So he took
her to dinner at a restaurant that both Chris and Eva had frequented. He had learned it was the last place where anyone saw
Chris.

When Jazz asked their waiter about her, he said he remembered
the police questioning everyone, but the woman who waited on
Chris worked only days. Maybe Jazz could come back tomorrow?

"We are leaving early tomorrow," Ben said.

"I thought it wasn't until mid-day," Jazz said. "What about
buying an outfit for New Year's?"

"I have a surprise for you. I bought you something. You're

going to love it. I had to. It turns out that because of the holiday, the planes Sebastian chartered are only available in the morning. You have to be ready by 8:00."

After stopping in two South Beach lounges where the music was loud and the information limited, Jazz and Ben headed back to the inn. Their rooms faced each other across the hall.

"Want me to come in?" Ben asked as Jazz searched for her key.

"Not tonight I have a headache," she said. And it was true. Her head was pounding. And her heart was solidly in Wit's corner. But there was no denying Ben's sex appeal. He pulled her towards him and kissed her. When his tongue started probing her mouth and his hand landed on her breast, she pulled away.

"Tomorrow you may feel differently," he said.

"Good-night," she said opening her door. So much for being a gentleman. In the room she looked at the bedside clock, ten after twelve. Maybe she could reach Wit at home. She picked up her phone. There was still a busy signal.

The next morning there was no time to call anyone. When she turned over and looked at the clock, she was horrified to see it was ten of eight. She jumped out of bed and into the shower. Ben was knocking before she finished drying her hair.

"I'll be down in fifteen minutes," she shouted through the closed door.

After flinging everything she brought with her into the overnight bag, she headed downstairs. He sat in a small chair in the foyer. He did not seem happy.

"We'll have to buy breakfast on the way and bring it on the plane," he said.

They stopped at a small Cuban market a mile from the airport. He bought coffee and a greasy egg and sausage sandwich. She ordered hot tea and picked out an apple and a cranberry muffin.

They carried the food onto the plane. As they got on she realized they were the only ones on board. "Anybody else coming?"

Ben asked the pilot.

"Just Ted Steinman," came the answer.

"I guess the others already left," Ben told Jazz. A taxi pulled up and Ted jumped out. "Sorry I'm late," he said rushing on board.

The pilot immediately started the engine and they were airborne. It was a beautiful clear day. The waters of the Florida Straits looked aqua. Jazz could see all the cars heading down the Overseas Highway towards the Keys. They were soon over open water.

She had tried finding Reef Key on a map, but none of the charts in her research showed its exact location. Numerous tiny islands dot the shores of Florida. The Keys are the most well known because most of them are accessible by car via the Highway.

Reef Key was barely accessible even by plane. Most of the time Sebastian kept the runway covered with cut palm fronds. From the air it appeared as if there was no place to land. When anyone wanted to fly in, they radioed ahead and Venta or Ralph removed the palm branches.

After looking at miles and miles of open water, Jazz finally saw an island. "Is that it?" she asked.

"I don't know," Ben said.

Ted looked at him strangely. "Of course that's it," he told Jazz. "What else could it be?" he said to Ben. "Cuba?"

As they approached, the runway became visible. It was bordered by big signs. When they got nearer, Jazz could read them. "Private property, keep out. Violators won't live to tell about it." The signs were also along the shoreline. "They certainly keep the curious away," she said.

From the air, she could see a white sprawling house beside a beautiful beach. A sailboat bobbed on a mooring. A smaller boat with an outboard was pulled onto the beach, a crystal white beach with palm trees ringing the edge. "It's lovely," Jazz said.

Behind the house, a jungle of greenery seemed to envelop the rest of the island. Only the runway down the middle was cleared. As the plane circled the island, she thought she saw another structure on the other side of the island. She started to say something to Ben, and then decided not to. Maybe she could take a walk over there.

The landing was bumpy. The runway was made of packed-down earth and heavy rains caused major ruts. When the plane finally came to a halt, there was silence. The two men made no effort to move. "Come on, let's see this place," Jazz said unbuckling her seat belt.

"This should be quite an experience for you, A.J.," Ted said. "Sebastian is a very special host."

Already out of the plane, the pilot unloaded the bags and the passengers. Then he waved and took off. The three were alone. No one was there to greet them. The jungle seemed impenetrable.

"How do we get to the house?" Jazz asked.

"Sebastian will send a golf cart," Ted said. Ben sat down on his suitcase. Jazz walked over to the nearest edge of greenery.

"The house is in the other direction," Ted said.

But Jazz didn't hear him. She walked into the woods. She was almost certain she heard something thrashing through the undergrowth. Her reporter's curiosity propelled her forward. The sound seemed to be coming from the direction where she thought she had seen the other structure.

Ben started after her. Ted stopped him. "What does it matter?" he said.

Jazz walked deeper into the woods. The thrashing was growing louder. Something was coming towards her. Nearer. Nearer. Maybe this wasn't such a good idea.

Maybe she should get out of here. But she couldn't move. The sound of thrashing and panting grew closer, and closer. Louder and louder. Jazz was frozen in place. Suddenly the foliage in front of her parted. A figure came crashing towards her. Then she saw the face. Staring at her was Paine Hayes.

CHAPTER 52

"Help me," Paine said, falling into her arms.

"Paine! You're Paine Hayes!"

From behind, Jazz heard an engine. A motorized vehicle was coming to the runway.

"JAZZ, JAZZ, where are you?" Ben shouted. She could hear his steps as he followed the path she had made in.

"I'll get help," she said to Paine.

"Don't trust anyone!" Paine gasped. "Not anyone."

"JAZZ WHERE ARE YOU?" Ben was getting nearer.

Jazz let go of Paine and rushed back to a clearing. "I'm over here!" she shouted.

Ben rushed through the underbrush. "What's going on?"

"Ben—oh Ben, look." Jazz turned to show him Paine. But there was no Paine. She had disappeared.

"What is it?" Ben asked

Don't trust anyone, Paine said. Not anyone. "I don't know," Jazz said. "I think it was a bear."

"A bear?" Ben started to laugh. "Jazz- please. Come on. The cart is here to take us to the house." He led her out, but not before she looked back. She thought she saw a pair of eyes meeting hers.

For five minutes Paine did not move. She couldn't believe that she had found someone on the island who wasn't a captive. Who was this woman? This Jazz? Was she there to rescue them? She knew who Paine was. She must be there to help.

Paine escaped only an hour before. She was trying to find the beach, when she heard the plane coming in. She decided to head for it. Maybe she could stow away on it. She had never been to this part of the island. She had never been anywhere beyond the grounds of the dark house.

She told Chris she was going to escape. With Sam and Eva dying, and now Jessica. She had tried to get Jessica to fight for her existence. But she was too far gone. In the last week of her life, the only words she had said were "Everybody thinks I'm dead, I might as well be."

It had been sport for the partnership to kill her. Ted told Paine how they set Jessica loose on the island, then hunted her like a deer. Arthur scored the winning shot. Hopefully she died quickly, Paine thought. Hopefully I will too, if the time comes. More and more, she thought of death. They all would soon be killed. The only chance they had was for someone to escape.

Chris cautioned her to wait. She argued they could go together when the time was right. But Paine saw an opportunity. Venta was moving some potted palms. He left the gate to the courtyard open. The security had become more and more lax.

During Paine's time to sunbathe, she was allowed to go back and forth to her room. As long as she kept tan, the partnership didn't care how long she was in the sun. And Venta didn't care what she did as long as she didn't talk to the others. Since they were locked in their rooms, that wasn't a possibility. If she tried to contact anyone, the monitors would show it.

Paine discovered the camera in the courtyard had been set up facing the sun. For a few minutes in the morning, the sun shone directly into the camera lens. If she escaped then, no one would see her leave. With it being New Year's Eve, Venta and Ralph were busy preparing the house for the party.

New Year's Eve, she thought as she watched Venta carry one palm and then another out of the courtyard. Last New Year's I was in Palm Beach at Donald Trump's. Now I may not live to see New Year's Day.

When Venta took one more potted palm out of the courtyard and headed towards the patio on the other side of the house, she raced out the gate, past his garden and into the woods.

When he returned, he assumed she was in her room. It could be hours before she was missed, maybe not until the party that night.

Because of the holiday, she hoped guests might arrive on the island. Guests could help her. Like this Jazz. Would she come back? Or would she bring someone from the partnership with her?

"Time to move," Paine said out loud.

Her skin was scraped and scratched from the underbrush. She wore just a brief cover-up over her bikini. How cold were the nights out here? Would she make it until night? Or would the partnership send out a hunting party? Paine Hayes dying in some rotten jungle, her body decaying in the mangroves. Wildlife would probably feed on it.

This was not the ending she had planned. She once told Megan that if anything ever happened to her to use Princess Diana's funeral as a model. "You're kidding," Megan said. She wasn't.

She realized she was hungry. Eventually she would have to find something to eat. Eat? She had forgotten about lunch. Venta or Ralph would bring a tray at 1:00 p.m. Where would they think she was? "Have to move, move."

She raced across the runway to the other side where she found a clump of bushes that she could hide behind. She would rest there, just for a minute. Maybe the plane would come back. She had heard it leaving. That's why she was racing toward it when she ran into that woman. That Jazz. Will you be our savior, Jazz?

CHAPTER 53

The shock of seeing Paine made Jazz almost speechless. Ben kept looking at her as they rode the golf cart towards the bright house. "She's not always this quiet," he said to Venta who was driving.

The day that started off with white fluffy clouds and abundant sunshine, now had turned gray. Dark clouds obscured the sun. "It probably will be just a passing shower," Ben said. Jazz didn't hear him. Her mind was racing. How to help Paine? Who to tell? How to get both of them off the island? What about the other members of the A-list? Were they here too?

After following a path carved through the thick vegetation, the cart lurched out of the jungle onto an expanse of white sand. They were on the other side of the island. The surf lay before them. The sand and aqua water reminded Jazz of Tahiti.

"What a beautiful spot," she said to Ben. To the right was the house she had seen from the air. It was an Old Florida house covered in gray clapboard. Its rambling porches were edged in an intricate white trim. It reminded Jazz of a gingerbread house, only gray instead of brown.

The house was built on a natural incline that elevated it from storm surges. Every porch offered a view of sea and large white wicker chairs in which to enjoy it. The entrance was located at the rear of the house facing the woods. A dozen wide steps led up to the door. Potted palms stood on either side like sentries.

It was all so picturesque that Jazz sat mesmerized in the golf cart. "Thanks Venta," Ted said hopping off.

"I will bring your bags in," Venta said as Jazz went to take hers.

"I'm not usually separated from my computer," she said. Ben grabbed her arm.

"Jazz, you are on vacation," he said. "And it will only be a few minutes."

Feeling foolish, she let go of the computer case and followed Ben and Ted into the house. Nobody greeted them.

"Where is Sebastian?" she asked.

"I don't know," Ted answered. "I'm sure he'll be here soon. Sit down. Relax. I'm going to get a drink. Anybody want one?"

"I'll have a beer," Ben said, sitting down on a big sofa that faced the ocean. Jazz was surprised at the ease in which he made himself at home. A beer at 11:00 in the morning? Didn't he at least want to look around? She did. She walked over to a curio cabinet and peered in. Lladro figurines filled each shelf. Most were of females, but there were two males.

"You like my china collection?" Sebastian Guyera had come up behind her.

"I find it interesting," Jazz said.

"I just bought another one in Miami that I was going to add. Why don't I put it in now? I'll be back in a minute."

He left as quickly as he arrived. "Very strange," Jazz whispered to Ben.

"There is no question he is different," Ben replied.

Sebastian returned with a box. As everyone watched, he carefully opened it.

"You may take it out," he said handing the box to Jazz. She undid the tissue paper and looked at the figurine. It was of a female with brown hair in a lavender dress.

"It's lovely," she said.

"I'm glad you like it." He put the figurine in the cabinet.

"Soon I'll have an even dozen."

Jazz looked at Ben and raised her eyebrows in a silent question mark. He smiled back at her.

"At last we officially meet, Miss Billings," Sebastian said taking her hand in his. He did not let go.

"We met at your father's party in October," she replied, pulling her hand out of his. He was even creepier than she remembered.

"But we really didn't get a chance to talk, to get to know each other. And now we have a weekend, a lifetime."

"When do your other guests arrive?" she asked.

"Not until late this afternoon. We're having difficulty with the planes I hired. The one you were on this morning? It had a problem when it got back to Miami. But I have been assured it will be fixed."

"Do I know any of your guests?"

"You will recognize many of them. It should be an exciting night for you."

A clap of thunder shook the room.

"It looks like we are going to have a little storm. Would you like to see where you are staying, A.J.? May I call you that?"

"That would be fine." He led her down a hallway. She peeked into each room as they passed—a dining room, a sitting room, two bedrooms. "This will be yours," he said bringing her into a bedroom at the end of the hall. It was decorated in the softest of yellows. The windows offered a panoramic view of the ocean.

"This is wonderful," she said as Venta walked in with her bags.

"And here is your luggage," Sebastian said. "Maybe you would like to get comfortable. Once the storm passes we can all take a walk on the beach, even go for a sail. I have a lovely little sailboat."

"That might be nice. Thank you, I think I will change."

When he left, she sat on the bed. Now might be her only time to plan what to do. She had to get off the island to get help for Paine. But how? Her mind spun. "Maybe if I say I'm really feeling sick. But there are no planes to take me off. I have to wait until the other guests arrive. I'll have to act as if nothing is wrong until then. Or should I start to get sick a few hours before? Does Sebastian know Paine is out in the woods? I'm over my head on this one. I think I should tell Ben. But Paine said 'Trust no one.' Oh God. Please tell me what to do."

The room seemed hot. She turned on the ceiling fan. No air-conditioning in The Keys. It was rarely needed. Maybe it was her blood pressure that was rising. She changed into shorts and a tank top, pulled her hair back with a rubber band and headed back to the living room. As she approached, she heard Ben's voice. He was arguing with someone. She stopped in the hallway.

"I think it should wait!" He was almost shouting. The other voice was so low Jazz couldn't make it out. "Listen to me!" Ben shouted again. And then he too whispered. Jazz strained to hear. But the voices were inaudible, and then there was nothing. The voices stopped. She sauntered into the room as if she was just enjoying a wonderful day. Ben was alone.

"Hi," he said. "I like the outfit. I don't think I've ever seen that much of your legs." He had changed too, into bathing trunks and a flowered shirt.

"I see you have legs too," she said.

"It looks like it's not going to rain. Let's take a walk on the beach, get the lay of the land."

"Okay. Do we need suntan lotion?"

"Ah, the New Yorker goes native. Yes, probably. I'll get it." He opened a drawer in a hallway table and took out the lotion. "We're ready, let's go."

Jazz followed him out, with a rising sense of unease. If Ben had never been here before, how did he know where the suntan lotion was?

CHAPTER 54

The clouds that had threatened were gone. It was a beautiful day again. "In New York we would have rain for hours," Jazz said as they walked along the shore. The sailboat she had seen from the air was still anchored off the beach. But the little boat that ferried people out was gone. "One of the boats I saw from the plane is missing," Jazz said.

"It's probably being used for something," Ben said. "What do you care? Are you planning your escape?"

"Should I be?"

"Jazz, loosen up. It's New Year's Eve."

"And we're supposed to be here working, not playing. Ben— prove to me you are an FBI agent."

"What? Do you think we have some secret password that only agents know? What is this all about?"

"You tell me you're an agent, but not to talk to any other agent about you. How do I know you're with the FBI? Are you carrying a gun? A badge?"

"Where would I put a gun? In my bathing suit? Actually I do have a gun. It's back with my clothes. And I do have a badge with me. It's hidden in a false bottom in my bag. I can show you it later, but it would be dangerous. I think Sebastian has the whole house monitored with video cameras. We have to be careful what we say and do in there. Trust me, Jazz I am an agent. I graduated from the academy thirteen years ago."

"Where is the academy?"

"Is this really necessary? The academy is at Quantico. Would you like to know the names of my instructors? What good would it do you? I could make them up. Would you like to know the name of my immediate supervisor in Miami? His name is Victor Tarrino. I can give you his phone number. He would be delighted to hear that an undercover agent is giving out all this information. Have we played this game enough?" He left her and continued walking.

"You've been here before." He stopped.

"What?"

"You seem too comfortable in the house. You knew where the suntan lotion was."

He stared at her. "While you were in your room I did some quick looking around. The table in the hallway was the first place I looked. I saw the lotion. When you asked for it later, I remembered where it was. Case solved?"

She wasn't sure. She couldn't decide whether to trust him. But what choice did she have? She had to get off the island to get help for Paine.

"Ben I need to leave immediately. Can you arrange that?"

"Why?"

"I can't tell you. But I promise I will tell you if you get me back to Miami."

"Not good enough. It took a lot to get us here. I'm not leaving unless there is a very good reason."

She wavered. "We need more help here than just you and me."

"Help with what Jazz? What have you found out?"

They had walked to the far end of the beach. Ahead the

mangroves met the sea. Jazz turned and looked back at the house. She didn't feel she had any choice. She had to trust someone.

"Ben, I've seen Paine. She's here."

"PAINE! Where? What are you saying?"

"Back in the woods where we got off the plane. She was running. She came to me. She said, 'Help me.'"

"Can you take me there?"

"If you can get me back to the runway. Can you get a plane so we can get out of here?"

"I don't know. I'll have to find out. Let me try to get the golf cart so we can see if we can find her. You stay out here. I don't want Sebastian to think you have anything to do with the cart or the plane. Let me go talk to him. Okay?"

"Okay," she said. He ran back down the beach towards the house.

She looked out at the water. "Hold on, Paine," she said. "Help is coming."

CHAPTER 55

Chris realized Paine was gone when it was her turn to sunbathe. Their rooms were next to each other. Paine would always knock on her wall, a signal that she was back and all right. She did it before she went to sleep at night. She did it when she awoke. She knocked whenever she left the room and returned. Chris's signal was to knock twice. It was their way of showing they were still hanging in there

Paine knocked on the wall that morning, but Chris hadn't heard any knock since. And now it was noon and time for Chris's turn in the courtyard. Paine's sunbathing ended at 11:00. Where was she?

As Chris lay on the chaise, she casually looked around. The captives knew their every movement was recorded by sick Sebastian and his cameras. But the courtyard camera had the sun shining on it. Paine could have escaped from here. But she also could have been taken somewhere. Paine had talked more and more of trying to get out. Maybe I waited too long, Chris thought.

She turned over on her stomach. She saw Venta out past the gate working in his garden. He loved landscaping. Chris figured it was his therapy for all the criminal activity. The gate was open. Had Paine gotten out? It was New Year's Eve. Everybody would be at the party that night. She knew she would be missed. Why go today?

Chris decided to test Venta by walking out to him. As she passed the gate, he turned from his weeding. "WHAT ARE YOU DOING?" he shouted. "You know you are not allowed out here."

"I wanted to see your garden," she said. "Please Venta, you work so hard on it and I love plants."

Venta remembered all the plants she kept in her apartment. He liked that about her. He liked a lot about this woman. No matter what his boss did to her, she never lost her sense of humor. And she seemed a kind person, like Sam. Sam's death had changed Venta. He had killed before, but he never had anyone ask God to forgive him. He had talked to Ralph about it. Was it not special, he asked, to know you are going to die and think of someone else? Ralph told him to forget it. "These rich people deserve what they get," he said. But Venta was beginning to feel sorry for the captives.

"All right, come over here. But don't tell anyone."

Chris took a quick look each way before walking over to the garden. It was her first time past the gates. In each direction were woods. Which way would Paine have gone? She didn't even know that Paine escaped. She could be imprisoned somewhere else. Or she could be dead.

Venta had just planted impatiens around the edge of his garden. "They do well this time of year," he said.

"They're lovely," Chris said. Is this how Patty Hearst lived, becoming friendly with your kidnappers? A plane flew overhead. It was coming in to land. "Are more people coming to the party tonight, Venta?"

"Just the usual," he said. "Oh, and maybe one new arrival." Chris's heart sank. Another victim. When would it end? Couldn't anybody in America figure all this out and help them? She looked so sad that Venta touched her arm.

"It's a beautiful day today," he said. "Look up at the sky."

"How long is this going to go on?" Chris asked him. She never had a conversation like this before with one of her captives. But maybe Venta was a captive in this too.

"I don't know," he said. "I don't know."

Then he turned and looked back at the house. "This is not good. You should not be here. Go back to your sunbathing. It is almost time for Jeff to come out."

CHAPTER 56

O n opposite sides of the island, Paine and Jazz heard the plane's engine. Darting further back into the foliage, Paine waited by the runway. Jazz headed back to the bright house. She had to find Ben and tell him about the plane. It was their way off the island. As she reached the steps to the front door, he came out. He had changed into long pants and a long-sleeved shirt. "I've got the keys to one of the golf carts," he said. "Let's go."

"Ben, I just heard a plane. If we could get to it—."

"Yes. But it's carrying another one of Sebastian's friends—Clorio. We don't want him to see us. We have to find Paine then get to the plane after Clorio gets off."

"And how do we get the pilot to fly us?"

"I brought two persuaders." He pulled from his pocket a gun and an FBI badge. "Happy now?"

Jazz felt a weight lifted. " Oh yes. Let's go."

They ran to the cart that was parked nearby. In a few minutes they were heading through the woods. "Can't this go any faster?" Jazz asked.

"No, they don't go over 20." It seemed to take forever to get to the runway area. Just as they were about to reach the clearing, Jazz saw the plane had landed and next to it, two men were boarding another golf cart. The cart started up and headed off—right towards them. "We've got to hide this thing," Ben said. He made a sharp right turn and drove into the underbrush. Jazz's face and arms, were smashing into greenery. "Stay down!" he ordered. Twenty feet into the brush he made another sharp right then killed the engine. "Don't say a word!" he whispered.

Paine was watching from the other side of the clearing. She hoped the plane was carrying some new people like the woman she had seen earlier in the day. When she saw Ralph arrive in the golf cart and Clorio get off the plane, she wanted to scream. Why was God testing her so? Her eyes caught a flash of white off to the right. It looked like another golf cart. But then it turned into the woods. Why? Could Jazz be on it? Maybe she was trying to hide, too.

Clorio and Ralph passed only a few feet from Paine and her hiding place. If she had a gun she would have killed them without a thought. But she had nothing. As soon as their cart disappeared into the woods, she turned her attention to the plane. The doors were open. The pilot had gotten out and walked to the edge of the woods. He probably has to pee, she thought. Now was the moment. If she could run to the plane, get there and climb aboard before he came back—. She ran out into the open.

The golf cart carrying Clorio and Ralph was stopped at the spot where Ben made the sharp turn. "Look's like somebody missed the path here," Ralph said, pointing to the tire marks and the knocked-down shrubbery.

"Probably Sebastian doing wheelies," Clorio said. "Come on. I am anxious to get there." Ralph started up the cart and they headed off.

Ben kept his finger to his mouth for Jazz to be quiet a minute longer. Then he jumped out of the cart and motioned for her to do the same. They ran to the clearing, just in time to see a figure racing down the runway towards the back of the plane.

"It's Paine!" Jazz whispered to Ben. They started running towards the plane too. But the pilot had gotten back first. Without seeing Paine, he closed his door, then realized the other door was open. He was reaching over to close it. Paine was only a few yards away.

"She's going to make it!" Jazz cried. Suddenly a shot rang out. Jazz froze. So did Paine. Jazz turned to see Ben with his gun pointed skyward. He had shot into the air. Paine turned and ran into the nearest woods. "Why?" Jazz mouthed to Ben.

"The plane was going to leave without her," he said.

"She was going to make it to the plane," Jazz said.

The pilot never saw Paine. He only saw a man with a gun at the edge of the runway. He started his engine and taxied away as fast as he could.

"Shoot again! Let him know we need him!" Jazz screamed. But it was too late. The plane gained speed and lifted off.

"I can't believe you did that!" she yelled at Ben.

"We have to find Paine," he answered. "Maybe if you go into the woods where we saw her enter, she will come to you. Tell her you're with an FBI agent."

Jazz ran into the woods. "PAINE! PAINE! I'M HERE TO HELP YOU!" There was no answer. "PAINE, I'M A REPORTER. I KNOW ALL ABOUT YOU AND THE OTHERS. I WANT TO HELP YOU!"

Paine was listening just a dozen feet away. She wanted to go to Jazz. Oh how she wanted to go, but Jazz obviously didn't know the danger she was in.

"PAINE, PLEASE COME OUT. I'M HERE ALONE."

Paine listened for a few minutes. It seemed that Jazz really was alone. She inched towards her. "Please, Paine." Jazz was no longer calling. She was simply pleading in a normal voice.

"I'm over here to your right," Paine whispered. "Don't look this way. Are you sure you are alone?"

"Yes. But there's help on the island. I have an FBI agent with me."

"The FBI? Thank God." Paine came out in the open. For a moment, she and Jazz just stared at each other.

"I'm Jazz Billings," Jazz finally said.

"I'm Paine Hayes."

"I know and I'm so glad you are alive. Are the others alive too?"

"Most of them. How are we going to get off the island?"

"Well that's a problem. But we have help. Ben has a gun."

"Who's Ben?"

"The FBI agent who is with me. Come, I'll take you to him."

"But what about Arthur?"

"Who's Arthur?"

"One of the partnership, one of the bad guys, Jazz."

"Partnership? I thought it was only Sebastian."

"No there are five of them. They take turns with us."

"Five? I didn't know about five. I don't know if they are all on the island now. Let's get to Ben. He'll know what to do."

"I'm already here, Jazz." The two women turned to face the voice.

"It's Ben," Jazz said.

"No," Paine said. "It's Arthur."

CHAPTER 57

"Technically you are both right," Ben said, pointing the gun at them. "My full name is Reuben Arthur Luvana. I'm not sure we were ever formally introduced, Paine."

Jazz felt sick to her stomach. "God, you told me you were an FBI agent."

"And I am, Jazz. It's just that some of us are more trustworthy than others." He took a two-way radio from his shirt pocket. "I have Paine," he said into it. "I have both of them. You can come for us. We'll be at the runway."

"Shall we take a walk ladies?"

Paine said nothing. She just headed towards the runway. Jazz followed. But the anger kept rising. "You are some piece of work, Luvana."

"I hoped things would be different, Jazz. I wanted more time with you alone. But you left no options once you found Paine. We thank you for that. These idiots didn't know she was missing until I told them. After you told me, of course."

"People know I'm here. They will come looking for me."

"Really? Like who? Carrie? Your message never got through, Jazz. Electronics is a specialty of one of the partners."

As they reached the clearing, a golf cart came towards them. Ralph was driving. "Ralph, have you met Jazz?" Ben said as the cart stopped in front of them. "And here is our friend Paine. Foolish Paine. She took a field trip but is anxious to return home to us."

The women were ordered to sit in the rear seat facing backward. "We better go straight to the dark house," Ben said to Ralph. "I'm sorry Jazz, your freedom just ended."

They headed back into the woods, in the opposite direction. Here the foliage was denser. It reminded Jazz of the Amazon jungle. As the cart bounced and lurched over roots growing in the path, Jazz looked at Paine. Paine's eyes were focused on something only Paine could see.

When the cart finally stopped, Jazz didn't know why. She couldn't see any house. Then she turned to the left and there it was. It looked like a tree house, so covered was it with vines and leaves. No wonder she hadn't seen it clearly from the air.

Jazz became the only captive who walked into the dark house. The others had all been carried in. They were drugged when they arrived. Sebastian and Ben decided it didn't matter with Jazz. The captives would be dead soon anyway.

Paine had never seen this entrance. She silently took notes of the hallway they walked down, and the number of steps leading to the basement where the small rooms were located. Maybe there would be another chance. As she reached her room, Ben shoved her in. "Get cleaned up," he ordered. "You're probably going to be the entertainment tonight."

He led Jazz to a room a few doors down. "Your clothes will be brought to you later," he said. "Not that you'll be needing them that often." He pulled her to him and grabbed her buttocks. She slapped his face. He pulled her tighter. "I hope the fight stays in you, Jazz. Welcome to your new home."

He opened the door and pushed her into a room containing a double bed, a chair and a full-length mirror. That was all. As she

225

looked around, the door locked behind her. She heard the sound and thought of how she would describe it. This was going to make an incredible story. Then it hit her. If the story were ever published, it probably wouldn't be her writing it.

CHAPTER 58

Chris was doing sit-ups when she heard the knock on the wall. Paine was back! Paine was alive! She returned the knock, tapping twice. Then Paine did something she had never done before. She started knocking and didn't stop. What did that mean? The knocking continued. Chris didn't know what to do. The wall was reverberating from Paine's knocks. Surely if Paine didn't stop someone would come and make her. Chris had to protect her. She started knocking on her wall. Jeff heard the knocking from his room and started knocking too. It became a chain of knocking. For a moment fear turned to anger. Everyone was knocking.

Except Jazz. She didn't know what to make of it. She lay on the bed and listened to the sound. The walls vibrated from it. It sounded like a tribal rite. It reminded her of the drums you hear just before someone is sacrificed.

At 7:00 p.m. Venta came to Jazz's room with her luggage. Her computer was missing. No surprise. "The party will start at 9:00," he told her. "Be dressed and ready to leave your room by then."

She hadn't eaten since the apple and muffin that morning. Here she was in a life and death situation and she was starving. "Could I have something to eat?" she asked.

227

"There will be plenty at the party." He slammed the door. Venta had decided he was getting too friendly with the captives. He was beginning to feel for them. Especially for Paine and what they were going to do to her that night. This new one, he would ignore.

The knocking had stopped. Jazz calculated it lasted about twenty minutes. She hadn't heard anyone order it stopped. It just slowly faded away. Strange.

She put her bag on the bed. In it was packed a long slinky purple dress. It must be what Ben bought. The top was so low she had no bra that would work under it. What kind of party was this going to be? There couldn't be anyone from the outside, not with her being held a prisoner.

How long would she be a prisoner? When Ben asked who she expected to rescue her, she hadn't mentioned Wit. Surely he would get help once he realized she was missing. But that could take days. Did she have days?

What about Graham? Had she misjudged him? It was Ben who was the bad guy, not Graham. She should have confided in him. She should have done a lot of things differently. If only she hadn't left New York without talking directly to someone and explaining where she was going. It could be weeks before people grew concerned. Some of the A-list eight were missing for months before she broke the story.

Fear began to rise in her. She tried to ignore it by taking a shower. One skimpy towel hung over the shower door. She would have to use it to dry both her hair and her body. She turned on the water. At least the spray was strong. She reached for the shampoo. It was her brand. So was the soap. This had all been planned. In spite of the hot water, she shivered as she stepped under the spray.

✫ ✫ ✫ ✫ ✫

What a lovely body, Sebastian thought as he watched Jazz soap herself up. The body was an added bonus. He had been attracted to the eyes the night he saw her at his father's party. Such a sparkle in them. Later, the mind. He couldn't wait to control that mind. But now there was this body too. Nice breasts, a slim waist, athletic legs. A.J. Billings was going to be as exciting as his first few times with Fanee.

He would have to deal with Arthur, of course. Arthur wanted A.J. too. But this was his house, his plan. Arthur would have to wait—as he would. The courting of A.J. would take a week or so, as it did with Fanee. There were always the others to satisfy his needs. Except Paine, of course. What a disappointment she had been, trying to escape. Paine would die tonight. They all would have to die soon. Arthur said Graham and the task force were making progress. It had begun investigating his employees, Venta and Ralph. It was only a matter of time before they would come to the island, perhaps in a few weeks.

Yes, he had to get rid of all of them, the captives and the partnership. All except Arthur. He needed Arthur for the stolen art network. Maybe in a few years, after everyone had forgotten about the missing A-list members, he could start over again.

He looked in the mirror. He was having a hard time deciding what to wear. This was going to be his best New Year's Eve ever. Should he go formal or informal? What would A.J. like? It was good that she was a prisoner already. He wouldn't have to play any social games tonight. She would be a little short-tempered at first. But once she saw how the others treated him, she would realize his power. And when she saw what he did to Paine—. Well, she would think twice about disobeying him. This was going to be a wonderful evening. He combed his hair back and smiled at the mirror.

Formal. Yes, the tuxedo. Women couldn't resist him in a tuxedo.

CHAPTER 59

For the first time in a long time, Jazz was ready early for an event. She put on the lavender dress, piled her hair in an upsweep, and finished her make-up, all by quarter of nine.

Now it was 9:30 and no one had come. Maybe this was part of the plan. Have her get all dressed up, then leave her alone. Maybe she wasn't going to any party. Maybe she would be alone in this room for days. She would not let Sebastian get to her. The room probably was being monitored. Ben said the house was. Why not these rooms? If the room had a camera, maybe the bathroom did too. She had taken a shower! She would have to remember to turn the lights off. But there was no light switch. The lights came on automatically. They probably went off automatically too.

She sat on the bed and waited. At 9:45, the door was unlocked. "They are ready for you," Venta said. She followed him down the hall. For an article, she once had taken a self-defense course. Maybe she could overpower him. But then what? Where would she go? She decided against fighting. At least for now.

At the end of the hallway, they went up a flight of stairs. At the top was another door. Venta unlocked it and they entered a wider hallway. Now they appeared to be in the main part of the house.

She saw a kitchen to the right, a dining room to the left. Ahead she heard music and voices. Venta stopped in front of closed double doors. "You go first," he said. She opened the two doors and entered a large room. Before her lay a dream scene. Only it was real.

A party was going on. Men and women in evening attire chatted in small groups. A couple slow-danced to *Yesterday*. It all seemed so normal. But the couple dancing was Jeff Worthington and Chris Whitman. They were alive! She wanted to run over and tell them that their families had been searching for them, that the world hadn't forgotten them, that she had written about them. Her head turned to the left, and there was Tracey Wise. Standing next to her were Kensington Washington and Spring Bellingham. All these months and they were here, alive!

Suddenly heads turned in her direction. Everyone stared at her. Jazz felt like she was looking at zombies. The captives were alive, but they showed no emotion. Except for Chris and Jeff. She saw them glance at each other, then back at her. Chris actually smiled. Jazz knew she liked this girl.

Sebastian arose from a couch, patting Kensington's behind as he passed by. "Well, our guest of honor. Miss Billings welcome to my other home, and Happy New Year to you. And what a New Year it will be for you." He glared at Venta who was standing behind her. "You can go. Keep watch over the entertainment. Do you think you can do that much?" Venta left, closing the doors behind him.

"Well A.J. I guess you recognize most everybody here. But they probably have no idea who you are. COULD I HAVE EVERYONE'S ATTENTION?"

There was silence. "This is our newest guest, A.J. Billings. A.J. is a reporter for the *New York Tribune*, a Pulitzer Prize winning reporter. There is talk that she could win another Pulitzer for a recent series of articles. It involves people who are missing. And now she has found them. Too bad she will not be able to tell her readers about it. A.J. has come to live with us. I think it best that for tonight, she not speak to anybody but the partnership. Is that understood? A.J., that means you will talk only to the men in the room except for Jeff. But he's not a real man, anyway. Are you?" Jazz could see the tension in Jeff's face. She smiled at him. With tight lips, he nodded back at her.

"So A.J. it is a party. You will dance, eat, and be merry. And I'm sure you will enjoy our special entertainment at midnight. Now dance with me. Clorio put on a slow song." He looked to the left and Jazz's eyes followed. A man was bent over a jukebox. When he found the song he wanted, he looked up. "How about Johnny Mathis?" he asked. Jazz felt faint. Smiling at her was Big Ears.

CHAPTER 60

Jazz was so stunned at seeing Big Ears, she didn't protest when Sebastian led her to the part of the room set up for dancing. "CHANCES—ARRRR" Johnny and Sebastian sang. As they danced, Sebastian's hands moved from Jazz's waist to her buttocks. She quickly pulled them back up. He laughed. Everyone was still staring and not moving. "EVERYBODY PARTY!" Sebastian shouted to the group. A few couples joined them on the dance floor. Jazz was counting heads. Just about everybody she wrote about was there, and more. Who was that dark-haired woman in the blue gown? But Eva wasn't there. Nor was Paine. Oh God, what had happened to Paine? A sense of dread passed over her.

The music ended, but Sebastian kept his arms around Jazz. "You are my special New Year's gift," he whispered in her ear. She glared at him. Then she felt hands pulling her out of his arms.

"My turn, Sebastian," Ben said. Jazz was now in his grasp.

"We talked about this," Sebastian warned, a dark look coming over his face. "But of course, dance with her."

Mathis was now singing *The Twelfth of Never*. Ben held Jazz close. She was beginning to feel like a piece of meat being divided among the lion pride.

"Try to enjoy yourself, Jazz," Ben whispered in her ear.

"Why?" she spat out. "Are you going to tell me you are just pretending to be a bad guy so we all can escape?"

"No, the games are over, Jazz. I am a bad guy, a very bad guy, and you do not want to fool with me, or Sebastian. I suggest you start thinking of pleasing us, the sooner the better." He grabbed her even tighter. Across the room Sebastian glared. Luvana was ruining his New Year's.

When the song ended, he whispered to Ted who headed over to Ben and Jazz. "Sebastian needs you," he told Ben. "I'll dance with our guest."

Ben and Sebastian were gone for fifteen minutes. When they returned, Sebastian was smiling. Ben was not. Sebastian had taken him to the video room and shown him excerpts from the "Arthur Tape."

It showed Arthur/Ben forcing himself upon Paine and other captives. Even more damaging it showed the FBI agent with a gun in his hand standing over the body of America's little darling, the Oscar-winning Jessica Lawrence. To a person off camera he yelled "one of my best shots." There were other scenes of Ben with stolen art, and taking money from Armando. "Enough," he said.

Sebastian turned off the machine. "There are copies with people who will release them if anything happens to me. Do we understand each other?" There was no answer. Sebastian opened the door to leave, then turned back. "I presume we agree. A.J. is mine until I grow tired of her."

Back at the party, Sebastian was almost gleeful. "Fanee," he called. "Come over here." The French woman quickly came to his side. "Chris," he called. "Come over here." Chris left Gary whom she was dancing with and dutifully walked over to Sebastian. He looked at Jazz to make sure she was watching. She was indeed. She wanted to speak to Chris, but couldn't get her alone.

"Now A.J. come over."

"Shove it," she answered back. A few of the captives nervously smiled. Jeff looked at Chris and raised an eyebrow. Sebastian marched over to Jazz and whispered in her ear. Only she heard him say: "Aren't you interested at all in what has become of Willie?" Her expression changed immediately. "He is alive and will remain so as long as you are nice to me."

"Now," he said in a voice all could hear. "Shall we try this again?" He walked back to the other two women. "A.J." he called. "Come here." She walked over to him. "Good, see how easy that was. Let's go sit somewhere. And where's the music? This is a party. Let's see some dancing. Jeffy-poo how about you dancing with Clorio?"

"Clorio likes the boys," he said to Jazz as they sat on the couch. "He especially liked Sam. Too bad about Sam."

"How about some Village People?" he shouted to Gary who was by the jukebox. "A little *Macho, Macho Man* for Jeff?" He began dancing in his seat, then put his arm around Jazz. Chris sat next to her. If only they could talk. "Is there a ladies room?" Jazz asked Chris.

"Can I show her?" Chris said to Sebastian.

"No, Fanee will take her." Fanee led Jazz out the door and down the hall to a small bathroom. "Do not try anything," Fanee said. "We all will suffer if you do."

"Where are you from? I don't know about you," Jazz said.

"Enough, just go in and come out quick."

The bathroom had no windows and no implements that Jazz could take for defense. When she came out Fanee was waiting for her. Another attempt at conversation failed. "Get back to the party," Fanee said.

"Have the captives become the jailers?" Jazz asked. Fanee ignored her.

By 11:30 the party was jumping in a ghoulish way. The members of the partnership were having the time of their lives, grabbing and groping every woman there. Ted pulled down the top of Tracey's dress as they danced to *Mony Mony*. More breasts were put on display. Panties were pulled off and tossed from captor to captor. All the women were being abused. Except for Jazz. She was Sebastian's prize. He would dance with her then leave her to fondle another captive. She felt like the virgin bride. But she knew her time would come. At one point she was near enough to Chris and Gary Dire to hear Dire say "Like old times, hey Chris? You and I together on New Year's Eve. I've already reserved you for the New Year's celebration." She wanted to tell Chris that Wit was looking for her, that he would never stop looking for her. But all she could do was offer a sympathetic smile. Chris smiled back.

A conga line formed to *Hot Hot Hot*. Sebastian grabbed Jazz and joined the group. Jazz went through the motions of dancing. What else could she do? She wondered where Paine was, and what happened to her.

It was ten minutes to midnight when Sebastian turned off the music and shushed the group. "My dear friends," he said. "It is almost time to say goodbye to the old year. Representing it is our surprise for the evening. Here she is, symbolizing the old, "Miss Paine Hayes."

The double doors opened and standing in the hallway was Paine in a see-through white flowing gown. Her blonde hair hung down over her shoulders. She was perfectly made up. Jazz had never seen her like this. "She looks like an angel," she said. On one side of Paine was Venta, on the other, Ralph.

"Come in my dear," Sebastian said. "As the old year, you need to say goodbye to everyone." Paine walked in and Clorio put on a recording of *Auld Lang Syne*.

"A bit early, Clorio," Sebastian said. "But a nice touch. Paine has offered to dance for us all. She was a naughty girl today. She tried to leave without permission."

Chris swallowed hard. The penalty for trying to escape was

death. Everybody knew that. They all heard what happened to Jessica. "Oh, Paine," she whispered.

"Now Paine wants you all to have a happy night," Sebastian continued. "She knows how displeased I am. So she has assured me she will do whatever I want so that none of you suffer. Isn't that right Paine?"

Paine nodded, and Sebastian looked at Clorio. He started the music. *Celebrate, Celebrate dance to the music*. Paine began to dance. As she did, she untied the front of the white gown and let it drop to the floor. She was completely naked. Men smiled. Women looked away. Each member of the partnership came up to dance with her. Like a Roman orgy they surrounded her, grabbing at her, and dancing suggestively in front of her. For Jazz, it seemed an eternity before the music ended. When it did, Sebastian said "one more surprise, but not until midnight. We have five more minutes." Paine was led out of the room. The music grew louder. "Everybody dance!" Sebastian ordered.

At the end of the song, he once again asked for silence. "Less than two minutes to go," he shouted, "everyone outside for fireworks!" They all hurried out the patio doors to the courtyard. The gate to the woods and Venta's garden was open. In a clearing, a platform had been hastily constructed. Paine stood on it. She was bound to a board with her arms outstretched. In each hand was tied a huge M-80 firecracker with a long fuse. M-80s were also at her feet. Jazz couldn't believe it. Paine was going to be the fireworks display. "One minute to go," Sebastian said. "Ralph, get ready to light our fireworks!"

"No!" Chris shouted. Paine looked at her, then whispered, "Please." She began to cry, "Please don't do this." She had finally lost control. As Paine cried, the other women screamed "No! Sebastian, no!" Members of the partnership looked at each other. This was getting out of hand.

"Ralph light the fuses!" Sebastian shouted. Ralph walked over to where Paine was tied.

"Sebastian," Ted said. "Maybe we should handle it another way."

"Thirty seconds to go," Sebastian shouted. "Light the fuses!" Paine began sobbing. The other women pleaded to stop this. Ralph had bent over to light the first fuse when a pop sounded. Then another. Paine gasped, then crumpled. Ralph backed away as blood spurted from Paine's chest. She had been shot. Everyone turned to see where the shots came from. Arthur was standing to the right of Ralph with a gun in his hand. "Paine's dead," he shouted to Sebastian. "That's what you wanted, isn't it? Now let's go in and enjoy the New Year."

Sebastian glared at him. But the others quickly headed back into the party room. The women were weeping. Jazz was crying too. For Paine, yes. But also for the others and herself. She now realized how sick Sebastian was. "Help will come," she whispered, as if saying it would make it happen. Jeff overheard her. "You better accept it," he said. "We're going to die before any help arrives."

CHAPTER 61

Paine's death marked the end of the New Year's celebration. Everyone but Sebastian lost the party spirit. Each member of the partnership chose a mate, or two, and headed to the small bedrooms for the rest of the night. Sebastian told Venta to take Jazz to her room. It was not a night for gentle courting. Instead, he partied until dawn abusing both Fanee and Spring Bellingham.

Jazz couldn't sleep. The last 24 hours kept racing through her brain. Finding Paine, Ben's betrayal, being taken captive, seeing all the A-list absentees and then Paine's death. Oh God, was she responsible for Paine's death, too? First Roger, then Sam, and now Paine. She told Ben about her. If she hadn't, would Paine still be alive? She thought of Charles Hayes, and the other parents offering their reward of five million dollars. What good would it do now?

Maybe somebody could be bought. Maybe somebody on this island was sick of Sebastian and the torture he was putting the captives through. Perhaps one of his employees. Or a member of the partnership. Maybe Ben? Oh right. He was a murderer. What good would the reward do? How about Ted—Gary—or Clorio? Clorio had obviously worn some type of latex disguise in Colorado. But his eyes and certainly his ears were recognizable. He was the only one of the group whose background Jazz didn't know. Could he be the electronics partner Ben was talking about? Did he kill Roger? Who killed Roger? Oh did it matter? They all were murderers and rapists. And they all would want the captives killed to hide their crimes.

How much time did she have? It was New Year's Day. She was supposed to be with Wit. When would he, or Carrie, or Joe, become suspicious about where she was? She tossed and turned. There was no way of knowing if it was night or day. With no windows in the basement bedrooms, time couldn't be measured.

It seemed forever before she heard a key turn in the lock of her door. It was Venta. "Here is your breakfast," he said. "It is 9:00 a.m. In an hour you will go outside to sunbathe. You'll take Paine's time. You will be outside for an hour. Then you will be brought back into this room. You will be spending a lot of time, alone, in this room. Get used to it. I will bring you lunch at 1:00. I do not know what your plans are for this evening. Maybe dinner with Sebastian." He turned to leave.

"I'm sorry," Jazz said. "I know I was told your name. But what is it again?"

"Venta."

"It's an unusual name. Is it a family name?"

He paused. He vowed not to be friendly any more with these people. Not after last night. He was tired of the games, of the killing. He wanted to go back to Argentina. "I am named after my grandfather's favorite bull."

Jazz couldn't help herself. She laughed. Venta found himself laughing too. "It is an odd choice, yes?" he said. "But this bull was a champion and strong, so strong, that my father wanted me to be the same. He thought the name would help."

"Venta, you don't have to be a part of this. There is a way out. There is a big reward being offered —."

240

"Stop. No more talking." He left, slamming the door and locking it.

Jazz was alone again.

At 10:00 a.m. Ralph came to take her to the sunbathing spot. Every question she asked was met with silence, except for one about suntan lotion. When she arrived outside, the sun was almost blinding. "I'm not used to the sun," she said. "Is there any suntan lotion?"

"I will get it," he said. When he left her alone, she looked around. The courtyard was walled and gated. She looked to see if the wall could be climbed, but it was too high. In one corner, she noticed a video camera. The red light was on. Showtime, she thought. A few minutes later Ralph returned, tossed the lotion to her, and left. She lay down on the chaise lounge and pretended to sleep. When Ralph returned an hour later, she realized she had been asleep and forgot to put the lotion on. Her face and chest stung as she was led back into the house.

CHAPTER 62

The partnership planned on partying all of New Year's Day. But Paine's public execution put a damper on the weekend. By noon, only Ben and Sebastian remained. After discussing business—more stolen art being shipped from Switzerland—Ben decided he, too would leave.

"I'd like to say good-bye to Jazz," he said to Sebastian.

"Be my guest," Sebastian said, handing him the key to her room. "But remember, no touching." Ben turned to leave.

"On second thought," Sebastian added, "touch all you want. I'll be watching."

Only Sebastian and his two employees had keys to the basement rooms. That gave Sebastian the power. Partnership members had to ask for permission to visit the captives.

Jazz was asleep when Ben unlocked the door. She heard it open and bolted upright.

"What happened to you?" Ben asked. "You look like a lobster."

"I was ordered to sunbathe. I forgot to put lotion on."

"Well you need some type of lotion to soothe that sunburn. I'll get some for you before I leave the island."

"Don't bother."

"I thought you would feel more kindly to me after last night."

"Kindly? You murdered Paine."

"I shot Paine so she wouldn't suffer. So you all wouldn't suffer watching her blow up."

"I am supposed to thank you for killing her?"

"She had to die anyway."

"No Ben, she didn't have to die. None of the people here have to die or be raped and humiliated. Everybody could be freed."

"Don't be naive, Jazz. I came to say good-bye. I'm going back to Miami. I don't know if I'll see you again. Sebastian doesn't advise me of all his plans. I'm scheduled to be back here next weekend. Hopefully you will be here too."

"Is that said to scare me?"

"No, just to warn you." He turned his back to the camera in the corner and pointed. She looked up and saw the red light. Sebastian was watching.

Ben sat next to her on the bed. "How about a good-bye kiss?"

"You've got to be kidding."

"Oh Jazz, is there any fear in you? I could take you right here. No one would come to your defense."

"Try it."

He put his hand out to touch her face. As she attempted to push it away, he grabbed one arm, then the other, and pinned them behind her back. The sunburn made it doubly painful. She winced but didn't scream out. She stared defiantly at him as he pulled down one side of her bathing suit revealing her breast. It was pale compared to the red skin above it. His fingers played with her nipple as he turned and smiled at the camera. She spat at him. He smiled at her.

"In a battle of strength, you know who would win, Jazz. But I will wait. Once Sebastian is through with you, you will look forward to me." He kissed her roughly on the lips. "Take care of that sunburn." He let her go, then saluted the camera and left. She quickly pulled up her suit and rolled over on her stomach. She grimaced as the sunburn hit the sheets. "Pig!" she said out loud. "You are all pigs."

Sebastian turned away from the monitor. He was going to have to do something about Arthur. But the insubordination didn't dampen his enthusiasm. He couldn't wait for tonight. The taming of A.J. Billings. What pleasure that would be.

At four o'clock his plans fell apart. He was soaking in the hot tub adjacent to his bedroom, when Venta rushed onto the patio. "Your father is on his way here," he said. "We just got a radio message from the pilot. We are to clear the runway."

Armando always came by helicopter, which meant he needed little landing space. But his pilot was cautious. The runway was always cleared for him.

"Damn, what does he want?" Sebastian and his father shared in the stolen art network. But Armando knew nothing about the guests in the dark house.

Venta and Ralph's loyalties were pledged to Sebastian, not Armando. They wouldn't have said anything. Had Ben? He would be foolish if he did. "Get Ralph and clear the runway. How long do we have?"

"He should be here in 15 minutes."

"Damn."

By the time he showered and dressed, he could hear the helicopter engine. He took one of the golf carts and headed for the runway. Armando had landed and was waiting impatiently when he arrived. Venta stood next to an empty cart. "I told Mr. Guyera I would take him to the house," he said. "But he wanted to wait for you."

"Well I am here my father, welcome."

"Happy New Year, my son." Armando reached out and hugged him. Sebastian tolerated the affection but offered none in return.

As they rode back to the bright house, Armando chatted about the weather and the party he attended the night before. "So many beautiful women," he said. "They would have loved partying with you."

"Why are you here?" Sebastian asked.

"In good time. I want to know first how you spent your New Year's."

Killing a naked woman, the son wanted to say. Instead—"I had a small party. Everybody has left by now."

"Who attended? Anyone I know?"

Sebastian smiled. Yes, dear father, you would know everyone. The rich bitches have been all over the news for the last few months. And they are just a soccer field away waiting for me and anything I want to do with them. "Some of my friends were here like Gary and Ted. Ben was here too. And of course some women."

"Sebastian you need to find a woman who means something to you. I need a grandson. G & G needs a future heir."

As they arrived at the house, Sebastian noticed Armando had not brought a bag. That was a good sign. The visit would be short. They entered the house and went into the living room. "Drink?" the son asked.

"A martini," the father said.

"It must be serious."

"It is."

Armando said nothing more, waiting until after he took a few sips of the drink.

"I spoke to Ben today," he said.

Sebastian stared at him. Would Ben have told? He couldn't be so stupid, could he?

"Yes?"

"He said the FBI is getting closer on the import operation. He tried to throw them off with what the Americans call a red herring. But an FBI team intercepted the Ghinello sculpture in a warehouse in Marseilles. Our people had not taken possession of it yet.

The warehouse people are under arrest and they may talk. The Campis called a meeting tomorrow morning in New York. They are not happy. We need to be there."

"Why we? Why can't you handle it?"

"Because this is a family business, Sebastian. I put you in charge of transporting the artwork. You should have known about the problem in Marseilles. But you are too busy hiding away on this island. How do you think we afford this island?"

"I have plans for the next few days."

"Well, cancel them. We have to leave before dark. We'll take the jet tonight to New York. Now go pack."

Sebastian did not like being ordered. For a moment he thought of putting his father in the dark house. This was his island where he was all-powerful. He glared at the man standing in front of him.

Armando didn't like the hateful look from his only child. "Sebastian, I'm sorry. I shouldn't have talked to you that way. Now, please, get ready to leave. You must realize how important Salvatore and Anthony Campi are to our operation. And the Ghinello sculpture was going in Anthony's private collection. So not only are they upset about the network, they are upset about this particular sculpture. They believe in family. They joined with us because we are a family business. Now, let's go."

Sebastian realized he had to. A.J. would wait. They all would wait. He went to his room and paged Venta.

"I have to leave," he said when the employee arrived. "Take care of our guests. Make sure no one tries anything. It may be a few days before I return."

Within a half-an-hour, father and son were on their way to Miami.

CHAPTER 63

It took four days to pacify the Campis. The first two were spent arranging the deaths of the two warehousemen being held in the Marseilles jail. That was what the Guyeras promised in their brief first meeting. The Campis refused to discuss anything else until that was accomplished.

Sebastian called the killer he used in Colorado. He was a professional assassin whom Clorio knew. As the killer was fluent in four languages including French, the job was not difficult to complete.

The second meeting with the Campis went better. A new network was arranged, a higher percentage for the Campis was agreed upon, and the Guyeras were invited to the wedding of Anthony's daughter later in the week. Armando immediately said yes, they would attend. Sebastian glared at his father. That would mean a week away from his island.

He was confident the notes he arranged from Jazz would take care of the first few days of her absence. But he had always planned for her to write another to both Carrie and Joe. It would say she was on a boat in the Caribbean working on a great tip for the A-list story, and Willie was staying with a new friend in Florida. The letter had to be written. Too much time was passing. He would have Venta make her do it.

After the Campi meeting broke up, he went to a pay phone down the street and called the satellite number. He talked in the special code he and Venta devised. Venta said he would take care of everything. Relieved, Sebastian walked to the corner to hail a cab. He had just made eye contact with a driver when Anthony Campi suddenly appeared at his side. "The meeting went well today," Campi said waving the cab off. "Your father is a wise man. I would hate for him to know how unwise you are."

"I don't know what you are talking about."

"Get rid of the broads on your island. I know all about your little harem. It's bringing too much attention our way. Get rid of them—soon. Do we understand each other?"

Sebastian turned to hail another cab. "I'm talking to you!" Campi snarled, grabbing his arm. "Get rid of them! Understand?"

"I have plans to do that," Sebastian said.

"When?"

"Soon. By next week."

"Good. Make sure it happens." He let go of Sebastian's arm and patted him on the shoulder. "I'll see you Saturday."

Sebastian watched as Campi walked back around the corner. As soon as he got into a cab he began thinking all the things he would do to Anthony Campi if he ever got him in the dark house.

Watching the cab leave were two men, each working for different employers. They knew about each other and were amused that two different parties had tails on Sebastian Guyera. Both found the public confrontation with Campi interesting. Neither, however, could hear any of it. They returned to their cars and using cell phones called their employers to report the latest on Guyera.

A subway stop away, Joe Nemond was in his office, talking on the phone to Carrie. "This isn't like her," he said. "Jazz always reports in, especially when she's involved in a story like she is now."

"Maybe she's in love, Joe. She said she would tell me all when she returned."

"But when did she say she would return?"

"Well she didn't really."

"What did she say?"

"She didn't say anything. There was a note on my door when I got home."

"And I got a note saying she'd be away for a week or two. But it's not like she's gone to the Amazon. She's in Florida. Why can't she call?"

"Joe, you sound like a parent. Give her some space."

"I would if I didn't feel some sense of danger. Roger was murdered. I'm worried about her. I was thinking of calling her mother to see if she's heard from her, but I don't want to alarm her."

"I wouldn't do that. Delilah would call out the National Guard. I suppose I could call Wit and ask him to have her call me. I just didn't want to bother them, you know. Something is always coming up, keeping her from a personal life. Let's just wait until the end of the weekend. I promise to call Wit on Monday if we don't hear from her."

"All right. Maybe I'm making too much of this. She hasn't taken a vacation in two years. She's entitled. But call me if you hear anything. I can't stop thinking about her."

★ ★ ★ ★ ★

In Washington, Wit was trying to forget he ever met A.J. Billings. He was tired of his emotions being played like a yo-yo. Why didn't she at least have the decency to tell him personally that she was dumping him for Ben?

He spent New Year's alone, watching the ball fall in Times Square while he downed scotches like water. He imagined her dancing with Ben like they had at Guyera's party. He imagined them doing all sorts of things until the scotch silenced the thought processes. Then he dreamed about her. Enough. He would immerse himself in his work and his continued search for Chris.

His private investigator had been tailing Sebastian. Wit had ended the surveillance on Jazz after their fight in Brooklyn. He learned Sebastian spent New Year's on his island in the Keys. But now he and his father were in New York meeting with the Campis. Very interesting. The Guyeras and a New York crime family? But still no lead on Chris. He started to think the unthinkable. In all likelihood, his sister was probably dead.

"The special committee meeting is in five minutes." His receptionist had knocked and entered, and he hadn't noticed. Congress wasn't in session during the holidays, but the crisis in Central America had brought committee members to the capitol for another closed-door meeting. It was possible the president was going to request that troops be sent in. "Too much going on," he said as he headed out the door.

In Georgia, Delilah was on her knees planting. She always worked in the garden when she was upset about something. And she was upset, and mad, that her one and only daughter had not called to wish her a Happy New Year. She left a rather abrupt message on Jazz's machine, voicing that sentiment, but so far no reply. If she didn't get a call back soon, she would have to talk to Carrie. Carrie understood the importance of family. Carrie would make sure Agatha Jasmine called her mother.

Wearing a wide brim hat to keep her fair skin even fairer, Delilah didn't see the man approach until he was standing next to her. She saw feet and gasped.

He kneeled down. "Sorry, I hope I haven't frightened you."

"You could have at least announced you were on my property."

"Now how does one do that, Deli?"

Deli. Delilah hadn't heard that nickname since her husband died. Jack Billings was the only one allowed to use a nickname in her house. And Deli was his nickname for her.

She stood up and stared at the stranger. He was about the age her husband would have been. Something about him was familiar. "Do I know you?"

"I need to talk to you about your daughter," he answered.

"But do I know you?"

A car passed slowly. He took her arm. "Could we go inside Deli? We need to talk about some things."

"Not until you tell me who you are."

"I'm Cracker, your husband's friend from Vietnam."

"Cracker? Oh my Lord, are you Cracker? Jack talked about you so much. You saved his life."

"And he saved mine. Now we need to talk—about Jazz."

"Agatha Jasmine? Has something happened to her?"

"I don't know. That's why we need to talk."

"Of course, come into the house. I'm sorry. I'm trying to remember your real name. Jack was always making up nicknames."

"Yes, he gave me mine. He and the other guys in Nam were the only ones who ever called me that. It came from my last name, Graham. Graham—cracker. Get it? I'm Ron Graham."

"Oh yes, now I remember. Ron Graham. What have you been doing with yourself all these years?"

CHAPTER 64

Before Graham could talk, Delilah had to serve lemonade. Her southern hospitality would have it no other way. They sat in rocking chairs in the sun room, sipping and rocking. It would have been a delightful reunion, if both didn't have so much on their minds.

"I'm with the FBI, Deli," he began. "I have been ever since Nam. Jack knew, but I was undercover for a long time so he wasn't allowed to talk about me. We kept in touch though. Even saw each other occasionally in New York. In fact I saw him a week before he died. He was so excited about Jazz at Northwestern. I didn't know about his death until a month after it happened. I called his paper and they said he was dead. I felt like I lost a brother. I tried to contact you. I knew how you would grieve. Jack told me so much about you and Jazz. But I was still undercover and every time I tried to call, you were out."

"I just wasn't answering the phone."

"I figured that. I had a friend of mine check things out. He said you were okay. When I finally did get a chance to visit you on Long Island, you had moved back here. Time just went on and I never made it to Decatur. But I knew you were doing fine. I had another friend in a bureau near here keep an eye on things. I've also been following Jazz's career. You see when Jack and I were in that cave in Viet Nam and neither of us thought we were getting out, we made a pact. We would look after each other's family if anything happened. I didn't have a family. I married later but it was brief. We never had children. But Jack—he had you and Jazz.

So I kept a watch on things through the years. You seemed to be doing fine without any male interference. And Jazz, well she's a powerhouse. I mean doing that story in the Amazon. I decided to take vacation time and follow her down there. But she didn't need me."

"You went after her? To the Amazon?"

"I promised Jack. Most of the stories she covers aren't dangerous. Until the Amazon. And now this."

"The A-list story?"

"She's way over her head, Deli. The Guyeras are involved with the Campi crime family. This is not some feature story. You know, it's so ironic. I had wanted to meet her, and you, to talk to you both about Jack and our friendship. But the time never seemed right. Then I was in Washington and Jazz was too. I went to the hotel she was staying in and she was rushing out. So I followed her. She went to the Capitol, to a press conference. I was curious to see about what, so I followed her in. That's one of the perks of the FBI. I can go anywhere.

"The conference was about the restoration of the Everglades. But Jazz asked a question about Armando Guyera. I couldn't believe it. He was part of a case I was working on. I thought I better warn her. But I also thought maybe she needed me more as an FBI agent than a friend. So I sent an unsigned letter to her hotel, warning her about Guyera and telling her to contact an FBI agent named Graham—me. She never did. I told the bellhop to tear up the letter if she didn't get it. I don't know if she ever did."

"I was working in Miami on the Guyera stolen art network

when Chris Whitman disappeared, the congressman's sister. The family's attorney is a friend of mine. He asked me to check into it. I discovered she wasn't the only one missing. I put together a report and sent it to Washington about other missing socialites and celebrities. Then all of a sudden I get a call from the congressman that a reporter A.J. Billings is getting involved. She calls and wants to meet with me. I didn't know what to do. Do I tell her about Jack and me? How much does she know about the case? Washington had decided to organize a task force. I was in line to head it. So I decided to take a wait and see with Jazz. I was torn between protecting her and helping her.

"And then there she was. She has Jack's eyes, you know. What a strange feeling to have her sitting there, interviewing me. I remember you writing Jack about her first steps. I tried to put her off. But she knew more than I thought she did. And the bureau had talked about releasing the information to the press. So I did. I gave her the scoop."

He paused. "But I didn't tell her about Jack. And I didn't tell her the other times I saw her. I was going to in Colorado after her assistant got killed. I knew they would eventually be after her. I tried to warn her. She kept barreling ahead. And now—."

"And now what?" Delilah grabbed his arm.

"And now she's missing, Deli. I promised Jack I'd look after her. And she's missing."

"Oh Lord. I knew there was something wrong when she didn't call me on New Year's Day. But when she's involved in a story, she goes away sometimes. Oh Cracker, where is she?"

"I don't know. I had someone tailing her. But somehow he lost her. She was at work and then she was gone. She left notes with her boss and her friend upstairs in Brooklyn that she was going to Florida."

"Have you spoken to them?"

"No, I don't need to. I have a surveillance system. It's best you don't know about it, Deli. But I know what's going on, or at least supposed to be going on in her life. She had gotten involved with the congressman—Whitman. She was supposed to be seeing him in Florida for New Year's Eve. But he was alone that night. I plan on talking to him after you. He has no idea that I know Jazz on a personal level. I have a feeling he thinks I'm pretty incompetent. I've been trying to keep him out of the loop. But it's time to talk to him. We've got to find her before —." He looked at Delilah. She was turning white. "We will find her Deli."

"What about Guyera? She thought Guyera was the key."

"What exactly did she say? That's why I'm here. Which Guyera?"

"The son, more than the father. We talked about how he felt about women. She thought he was a creep."

"He is much more than that. He could have taken Jazz."

"Then follow him."

"We're already doing that. We're monitoring his phone calls. I want to search his apartments and visit his island in The Keys. But the Guyeras, slime though they may be, still have ties to very prominent people. We have to move cautiously."

"There is no time to move cautiously. I want my baby back." Delilah began to cry. Graham awkwardly reached out and held her hand. "I'll find her Deli, I promise, I'll find her."

CHAPTER 65

On Reef Key, the imprisoned Jazz was close to desperation. You couldn't be a people person if you never saw any people. For days she sat alone in her cell, as she now called the small room. Isolation was destroying her psyche. Venta was the only contact with the outside world. When she asked for something to read, something to do, he told her to exercise. That's what the others did. So she did push-ups and sit-ups. She felt like she was training for a WWF wrestling show. But the jokes weren't coming as easily anymore. There was a good probability she was going to die, and soon. Before that would come physical abuse.

She tried to prepare her mind. But the fear kept rising. To switch it off, she did deep breathing exercises. She tried to focus her thoughts on escape, or anger and how she would pay Sebastian back. But always the fear returned. She never realized how much of it was inside her. Was it in everyone? Paine had let go only at the end. Would she last as long?

Food arrived three times a day. The meals were basic, but not meager. Cake and cookies were even served for dessert. Sebastian must like his victims on the plump side. She felt like Gretel being fattened up by the wicked witch before being stuck in the oven.

Not a good thought. She switched to another. There were so many thoughts as she stared at the walls of her cell. The only diversion was sunbathing. She saw Chris as they exchanged places in the courtyard. They weren't allowed to talk, but one time Chris sang *Knock three times on the ceiling if you want me.* Jazz figured that was a signal. When she returned to her room, she knocked three times on the wall. From a few doors down she heard a return knock. Then another knock, and another. The walls of the basement echoed with knocks from each room. The knocking became her lifeline.

But it couldn't stop the dark thoughts from returning. What about those she would leave behind? Her Willie-boy. Where was he? How was he being treated? He needed so much love. He was so trusting. Her heart ached for him.

And for her mother. Did Delilah realize she was missing? How would her mother deal with losing her? She would be devastated. The only thing that kept her going after her husband's death was her daughter. Without me—Jazz stopped that thought, too. What were Carrie and Joe thinking? And Wit. She could have spent New Year's with him. They could have been a couple by now. Oh Wit, I blew it. Would he blow it too? He was her only hope. He knew where she was. Why hadn't he done something? More dark thoughts as the lights went off, signaling the end of another day of isolation.

Sebastian had arranged to leave the wedding reception early so he could fly back to Florida before nightfall. He had to get to Reef Key before dark. The island's runway had no landing lights. In Miami he borrowed his father's helicopter and ordered the pilot to radio Venta that he was on his way. The pilot was not pleased. His orders were to fly only Armando Guyera. He didn't particularly like the son. But when the son threatened to have him fired, he did what he was told. Tomorrow, he would talk to the father.

Sebastian didn't care about the pilot. All he could think of was his new prize, A.J. Billings. After Campi's comments, he knew he would have to get rid of the captives. But for a few days he could concentrate on A.J.

Since it was Saturday, the rest of the partnership would be partying on the island. That could cramp his courting style. He would have to leave the dark house to them and bring A.J. to the bright house. His courtship had to be done privately. He didn't want the others to see him being attentive. It might be considered a sign of weakness. Next Saturday he and A.J. would go to the party as a couple.

The more he thought about it, the more he realized next weekend would have to be the final one for the A-list captives. They would go out with a big bang, and so would the partnership. Tomorrow he would plot it out with Venta and Ralph. The plan would be ready in case everyone had to be killed earlier in the week.

The sun was setting as the helicopter touched down on Reef Key. Venta waited with the golf cart. "I brought you bug spray," he said as Sebastian climbed aboard. Twilight signaled the onslaught of the no-see-ums and mosquitoes. Traveling through the thick undergrowth at dusk was something no one wanted to do. The bugs practically carried you away.

By the time they reached the bright house, both men were swatting and scratching. They ran into the house. "Where is everybody?" Sebastian asked.

"They're having a dinner party at the other house. They didn't think you would be back."

"They probably hoped I wouldn't be back. But it's just as well. Wait until it's dark. Then bring A.J. Have her dress in something formal and sexy."

"She doesn't have many clothes."

"Then borrow something from somebody else. Take some of Paine's clothes and give them to her." He went into his bedroom to change, but more importantly to view the monitors. Clorio had devised a system where Sebastian could see what was happening in the dark house from the comfort of his bedroom in the bright house. There wasn't a room on Reef Key that he couldn't spy on. And with his three recording machines, he could spy at his leisure.

In the dark house Ben was visiting Jazz. She was so starved for human contact, she was almost glad to see him. "I don't think we'll see Sebastian until tomorrow," he said. "That means you are mine tonight."

"Lucky me. I thought you were forbidden to see me."

"Nobody forbids me anything, Jazz. I could give you to Ted or Gary tonight. Consider yourself lucky to have me."

"How long have you been a criminal, Ben?"

"Ah you want more of my history. Is this what you consider journalistic foreplay? Let's see, I seized the opportunity to make more money than I ever dreamed of about five years ago. I began an association with some people in New York. They were anxious to know what the FBI knew. They actually introduced me to Sebastian about two years ago."

"Do you kill for him?"

"I kill when necessary. For the government as well. But that is not my main job for the Guyeras. I keep them informed of what the government is doing. I also keep the government informed of what the Guyeras are doing. I'm just not as truthful with Washington."

"And you don't think they will find out? They are probably on to you right now."

"That could be. I suppose I should enjoy myself quicker." He reached for Jazz. She pushed his arm away. "It would be nice if you wouldn't fight me every time."

"What are you going to do, Ben? Rape me?"

"If it's necessary. I was hoping it wouldn't be necessary." He began to unbutton Jazz's blouse. As he unbuttoned, she rebuttoned.

"This is kind of fun," he said. "But too time consuming." With one hand he ripped the front of the blouse open. Jazz tried to jump off the bed. But he was on top of her. She couldn't move as his mouth found her breast.

"Stop it, you make me sick!"

He laughed. "You are about to become my woman. Do you want it rough? I can make it very rough." He grabbed the elastic waist of her shorts and pulled down the shorts and her panties. He was so focused on her, and her fighting, he didn't hear the sound of the door opening behind him. As quickly as he was on her, he was pulled off. Venta and Ralph pinned him against the wall. Jazz attempted to cover up. Then she noticed the open door. Standing in the hallway was Sebastian, with a gun in his hand.

CHAPTER 66

W it was in Naples when Graham called saying he was in
town and had to meet with him. "Is there something new
on Chris?" he asked as soon Graham entered his office.

"No. It's not Chris I'm here to talk about."

"Then who?"

"Jazz Billings."

"Something's happened to her?" Wit's voice lost its bravado.

"It sounds like you care about her."

"It's complicated."

"She's complicated."

"I know."

"Congressman, Miss Billings is missing. I was hoping you
might have a lead on where she is. She sent notes to her friend
Carrie and Joe, her editor. But I don't buy them."

"What do the notes say?"

"That's she on a boat in the Caribbean working on some great
angle for the story."

"Well if she is in the Caribbean, she's with Ben Luvana."

"Why do you say that?"

"Because she called and left a message with my press secretary,

Betty Norris. She said she couldn't see me New Year's because she decided to go out with Luvana. That's something isn't it? She didn't call me. She left a message with my press secretary."

"Did she say where she was going?"

"I doubt it. It doesn't really matter to me."

"Well it matters to me. Where is Betty Norris?"

"In Washington."

"Please get her on the phone."

"Do you think Luvana has taken Jazz somewhere?"

"I'll explain a few things after we speak to Norris."

Wit dialed Washington. When Betty heard it was the congressman, she quickly got on the telephone. "I'm putting the call on speaker, Betty," Wit said. "Ron Graham from the FBI is here. We need to talk about A.J. Billings. What did she say when she spoke to you?"

"Well I didn't exactly talk to her, Wit. She called the Naples office and left a message." That was a different story than what she had first told him. "Betty, I want to know everything she said."

"Just that she couldn't make New Year's because she was spending it with Ben Luvana."

"Miss Norris, this is Ron Graham. Did she say where she was going?"

"I—I don't remember." Damn that Billings. Betty couldn't decide what to answer.

"Miss Norris, I have reason to believe Miss Billing's life is in danger. If you know anything tell us now!"

"She might have said something about an island."

"WHAT?" Now Wit was angry. "What island? You didn't say anything about an island."

"I didn't think it was important. I think she said she was going to Guyera's island with Luvana. What is the big deal?"

"Anything else?" Graham asked. "Anything?"

"No."

Wit took the phone off speaker. "I'll talk to you later," he said to Betty and hung up.

"What do we do now?" he asked Graham.

"Well Luvana is back in Miami with no sign of Jazz."

"How do you know that?"

"Congressman, Luvana is one of our agents. He's been working undercover on the Guyera import case."

Luvana a FBI agent? Wit had to digest that fact and how it related to Jazz. It would be easier for her to be romantically involved with a government agent than a seedy friend of Sebastian's. That meant she could be serious about Luvana. But at least she wouldn't be in danger with him.

"Then Jazz should be safe if she was with an FBI agent," he said to Graham.

"Well I have my suspicions about Luvana. We've started investigating him. I think he may be playing both sides of the street—giving us false information while taking payoffs from Guyera and Campi. Your P.I. may not have that information. The Guyeras are hooked up with the Campi crime family from New York."

"I know. They all met in New York this week."

"I'm impressed with your guy. Maybe we should hire him."

"I took him off of Jazz. She got so mad, I told him to stop following her. That was stupid. I knew she was in danger."

"You should have kept on having her followed. We've got to find her and soon." Graham seemed shaken.

"Why are you so concerned about her?"

"It's a long story Congressman. Maybe I should have told you a while back. Maybe I should have told her. But I didn't. I knew her father in Viet Nam. We were best friends—saved each other's lives. Once when neither of us thought we were getting out alive, we made a pledge to take care of each other's family. I never had a family. But Jack had Jazz and Deli—Delilah. After he died, I watched over them from a distance. They didn't really seem to need me. I told Deli the other day that Jazz never did dangerous stories until the Amazon, and now this."

"If you know Jazz's mother, why doesn't Jazz know you?"

"I didn't meet Deli until two days ago. She knew about me. I don't think Jazz ever heard of me. I probably should have told Jazz the first time she walked into my office, but instead I decided to help her. That was dumb too."

"She didn't trust you. Neither did I."

"I know. There were things that neither of you were cleared to know."

"I'm a congressman!"

" You're not the president. We have two important cases intertwined here—Guyera and Campi and the stolen art smuggling, and Guyera's possible connection to the missing socialites. If we move on one, we may ruin the chance to solve the other. So we're proceeding cautiously."

"But there may be no more time if Jazz is being held on the island."

"We don't know that."

"And we don't not know that. You need to talk to Luvana about New Year's Eve."

"I know. But I'm not his favorite person. We had a run-in already on the smuggling case."

"I'm not sure I should be the one to do it, either. Maybe we should have Carrie, or Jazz's mother contact him."

"Deli's not a bad idea. She is a good judge of people. I'll ask her to call him."

"And soon."

"I agree. I'll arrange it today." Graham stood up to leave. Wit reached out his hand. "I'm glad we're on the same side now."

"We always were, Congressman," Graham said, shaking his hand. "It's just that we prefer doing the investigative work ourselves."

"Sometimes it pays to listen to others. If you had, Jazz might not be in danger."

"I don't dispute that. I'll be in touch." Graham walked out and Wit picked up the phone. "Get me Betty," he said.

CHAPTER 67

In Jazz's room, all eyes were focused on Sebastian and his gun. "I thought we had an agreement, Arthur," he said. "I've given you everything you want here. And this is how you repay my hospitality. Miss Billings is my guest, remember?"

He put the gun under Arthur's chin and Jazz closed her eyes waiting for the explosion. After a few seconds of silence, she opened them. Sebastian had turned towards her. "I'm sorry," he said, "this is upsetting you. We will take this discussion elsewhere. I'd like you to get dressed for an elegant dinner party. Venta will come for you in a half-an-hour. Be ready. I don't like to wait for my dates." He motioned for his men to escort Ben out. He followed, the gun still in his hand.

Jazz heard the door lock, footsteps lead away and then silence. She was alone again.

At the dinner party upstairs, Chris was trying to get Jeff's attention. They had been seated diagonally across from each other. She was Ted's date tonight. Jeff was ordered to accompany Kensington Washington. Clorio was mad at him. No matter how he treated Jeff, kindly or roughly, he couldn't get any emotion from him. It just wasn't the same since Sam had been killed. Clorio was still mad at Sebastian for ordering that. If this game was to continue, they would have to abduct another gay man. Tonight Clorio was playing host. He organized the dinner and cooked it, with the help of Fanee. The menus were always simple. Sebastian couldn't chance bringing in a trained chef. Ralph, Venta, or members of the partnership, usually prepared the meals. Because the captives might put something in the food, they were asked to help only occasionally, and they always had to taste the dishes first.

Tonight Clorio was cooking an Argentinean stew. The appetizer, conch fritters, had been served when Chris finally made eye contact with Jeff without anyone else seeing. She shifted her eyes toward the bathroom. Jeff understood. After so many months of captivity, they had a series of signals.

Chris asked to be excused to go to the bathroom. Ted signaled for Venta to accompany her. As a holiday bonus, Ralph had been given the night off, and for the first time the use of a captive. He chose the most timid—Spring Bellingham.

"Venta, please," Chris said as they exited the dining room. "I can go to the bathroom myself."

"All right," he said. "I will wait here." He sat down in a chair in the hallway.

Jeff soon approached.

"Have to use the john," he said.

"Chris is in there."

"I'll wait in the hall." Venta watched him walk towards the bathroom. He knew nobody would try anything after what happened to Paine. As he sat, his pager went off. The message read "Bring Jazz." He went back into the dining room to tell the partnership he had to leave and that two of the captives were by the bathroom.

When Jeff saw him go he ran to the bathroom door and knocked twice. Chris opened the door. They had been able to meet like this once before.

"We don't have much time," Jeff said. "I don't know where Venta went."

"We have to make contact with this new hostage, Billings."

"But how?"

"I pass her each day going into the courtyard. If you could make some diversion—I'll knock to tell you when—then I might have time to talk to her."

"When do you want to do it?"

"Tomorrow."

There was a loud knock on the door. "Get out of there, now!" It was Clorio. They had no choice. There was no lock on the door. Chris walked out first adjusting the back of her dress. "I needed someone to zip up my dress," she said. "He was around." Jeff looked sheepish as he followed her out.

"Get back to the party," Clorio ordered. Should he tell Sebastian? He would think about it.

Riding the golf cart towards the bright house, Jazz once again tried to entice Venta to help her. "Isn't this tiring for you?" she asked.

"What?"

"Having to deal with us every day and night. It could all be over and you could be a rich man if you would only consider the five million dollars reward. You wouldn't even have to be involved. I could get the money to you."

He didn't say anything. That was a good sign. "I've been think-ing, Venta. If I could somehow get off this island, either in a boat or a plane, I could get help for the others. Nobody would have to know you were a part of the escape. And everybody could live."

She didn't know plans were already underway to kill them all. Venta felt bad about that. This one seemed feisty like Paine. He couldn't get over the way Sebastian had planned to kill Paine. And now the way he wanted to kill the rest. Venta didn't know if he could watch that. Then there was the offer of money. What his family could do with that amount of money.

He said nothing. Jazz's heart leapt. Normally he told her to shut up. "Please consider it, and soon," she said. "I don't think we have much time."

"No, you don't."

They had reached the house. "Do what he says," Venta told her. "It will go easier on you."

CHAPTER 68

Sebastian was waiting in the living room. He had decided to dress formally. The dark Armani jacket and black shirt made him look taller and stronger, he thought. Jazz thought he looked ridiculous, dressed in the tropics as if he was going to a New York disco.

"Good evening A.J., welcome once again to my home."

She said nothing. He gestured toward the sofa. "Please sit down. I thought we would have a little champagne before dinner. Champagne always makes me think of some special occasion. Don't you feel the same?"

"Is this charade necessary?" she asked.

For a moment his eyes flashed anger. But then he relaxed. It would take time. A.J. would learn to submit. He had so many ways to make her. First, there was the dog. If that failed there were her friends and her mother. It had worked on the others. It would work on her.

"Willie was crying for you the other day. I'm sure he would like you to play these charades."

At the mention of Willie, her arrogance disappeared. "Where is my dog?"

"In a safe place, today. But tomorrow, well—."

"Please don't hurt him. He's just an animal."

"One that is very useful to me at the moment. Let's keep him useful, and alive, shall we? Now would you like some champagne, or something else?"

"Champagne would be fine."

"Good. Good. Sit down next to me."

She sat as ordered. Her mind started planning. One karate chop, or whatever her defense teacher called it, and she could have him on the floor. Would that be the end of it? What would the others do if she hurt Sebastian?

"You look as if you want to kill me, A.J. That is not the look I had in mind. Be aware that if you plot to do me in, I have safeguards in place. For you it involves those you love—Willie, your mother, Carrie. They mean nothing to me. But everything to you. If something happens to me, or you displease me, they will die.

"I have a hired assassin on retainer. I pay him whether or not he kills anyone. I like to get my money's worth. He hasn't murdered anyone this month. Of course last month, he took care of three—all in Colorado.

"Oh God—Roger."

"Well, I can see that's still painful. Let's not go there. I just wanted to make sure we had an understanding. Do we A.J.?"

She was trapped. "Yes."

"Good. Now let's enjoy ourselves. Talk to me of your work. I find it so fascinating, although you got it wrong regarding the absent eight. There were actually ten—nine of them Americans. You never knew about Jessica Lawrence. I'll tell you about her sometime. What do you think your next story would have been regarding our missing friends?"

"That their kidnapper was found chopped up in little pieces in a Florida swamp." She couldn't help herself.

"Ah you have always been a sarcastic person." He put his arm around her shoulder. "I think I need you more docile for a while." He stroked the back of her neck. She stared straight ahead. The thought of looking at him made her feel ill. He leaned over and kissed the back of her neck. She clutched the sofa cushion. Deep breathing. She would try deep breaths.

"I will go slow with you, A.J. I could have you anytime I want. But I want you to desire me to." His hand moved up her thigh, past her waist, to a breast. He used his index finger to trace its outline. She didn't move.

"I am excited just touching you. Do you feel it too? I think I will touch you some more after dinner. Are you hungry?"

She felt like throwing up. But anything was better than being this close to him. "Yes. What are we having?"

"Well, we are limited with our menus as you know. Can you cook? No, I think not. I brought back from Miami today some wonderful Mahi Mahi. That's dolphin you know." Jazz looked askance.

"That's a fish, not Flipper. Venta fixed it in a wine sauce. All I have to do is heat it up. Normally he would serve but he's busy over at the other party. So much going on this weekend. Next weekend we'll join the others. I thought we should enjoy each other first."

He led her to a small table set up in front of the patio glass doors. Beyond, torches illuminated a path down to the beach. The ocean was just a few hundred feet away. She could hear the waves crashing on the shore.

"What happened to Ben?" she asked.

"Why would you care about him after what he attempted to do to you?"

"I'm just curious."

"He's alive. I need him. He is very useful to our operations. I will have to tell you all about them. Your reporter friend Joanne got so much wrong. Of course she knows so little. But having an

FBI agent on your payroll, well, that is very helpful. Ben was given a reprimand tonight. He has been made to understand he will not be seeing you alone again. It's just you and me, A.J. You will be my last conquest for a while."

As she picked at the salad, he went into the kitchen to get the fish. She thought of poison. She thought of all the ways she could kill him.

Even though she wasn't hungry, she had to admit the fish was delicious. While they ate, Sebastian chatted about his childhood. She spoke as little as she dared. It seemed so ludicrous. She realized he was actually trying to court her. It was almost charming in a ghoulish way.

Maybe she should take another tack. Maybe she should play the game too, act as if she cared. She had taken a drama course in college. She could act. Why not now?

"The food is delicious," she said.

"I'm so glad, and wait until you taste dessert." He began to clear the table. She got up to help.

"No, no, this is my night to wait on you. Sit down, I'll be right back." He went into the kitchen and returned with the dessert. "Surprise!" He was holding a cake. On the top was crudely written "S.G. and A.J." The initials were enclosed in a big heart. "Do you like it?"

"It's very sweet," she answered.

"Then you must cut the first piece. It will be good luck."

Good luck? Killing you would be good luck. Smiling, she took the knife he handed her and hesitated. She was holding a knife. She didn't notice his hand close tightly on the small gun he had placed in his pocket while in the kitchen.

For a second longer she held the knife, then she cut a small piece of cake. "Have to watch the waistline," she said.

"I think your waistline is perfect. Forget the cake for a minute. Let's dance. I understand you love to dance." He pulled her out of the chair and led her to the entertainment center in the living room. A push of a few buttons and Tony Bennett filled the room. "I love the old ballads, don't you?"

"Yes." Actually she did. She had imagined dancing with Wit to them. Awkwardly, Sebastian took her in his arms. She felt like she was back at Miss Reed's dancing school. In fact he wasn't much taller than the boys she danced with at Miss Reed's. But his box step soon gave way to the grind. He took her arms and put them around his neck. *I LEFT MY HEART IN SAN FRANCISCO* he sang in her ear as his hands moved down her back. He began rubbing against her. She endured it. After all this was a play, and she was the leading lady.

"I would like you to kiss me A.J."

"Where?"

He laughed. "Oh I knew you would be fun. Let's try the lips to start."

So she kissed him. And then his tongue probed her mouth. The nausea rose, but she fought it back. She let him kiss her until she thought she would suffocate. She gently pushed him away. "All this on a first date?" She was joking. He wasn't. "You're right. This is only our first date. We will go no farther. Let's have dessert."

As she ate the cake, he stared at her chest. She didn't like where that could lead. "Got any good movies to watch?" she asked.

"I want you to sleep in my bed tonight, A.J. We will not make love. But I want you near me. I want my head on your breast. I want to part your legs and put my fingers inside you."

It's a play. I'm an actress, I can do this. But she didn't know how she could not act repulsed being in the same bed with him. This was the man who ordered Roger and Paine killed.

He got up from the table. "Let's watch a movie first, as you suggested. I'll let you pick it out." She started to take the dishes into the kitchen.

"No, no, leave that for Venta."

They went back into the living room and he showed her where the DVDs were stored. She chose *Live and Let Die*. It seemed appropriate.

CHAPTER 69

Delilah would do anything to help find her daughter. So when Cracker called and suggested she telephone Ben, she said only one thing. "What's the number?" As she dialed it, Ben was in a small plane flying back from the island. The punches to the stomach and ribs could not be seen, but they certainly were being felt. Every bounce from air turbulence made him grimace. He was enraged at the way Sebastian had treated him. But he knew he had to bide his time. He needed Sebastian more than he needed Jazz. She was a diversion. Guyera was his fortune.

When he arrived back at his apartment, the message light on the phone was blinking. Several people had called. But only one intrigued him. Jazz's mother. He immediately dialed the number.

Delilah had been unable to focus on anything waiting for the phone to ring. When it finally did, she almost jumped out of her chair. It took two rings for her to regain her composure.

"Hello?"

"Mrs. Billings, this is Ben Luvana."

Calm down, she thought. Use that Southern charm. "Well thank you for getting back to me, Mr. Loo-van-ah. How is the weather down there in the tropics?"

"Balmy, Mrs. Billings. It was a lovely day."

"Well we have had a nice day too. Warm for January, but not balmy. I'd say more mild than usual."

"What can I do for you, Mrs. Billings?"

"Well I seem to have misplaced my daughter. I have something I need to go over with her and I haven't heard from her in a while. Her friend in New York, Carrie, said she went to Florida and is now in the Caribbean. Agatha Jasmine spoke so highly of you— I was looking forward to meeting you—and you being in Florida, I thought you might know where she is."

"Sorry, I have no idea."

"When was the last time you spoke to her, Mr. Loo-van-ah?"

"I can't remember, maybe two weeks ago."

"But what about New Year's Eve? You were supposed to be with her."

"Who told you that?"

"Well Agatha Jasmine told someone. I can't quite remember who. But she was emphatic she was spending New Year's with you."

Damn! Ben tried to remember. When did she get away from him long enough to call? The phone booth across from the hotel! Who had she called? What did she say? "Actually, Mrs. Billings I did ask her to spend New Year's with me, but at the last moment she said she had other plans. She never told me what they were. If she told someone she was going to be with me, than she was covering up for something. Maybe she is seeing someone she doesn't want you or her friends to know about."

"My daughter does not date riff-raff. If she did, she would tell me."

Ben smiled. Mother and daughter both had a way with words. "I'm sorry I don't know where she is."

"Well I need to speak her. If you hear from her, would you ask her to call me right away? Otherwise I am going to the

277

authorities."

"I'm sure you'll hear from her soon. I wouldn't worry about her. She seems very self-sufficient."

"Well thank you for your time, Mr. Loo-van-ah."

"The pleasure is all mine, Mrs. Billings. Good-night."

As soon as they hung up, each immediately called others. "Sebastian," Ben said, "We've got a problem." He switched to the code.

"Cracker," Delilah said. "He's lying up his nostrils. He knows where she is."

Graham had been considering doing something not by the book. Deli's phone call convinced him. He spent his whole career obeying the rules. Now it was time to ignore them. He would put a tap on Ben's phone. He had asked officially for it. So far it had- n't been approved. The tap couldn't wait any longer. He was in Miami, and he would visit Ben's apartment the next morning. He knew that Ben was scheduled to meet with his supervising agent.

He told Delilah all that. She was impressed. Cracker seemed a man of action. But was it too late? She couldn't sleep that night worrying about where her baby was. Was she hurt? The thought kept her awake until almost dawn, when she fell into a deep sleep. From somewhere came a ringing. What was it? Her mind drifted in an out of sleep. The ringing continued. It was coming from the phone on the nightstand. She groggily reached for it. "Hello?"

"Mom?"

"Who is this?"

"It's Jazz."

CHAPTER 70

Was it a dream? Was her daughter on the phone?

"Mom, I can't talk long. I've borrowed someone's cell phone. I just wanted you to know I'm all right. I'm on a boat in the Caribbean. I've got the big break in the story. But I can't tell you over the phone."

"Agatha Jasmine. Are you sure you are all right? I've been so worried about you. Cracker suggested I call Ben to see if he knew where you were."

"Cracker? Who is Cracker?"

"He's a friend of your father's. He's been so helpful. I was so afraid that something had happened."

"I'm okay, Mom, really. It's beautiful down here."

"But everybody is worried. Where is Willie?"

There was a pause. "He's okay. A friend is taking care of him. Now I've got to go. Please tell Carrie and Joe I'm okay. And I will try to call you again soon. Okay? I love you. Bye, Mom."

"Agatha—." She was gone.

She's alive! Delilah was awake now. Thank you Lord. She's okay. She's fine. I've got to call Cracker.

Jazz's hand was shaking as she hung up the phone. She realized it could be the last time she spoke with her mother.

"You did very well, my love," Sebastian told her. "Now come back and snuggle with me."

He had kept his word. He didn't force himself on her. But he did watch her change into the white nightgown he selected for her. She avoided his eyes as she took off her clothes. She tried to ignore all the lewd comments he made. A few kisses, a few gropes and he was fast asleep.

At first, she couldn't get to sleep lying next to him. But at least she didn't have to act. And then exhausted from the stress, she had fallen asleep, until Ben contacted Sebastian.

"Who did you telephone?" Sebastian shouted, shaking her awake. "Who did you tell about Ben and New Year's Eve?"

"No one," she lied. "I didn't tell anyone. There was no time to call."

Sebastian wasn't sure. Could A.J.'s mother have made it up? Could she be that devious? She said she was going to the authorities. He and Ben agreed the only way to stop any investigation was for Jazz to call her. Jazz was reminded about what was at stake. If she didn't say exactly what they planned, someone she loved would die. The call was made at 5:00 a.m. Sebastian assumed Delilah would be groggy then, and she was.

The telephone call would give him another week. The last week he would have with her and the others. Too many parts of his plan were unraveling. The A-list parties had to end. It was unfortunate he couldn't keep A.J. longer. But that would complicate matters. He would simply have to move up the courtship timetable with her. The next morning he sent word to Ted, Clorio and Gary that he wasn't feeling well and would have breakfast in his room. He had Venta tell them not to disturb him when they left.

"He's getting stranger," Ted said.

"He's always been strange, " Gary added. Clorio said nothing.

He knew every word and action was being recorded for future viewing.

By 11:00 a.m. all of the partnership was on its way back to Miami, except for Sebastian. He was having breakfast in bed with Jazz.

"I'm going to leave you for a few hours," he told her. "I have business on the mainland. But you can spend the morning getting a little more sun. I want your legs to be brown and—." He pulled up her nightgown to expose the top of her thigh. "I want a bikini line. I sent to your room another bathing suit. I don't like the one piece you brought with you. Tonight I will have a special surprise for you. Now get dressed." He slapped her on the rump.

She got out of bed and turned her back to him. He watched as she put on her underwear, then the dress she wore the night before. "Such a lovely body, A.J. Tonight I will explore it as no other man has." He sighed. "But now I must get ready. Venta will take you back to your room in the other house."

CHAPTER 71

She rode in silence on the golf cart. Venta kept looking at her, wondering how bad it had been. Finally she spoke. "Have you thought any more about helping me?"

Venta sighed. "He would find out."

"No he wouldn't. But even if he did, what would it matter? He'd be arrested. He would be out of your life."

"I don't want to talk about it today." They rode the rest of the way in silence.

As he opened the door to her room, he looked at his watch. "He wants you to get sun today. So get ready. Chris is just finishing up. You can follow her."

Jazz put on the two-piece suit lying on the bed. It was so brief she felt as if she had nothing on. Parts of her body would see sun that had never seen the outdoors.

As she dressed, Venta went to the courtyard. Chris was lying in the chaise, asleep. Just as he was about to wake her, Ralph came around the corner. "I need to talk to you," he said. They both looked at Chris. "Leave her here," Ralph said. They walked out past the gate to Venta's garden.

"Sebastian has moved up the timetable," Ralph said. "They are all going to die on Saturday."

"Have you heard how we are supposed to kill them?" Venta asked.

"Yes."

"And you can do that?"

"I've done worse."

"It makes me sick."

"Venta, don't get personal about this. We just do it and move on. But we need to get all the materials. We need to work on it now."

"I've got to take him to the runway."

"After, then. Come back here and we'll make a list of what we need."

They walked back into the courtyard. Chris still lay with her eyes closed. The two men headed off in separate directions, Venta into the house, Ralph back out the gate. After a minute of silence, Chris opened her eyes. She had heard the conversation. It was all she could do not to cry out when she heard her death sentence.

As soon as she saw Jazz appear from the house, she wanted to shout it to her. But Jazz was followed by Venta.

"You are supposed to be finished," he said to Chris.

"Please Venta," Chris said. "Just a few more minutes. I was having such a nice dream."

He looked at the two women. What did he care? Let them have a few minutes together. "I will be back for you in five minutes."

Jazz sat down in a chair next to Chris. "I can't believe he's leaving us alone."

"He figures it doesn't matter," Chris said. "I just heard him and Ralph. We're all supposed to die on Saturday."

"That's only five days away. We don't have much time."

"For what?"

"To plan an escape."

"You sound just like Paine, and look what happened to her."

"What's the alternative, Chris?"

"There is none. I want to hear your ideas. But first, please, tell me about the outside. Did you have contact with our families? Have you seen my family?"

"Yes, they miss you terribly. I've come to know your brother fairly well. Your mother and I don't see eye to eye."

"There aren't many people that my mother likes. Are they both okay? How are they taking this?"

"Wit is committed to finding you. I'm hoping he'll come looking for us when I don't show up."

"How well do you know my brother?"

"Chris, we can talk about that later. We've got to devise a plan. The only way off this island is by plane or boat."

"I've heard the planes. But there is no boat around. Where are we?"

"We're in the Florida Keys. And yes there is a sailboat by the other house. I saw it when we were coming in for a landing."

"You know about the other house?"

"I was there. Sebastian lives in it. It's on the other side of the island. The boat is near there. I saw it this morning. The problem is I don't know a thing about sailing."

"But I do. I even won races when I was younger. You get me to a sailboat and I'll get you to civilization."

I'm trying to convince Venta to help us."

"Why would he?"

"Because there's a reward of five million dollars for all of you."

"It's hard to believe people still care. It's been so long."

"You've been the biggest story for months." She heard a door slam. "There isn't much time. We've got to plan how to meet again."

"And we have to bring Jeff in on it. He will help. I know he will."

Venta was back. "Enough Chris, back to your room."

"Thank you Venta. You have been very kind." She smiled at Jazz and walked back into the house.

As the sun beat down, Jazz thought more about the escape plan. They would need the small boat to get to the larger sailboat. They would have to escape at a time when they would not be missed. Every room had a monitor. How could they leave unnoticed? The questions kept coming. What about outside help? Surely by now Wit realized something was wrong. Maybe he and others were already on their way. Maybe the Calvary was coming. By tonight she could be back on the mainland. Or she could be raped.

CHAPTER 72

There was no Calvary coming. After speaking to Delilah, Graham called Wit.

"Jazz called her mother," he told the congressman. "She said she was fine."

Of course she's fine, Wit thought. She's making a career out of dumping on me. "Then I guess we shouldn't do anything."

"Not right now. You keep your tabs on Sebastian, though."

"And what about you?"

"I've got some ideas, I'll let you know if they pan out. I'll call you next week."

The agent didn't tell Wit that he planned to put an illegal wiretap on another federal agent. Some things were best left unsaid.

In Miami, Sebastian had just finished a meeting with his father to work out details on transporting another piece of stolen art. He was headed to the airport when his pager went off. It was Clorio calling from his apartment in Miami.

"We need to talk," Clorio said. "In person."

"I was on my way back to the airport to go to the island."

"Stop off and see me. It's important."

Clorio was one of the few people Sebastian trusted. They had been allies since prep school. Friend was too strong a word. Sebastian had never learned how to be a friend. Clorio never cared about having any. They both wanted power and both took it. They shared a bond for cruelty. It was Clorio who found the assassin. Although Venta and Ralph killed when ordered to, Sebastian realized their hearts might not always be in it. Especially Venta's. Sebastian wasn't sure Venta could carry out his plan to eliminate the captives. So he had called the assassin and scheduled him to come to the island early Saturday morning.

Clorio's apartment overlooked the Atlantic. It took 20 minutes to get there. "This better be worth it," Sebastian said.

"Sit down, you are always in such a hurry."

"I'm on a schedule."

"Yes, I know. The grand finale to our parties. It all ends Saturday, doesn't it?"

"I was going to talk to you about that. How did you find out? Ah yes, our killer. I must check his allegiance."

"He assumed he worked for all of us."

"What do you want, Clorio?"

"I want to offer an alternative to killing them."

"Clorio, have you grown a heart that I didn't know about?"

"No, I'm thinking in financial terms. I have a friend from the Middle East. He is involved in an underground network of buying and selling companionship. That would be the politically correct term. You and I would call it the slave trade. They sell slave-girls. I prefer the slave-boys. The seven we have are worth at least five million dollars each. And don't forget. We have a George Washington descendant. Do you know how much others would pay to have a relative of the founder of America as a slave? We could hold an auction."

The idea had appeal. "But the logistics, Clorio."

"If you got them on the island, you can get them off. And you have a perfect transportation system to ship them anywhere in the world."

"I would have to think about this. I had plans."

"I'm sure you did. I haven't approached my friend yet about who we have. I just told him I might know somebody who had access to some attractive people. I made it vague. But he was very interested. Money is no problem with these people."

"Money is no problem for me, Clorio."

"I know that. But I also know it comes to you at the impulse of your father. With this, you could have twenty million as pocket change. We could split at least forty million, just the two of us. No need to bring in the rest of the partnership."

"The rest of the partnership may not be around after Saturday."

"I would expect nothing less from you."

CHAPTER 73

Sebastian told Clorio he would think about it. Whatever was decided, it would have to be done soon. Clorio said he would check with his friend, but he didn't see that as a problem.

Slaves. That would be an interesting end for the rich bitches. And for Jeff and A.J. The only problem was that as long as the captives remained alive, they could link him to their abductions and the murders of Sam, Paine and Jessica. He would have to think about this.

At 4:00 p.m. he reached the island. Venta was waiting.

"Are we moving on the plans for Saturday?"

"Yes. Ralph ordered some things. One of us will fly to Miami tomorrow and pick them up."

"I want to plan the Friday night party. I want it to be special. My birthday is next week. Let's have a birthday party. Tell everyone I want gifts. They can do the same as for Christmas. They can make them up and we'll record them. And I want a big cake. I want party favors. Let's have it outside in the courtyard. Now take me to the dark house. I want to visit Kensington Washington. I have been thinking about her."

An hour later he had finished with Kensington and unlocked

Jazz's door.

"Surprise! I am back." He jumped on her bed. "I want to tell you about my birthday party. We are going to have it Friday night."

Jazz tried to move to the far side of the bed. Parties and sex seemed all Sebastian was interested in.

"I want you to give me a special present," he said, pulling her close to him.

I've got a special present for you, she wanted to say. Instead she was silent. She was getting good at holding her tongue. If she ever got back to the real world, she would be a new person.

He was going on about the party. At least when he talked he didn't grope.

"Come with me." He suddenly jumped off the bed, and opened the door to the hallway. Should she try to flee? But flee where? She followed him. He went a few doors down and unlocked one. They entered another small bedroom. A painted skyline of New York adorned one wall. "This was Paine's room." He said. "And these"—he opened the closet—"these were Paine's clothes. I want you to try some on. I don't like the clothes you brought. And I'm afraid we can't go shopping."

Jazz looked at the dresses. They still smelled of Paine's perfume. "I couldn't," she said.

"Ah, but you will. You are about the same size. Maybe you have smaller breasts. Paine had an incredible body, don't you think?"

Oh, it was time for the karate chop. This man was such a sicko. But she took the dress he handed her. It was a yellow sundress with tiny straps. "Try this on," he said.

He sat on the bed as she took off her shorts and top and put the dress over her head.

"Without the bra, A.J."

She removed the bra without removing the dress, a trick she had learned in eighth grade gym class. Slide the bra straps down your arms and pull the bra out. The dress fit her. "I have definitely lost weight," she said.

"And it is becoming," he replied. "Come here A.J."

She wanted to scream, "Get away. Leave me alone!" She wanted to scream every time he came near her. He pulled her down on the bed and jumped on top of her. Fully clothed, he began rubbing against her, pumping back and forth, simulating the sex act. "Tonight I will possess you," he said, moving his hands over her body. "And you will respond to me. Won't you?"

She stared at the ceiling. Had Paine stared at this same ceiling with men on top of her? He moved faster and faster. He was going to have a climax with his clothes on. Her eyes filled with tears.

CHAPTER 74

The howling in the warehouse never stopped. One dog would start and the others would follow. By the time the first dog grew tired of crying, a dozen others had taken his place. Willie howled along with the rest of them. He never had howled before but it became his way of saying "I'm here." With his cage wedged behind some cartons, he couldn't see the other dogs. But at least with the howling he knew they were there and as miserable as he.

Once a day, for ten minutes, he was taken out of the cage and allowed to move around in a fenced-in space behind the warehouse. The area was strewn with debris that had either blown there or been tossed over the fence by kids who walked by. Willie could hear them laughing as they passed. He barked and barked but nobody paid any attention.

Where was Jazz? Why was he here? His legs had grown stiff from being in the cage. To get some attention, he tried licking the hand of the person who left food. But the teenage boy ignored him. The boy allocated 15 minutes each morning to feed 24 dogs before taking the subway to school. If he was running late, the 21st through 24th dog didn't get fed. Fortunately Willie was number 17. He received a small cup of dry food and a bowl of water. But he didn't have what he needed most—human companionship. After ten days of captivity, he became lethargic. He spent his days just lying in his cage.

"I think there is something wrong with the big black one," the boy said when the owner came in one day to pay some bills.

"The guy who left him was supposed to be back by now," the owner said. "Maybe I should call him." He opened an old black file cabinet and pulled out a folder. In it were several scraps of yellow paper. On one he had written number 17 and the name Rodriquez with a phone number. He dialed it. An answering machine picked up. "This is Angelo Suaren in the Bronx," he said. "I still have your dog and I don't think he's doing so well. Call me."

The phone rang in a warehouse in Miami. It was one of many phone lines used for dummy offices at G & G. It took two days for the message to be received by Sebastian. The first person who took it assumed it was a wrong number. Fortunately for Willie, the message taker mentioned the call to Ralph who had stopped by the warehouse to see about the explosives he ordered for the Saturday massacre. Ralph knew about Jazz's dog. He called Sebastian.

Sebastian decided he didn't need the dog for much longer. It certainly didn't matter if it died. But to be on the safe side, he would keep it alive until Saturday. As Clorio had dropped the dog off, he asked Clorio to call the Bronx warehouse.

"You called about my Lab," Clorio said to the owner.

"Yes, Mr. Rodriquez. He is just lying in his cage. He won't eat. He is, how do you say it, moping. I wondered if you wanted me to bring him to my brother. He went to veterinary school."

"No, I'm sure he'll be all right. I should be back for him by Monday."

"He really does not look well. But all right. As long as you know I cannot be blamed if he gets sick. I think he misses you."

"Yeah, well I miss him too. See you next week."

Clorio laughed as he hung up the phone. In a dump like that, the guy's a bleeding heart. Who would have thought?

Fifteen hundred miles away from him, Jazz was thinking of Willie. She knew she would probably never see him again. Sebastian acted like he was still alive, but when she asked for proof, he just laughed.

She was losing hope for anyone surviving. Venta hadn't said he would help. There was no sign of Wit or the FBI And she had no way to speak to Chris about the possible escape. She decided she would have to try something on her own that night.

Sebastian swam each day in the ocean. Although he was thin, he did have muscles. Still Jazz was confident she could take him with the element of surprise. She had been the star of her defense class. "Such hostility," her teacher said. "You could be a champion mugger."

It was Ralph and Venta who worried her. And what she would do once she overpowered Sebastian. The partnership wasn't due back for two days. That meant no plane, unless Sebastian was going back to the mainland. She couldn't take the sailboat by herself.

Her only hope was some kind of communication—a phone or radio in the house. Sebastian had handed her a cell phone to call her mother. But she hadn't seen it since. And how had Ben communicated with Sebastian the other night? She thought she heard something ring. But she had been so sleepy.

Venta came for her about 5:00 PM. She knocked on her wall twice as she left. She didn't care that Venta saw her. She was confident he would say nothing. Chris knocked back.

"I'm hoping you realize time is running out," she said as they rode to the other side of the island. "You've got to help us."

"I have been considering it," he said.

Her heart began to pound. "Venta it's time to commit, we only have two more days."

"If I helped you, would you say in your article that I was a good person?"

Now was not the time to think of ethics. "Absolutely. What we need are the boats. We need to take the little boat out to the sailboat. We need the keys, we need supplies. But most important we need to get out of our rooms."

"You would be out of your rooms at the party Friday night."

He was considering it. "But we couldn't sail away in the dark. It would have to be during daylight. Maybe Saturday morning, early."

"It would have to be before Saturday." He didn't want to tell her about the funeral pyre Sebastian had planned for Saturday afternoon. "How would I get the money?" he asked.

"After we left and returned with help, you would have to be arrested. That would help your cover. But you have my word that I would explain everything to the authorities and I would help get you the money."

"That is not much to believe in."

"Venta, my word means everything to me."

"Swear on your mother's life." He didn't know how tenuous Sebastian had made that.

"I swear."

"Then I will think about it."

She felt her heart sink. "Please Venta, commit. We have to make plans."

"I will think about it. That is all."

They had arrived at the bright house. She had a decision to make. Should she try something tonight and possibly be killed? Or should she wait for Venta, and still possibly be killed?

The decision was easier than she thought. Sebastian met her in a towel. "We are going in the hot tub," he said.

"I don't have a bathing suit."

"You don't need a bathing suit. It's time A.J. we got to know each other."

CHAPTER 75

As they headed toward the hot tub, A.J.'s mind raced. She couldn't give in to this man, this man who had Roger killed. And if she didn't give in, he would kill her mother—her dog—and her.

She had been taught in the defense class to strike when the opponent least expected it. There was no finer moment than when about to step into the hot tub, Sebastian removed his towel and stood before her naked. Everything about him is small, she observed.

"Let's undress you," he said reaching his arms out to her. With one quick movement, she grabbed his arm and tried to flip him. He staggered. She gave one chop, the side of her hand hitting his throat. She was a little off the mark, but the surprise of the blow sent Sebastian reeling backward. He fell against the side of the hot tub. She aimed a kick at his head. That too was not perfect—it had been a long time since that defense class—but the kick connected with his head so that it snapped back, and landed hard against the hard tile floor. Sebastian lay motionless on the floor.

"All right! "Jazz shouted out loud. Her adrenaline was pumping, her heart racing. She bent over him. He didn't seem to be breathing. She tried to find a pulse. Nothing. "Oh God, I killed him." With a fluky kick, she had killed him! Should she pull his body into the hot tub and make it look like a drowning? She could do that later. First she had to find some form of communication with the outside world.

She ran down the hall into the living room. She pulled open drawers, rummaged through cabinets, looking for the cell phone or a radio. Nothing. She did the same in the dining room, the kitchen, and every spare bedroom. Then it hit her, his bedroom, of course. Back down the hall and into the master suite. When she stayed there the other night, she hadn't noticed any communication equipment. It had to be hidden. His clothes were lying on the bed. She searched through them. In the pocket of his pants, she found a pager. She put it in her pocket and went to the closet. All she found were clothes neatly hung. She looked in the bathroom then back into the bedroom, opening all the drawers in the dresser. She looked under the bed. Nothing. He had to be able to talk to the mainland. Where was the phone? She looked behind furniture, under it. Think, think. Where was it?

Ben had said Sebastian monitored everything that went on in both houses. Where were the monitors? They would take up room. She went back into the closet and began moving clothes around. Not able to see behind them, she took shirts and pants and threw them on the floor. And then she saw it, a door, inside the closet. She tried the handle. It was locked. Damn. Now she had to find the key. But wait, there was a set of keys in the nightstand she had just emptied. She pushed things aside on the bed trying to find the keys she had tossed there. She didn't hear the sound from the front door. Someone was coming in.

She found the keys. Was the right one there? She raced back into the closet, trying each key. It was the next to last one. In it went and the door opened. Before her was a tiny square room. On the left wall were a set of monitors and several video recording machines.

Next to the far wall was a small desk with a folding chair. The desk held a radio with a microphone, a satellite phone and some type of receivers.

Oh God, she thought, how do these things work? Where was the cell phone? That she could handle. She started pushing buttons. She pushed the on-off button on the satellite phone. There was no dial tone. Did you have to call some number before dialing the one you wanted? She turned on the radio. She spun the dial until she could hear someone talking. She picked up the microphone. "May Day, May Day," she shouted.

The bedroom door opened.

Jazz kept clicking the microphone. "Can anyone hear me?" Silence. "This is an emergency, can anyone hear me?"

A male voice came back. "I hear you, emergency. Who are you? Where are you?"

"I'm A——. The blow came suddenly. She felt an incredible pain in the back of her head, and then, darkness.

CHAPTER 76

Delilah and Graham spoke almost every day. Although the tension lessened after Jazz's phone call, Delilah said she wouldn't be at ease until she saw her daughter again. Graham told her the wiretap on Ben's phone hadn't produced anything new. Luvana was still in Miami. Sebastian was on his island.

"When will you arrest them on the stolen art?" Delilah asked.

"Possibly by the end of the month."

"Good. Jazz should be back then. She can write about it."

Graham was reluctant to say how troubled he felt about the phone call. It had been too rushed. And why hadn't Jazz contacted Carrie and Joe as well? She had a job. Surely she would call her boss. And she shared everything with her best friend. But neither Carrie nor Joe heard any more from her. He checked every day. So why only Deli? Because she called Ben?

He was too cynical. Of course Jazz would contact her mother first. If her call had been made under duress, Jazz would have tried to put some secret message in it. He knew her well enough for that. But Delilah hadn't said anything sounded unusual. Still, he decided to go over the conversation one more time.

"Deli, tell me again what Jazz said that morning."

"Why Cracker? Do you think something is still wrong?"

"I get paid to think like that. Humor me, okay?"

"All right. I was sleepy so it's hard to remember everything. I said 'hello.' She said 'it's Jazz.' I asked if she was all right. She said she was.

"I remember saying that Cracker and I were talking and you suggested I call Ben. She asked who Cracker was. I said he was a friend of her father.

"I said everybody was worried about her.

"She said she was on a boat in the Caribbean and had discovered something big on the story. I asked where Willie was. She did pause there. But then she said he was with a friend. And she said not to worry and hung up."

"And that was it? You're sure."

"Let's see. Well, she did say at the end 'I love you Mom.' I thought how sweet of her even if she never calls me Mom. She rarely tells me she loves me. But then I rarely tell her too. We'll say that more often when she gets back. In fact I think I'll have a big party when she—."

"Deli," he interrupted, "what did you say about her calling you Mom?"

"She said 'I love you Mom.' She hasn't called me that since she was a child. I told her I don't care for it. I prefer Mother. I think it's more respectful. So it's always been mother."

"But she called you Mom in this phone call."

"Well come to think of it, she called me Mom several times in that call. I think she first said 'Hello Mom.' Because I asked 'Who is this?' I never answer to Mom. So I didn't even realize it was her."

"Deli, why didn't you tell me this before?"

"Do you think it's important?"

"Yes, I do. I think I better have a personal talk with our friend Luvana."

"Now Cracker, don't get yourself in trouble."
"It's Luvana who is·in trouble, Deli."

CHAPTER 77

Ben wasn't at his apartment when Graham arrived. He had learned disturbing news for Sebastian and had to deliver it in person. When he tried reaching the island by satellite phone, nobody answered. When he tried using the radio in the helicopter he rented, nobody answered. What was going on? Sebastian had a pager that was connected to all his communication lines. He always knew when someone was trying to reach him.

The helicopter pilot thought Ben was crazy when he was told to land on the small key near nowhere. After seeing all the "Keep Out" signs, he was even more concerned. But Ben said he had friends on the island and it would be fine. As the runway was covered with the green camouflage, they had to land on the beach. The pilot balked at that, until Ben offered him another $1,000. Fortunately, it was low tide. There was enough room to touch down and allow Ben to hop off.

He jogged down the beach to the bright house. When he arrived, the front door was unlocked and no one seemed around. He started down the hall, then heard a noise coming from Sebastian's room. He headed there. As he entered, he noticed the ransacked condition. Then he heard a voice coming from the closet. "Mayday, Mayday." It was Jazz. Where was Sebastian? He raced into the closet and saw her in the communications room. That's why nobody answered. She must have pushed the main switch disconnecting the pagers to Sebastian and Venta.

"I hear you emergency. Who are you? Where are you?"

He took out his gun. But he couldn't shoot her. Instead he took the butt of the gun and smashed it against her head.

Jazz awoke tied to a bed. Her head felt as if it would burst from the pain. It was hard to focus. She tried blinking to see where she was. It looked like her mother's room in Decatur. She was in Georgia. It had all been a dream. But then she saw the patio doors facing the ocean. A figure was sitting in a chair staring at her. As she stirred, the figure rose. It was Sebastian, a bandage wrapped around his head.

"Surprised to see me?" he asked.

"I'm sorry you're alive," she said.

"At the moment that's exactly how I feel about you. I don't know why Ben didn't kill you. You disappoint me A.J. I thought you were smarter than what you tried to do. I've been waiting all day to tell you that. Now I will have to punish you. I think Delilah should die first, don't you? Of course you will die too. But not before I kill off everybody that means anything to you. Oh, by the way, Willie is no more. That was the easy one. He whimpered when he died. Not much of a stud dog."

Jazz closed her eyes. The tears began to flow. She tried blinking to stop them. She didn't want the bastard to see how much she hurt. Why hadn't she put him in the hot tub and drowned him? Poor Willie. Her baby.

"By the way, A.J. your karate skills need some updating, don't you think?"

He started to walk towards the bed, grimaced and sat down in a nearby lounge chair. "I think we both may have concussions. Mine, however, is due to hitting the floor, not to any great power you think you possess. I will show you. I'm going to rape you A.J. And then I'm going to allow every man on this island to rape you." He got up, but again the dizziness made him sit down. "My personal punishment for you will have to wait for an hour or two."

Hearing voices, Ben walked out of the closet. He looked at Jazz, helpless on the bed. "You couldn't play the game, could you?" He motioned for Sebastian to meet him outside. Sebastian shook his head. "That won't be necessary Ben. Anything A.J. hears will never be repeated. Have you made the calls?"

"Yes. They will all be here by tomorrow afternoon."

"Good. I'm sure I'll feel fine by then. I doubt A.J. will ever feel better. Now if you could help me into the communications room, I need to talk to my father."

He slowly got up as Ben held his arm. As they walked near the bed, Sebastian stumbled against it, causing a figurine to drop out of his pocket. It was of a brown-haired woman in a lavender dress. The Lladro he put in the curio cabinet, when I first arrived, Jazz realized. She watched as he picked it up and held it gently for a second. Then he tightened his fist around it and hurled it against the wall. It shattered in a dozen pieces. "Think about dying, A.J. But think of lots of pain before, and think of the pain your mother is going to feel. Sweet dreams."

CHAPTER 78

The timetable had been moved up. Instead of Saturday, the A-list members were to die Thursday, two days earlier. Sebastian decided not to sell them into slavery. Maybe he would do that with someone else, some other time. There were too many loose ends with these captives.

They had to be disposed of sooner, because Ben told him the FBI was closing in on the stolen-art network. The bureau knew the location of the Miami warehouse. They were going to raid it that night. There was talk of searching the island on the weekend.

Sebastian called the warehouse and told the workers to eliminate whatever they could. Phone lines were being disconnected. Artwork was being moved. By the time the FBI arrived, there would be little left to incriminate anyone. But the island? If they came to the island and found the captives—.

His head splitting, his empire under attack, he had no time for Jazz. He told Venta to take her back to her room in the dark house. He would deal with her later. And what dealings. He smiled as he thought of how he would abuse her. After, he would call the assassin in her presence, to let her hear the orders to kill her mother.

For Jazz, the ride back to the dark house was agony. Every bump felt like a hammer hitting the back of her head. Still she persevered with Venta. "We have no more time, we have to do it, tomorrow."

"I know," he said. Sebastian had told him about moving up the schedule. "But you are not well enough to try to escape."

"I'll be fine," she said, although she wasn't certain she meant it. "You've got to get me together with Chris and Jeff Worthington."

"You said nothing about needing him too."

"Chris thinks he's important in helping us."

"This will be difficult, getting you all out at once."

"You just need to unlock our doors and fix the monitors so they go on the fritz."

"Fritz?"

"So they don't work. Then you need to leave us the little boat with supplies and the keys to the engine on the sailboat. Tell us where you leave the boat and we can handle the rest."

"I don't know. I don't think you can succeed. And if you don't, he will kill me and members of my family."

"And how do you know he won't do that anyway? He's a psychopath you know."

"He needs me."

"Oh Venta, he doesn't need anyone. He buys loyalty. Please don't let all these people die."

He didn't answer. They had reached the dark house. He escorted her down the hall in silence. As he unlocked her door, she touched his arm. "The monitors have to go out first." He said nothing. She heard the door lock behind her.

CHAPTER 79

Jazz knocked on the wall twice. Nothing. She knocked on the wall again. Still no answer. Where was Chris? Had something happened to her as well?

All the captives, except Jazz, had been herded into the party room, where they were lined up in front of a video camera. Ralph told each one to say their name, where they were from, and then offer a birthday wish to Sebastian. As they were going to die before his birthday next week, Sebastian decided he would have the tape to remember them by.

Ralph noticed Jazz wasn't there. Not knowing of the conflict at the bright house, he went to her room and ordered her to follow him. She took a spot in the line next to Chris.

"You look terrible," Chris said. "Are you all right?"

"I had an altercation with Sebastian. He doesn't look much better. It's the back of my head. Do you see a bump?"

"I see Mount Everest. You should be lying down."

"I don't have time. They've moved up the schedule. If we are going to save everyone, including ourselves, we have to leave by tomorrow morning."

Venta was watching them from across the room. It was Chris's turn to stand before the camera.

"I'm Chris Whitman from Palm Beach and I want to wish Sebastian Guyera a very special birthday. You just don't know how much I'll be thinking of you on that day. I hope to give you a very special gift." She smiled then gave a cutting motion across her throat. "Oh that was for the cameraman, not for you, Sweetie."

Jazz was next. "Happy Birthday," she said and started to walk away.

Ralph turned off the camera. "That's not enough," he said. "Say your name, where you're from, then say something special about his birthday." Jazz moved back into camera range. "I'm A.J. Billings from New York. I wish that this birthday is like no other for you Sebastian." Ralph rolled his eyes. That was probably as good as he was going to get. And this from a writer? "Fanee, you are next," he said.

Chris and Jazz moved over and stood next to Jeff. "It's got to be tomorrow," Chris whispered to him.

"Why?"

"Because there is no more time," Jazz said. "They are getting rid of us the day after tomorrow. I've tried talking Venta into helping us. He's on the verge. I've told him what we need—the boats, the supplies. He said he would think about it. I also told him he has to knock out the monitors, unless of course we're all together in a room like this. Then we could just slip out."

"We could get into a group," Chris said. "We could tell Ralph that we would all like to sing "Happy Birthday" together."

"But how much time would that buy us?" Jeff asked. "It's better we leave early in the morning. We'll stuff our beds with clothes so it looks like we're sleeping. If he can't knock out the monitors, then in the middle of the night, you throw something over the monitor and quickly make up the bed so it looks like someone is in it. Then uncover the monitor. I'm the first one out in the court-yard at 9:00 a.m. I'll try to overpower whoever lets me out, then

I'll open your doors."

As Jeff talked, Ralph joined Venta. "It looks like they are planning something over there," Ralph said pointing to the three. "Maybe we should break it up."

Venta said nothing. He had made his decision. It was the best thing for him and his family. He would tell Jazz when he escorted her back to her room.

The three were too busy plotting to notice their captors' looks. "What good is our getting out if we don't have the boat?" Chris asked.

"There is a radio and a satellite phone in Sebastian's bedroom closet," Jazz said. "I had just made contact with someone when I got beaned. I thought I had killed Sebastian. Obviously I miscalculated my strength."

"You are as crazy as Chris," Jeff said. He looked at Chris and she at him. For the first time Jazz noticed the sparks. No wonder Chris wanted Jeff with them. How the two could fall in love in this atmosphere. But that look said they had. "All right lovebirds," she said. "Let's get back to the plan."

"Lovebirds?" Chris said. "Oh no, Jazz, you've got the wrong idea."

"No, she hasn't," Jeff said. "But we don't have time to talk about it." Venta was walking towards them. "If Venta agrees to help us Jazz, knock four times on the wall. We'll then wait for you to start things moving. If he won't help, knock just once and we'll fix the beds in the middle of the night. Tomorrow morning, hide in the corner by the door and wait for me."

Venta had reached them. "Ralph wants everybody back in their rooms."

"And why aren't you in charge?" Jazz asked.

"Only Sebastian is in charge," he answered. "Let's go." The three headed towards the stairs leading to the basement. "Venta, we need to know," Jazz said.

"I speak only to you," he said. He locked Chris in her room, then Jeff.

As he unlocked Jazz's door, he whispered his decision to her. When he finished, her heart was pounding. After he left, she sat on the bed, her head in her hands. Tears welled in her eyes. Then she walked over to the wall and knocked—four times.

CHAPTER 80

Carrie had made it a policy to check Jazz's apartment every afternoon to pick up the mail and check for telephone messages. Both were piling up. When was that girl coming back? As usual the message light was blinking when she entered the bedroom. She pushed the play button as she sat on the bed to look at the mail. A reporter wanted to talk to Jazz about a story he was working on. A television station wanted to know if she would appear on a news program. A charity organizer wanted her to sit on their board. A man wanted to talk about Willie. What was that? Carrie pushed rewind, then play.

"Miss Billings, my name is Doctor Xavier Gorman. I want to talk to you about your dog, or maybe it's not yours. I am a veterinarian in the Bronx. I have a very sick dog here and the tattoo on his ear shows he belongs to you. But the person who brought him in says a man owns him. Could you call me at 555-6892."

Carrie wrote down the number and immediately called it.

"Could I speak to Dr. Gorman?" she asked. "It's important."

"Who is this?" the receptionist asked.

"A friend of Miss Billings. He called her."

"Just a moment." Minutes went by. Carrie could barely stand it.

"Hello."

"Dr. Gorman?"

"Yes."

"I'm Carrie Farley, a friend of A.J. Billings. You called about a dog."

"Oh yes. Well, I don't know if it is her dog. But something didn't seem right when he arrived."

"Is it a male black lab?"

"Yes."

"With a beautiful head and very friendly."

"He certainly has a beautiful head. I'm afraid he's too sick for me to know about his disposition."

"Dr. Gorman, my friend has been gone for awhile. And I'm not sure everything is okay. Could you do me a favor? Could you go to him and say the name Willie and see what happens?"

"All right. Hold on Miss Farley." Again she waited. She looked at her hands. They were shaking. Finally, "Miss Farley?"

"Yes?"

"I called him Willie. His tail wagged a little. I think this may be your dog."

"Where are you located? I'll get a baby-sitter for my son and I'll be right there." He gave her the address. She thanked him and immediately called her friend Madelyn who lived across the street. When Madelyn was told about the situation, she said she would be over in five minutes. In ten, Carrie was in her car, on her way to the Bronx.

The veterinarian clinic was not in a good area. But Carrie could care less. She parked her car on the street and raced into the building. "I need to see Dr. Gorman right away," she said.

"Who are you?" the receptionist asked.

"I'm Mrs. Farley. It's about the black lab."

Dr. Gorman came right out. "Follow me, Mrs. Farley." They walked down a dark hallway past examining rooms filled with people and their pets. They stopped in front of a room lined with cages, three levels high. As they entered some dogs started barking, others just lay there. "He's back here," the vet said.

Lying in a bottom cage was a lump of black fur.

"Willie?" Carrie said, crouching down. The head facing the back of the cage lifted.

"Willie, is it you?" The tail began a slow thumping. The body tried to turn.

"He's severely malnourished," the vet said, "and he's got some type of intestinal infection. He's pretty weak. I don't think you're going to get much of a reaction." But the doctor didn't know Willie. As Carrie said his name again and again, he found his last inner reserve of strength. On legs that could barely hold him, he stood up and tottered towards her, his tail now moving like a fly swatter.

"Please, can I touch him, can I hold him?" Carrie began crying. Willie was trying so hard to reach her. He stumbled and fell on his side.

"Sure." The cage door was opened. She reached in and held his head. He licked her hand again and again. "Oh Willie." She was sobbing now. "Oh poor Willie. What have they done to you?"

"We have to talk about that," the vet said. "I think we need to call the police."

"I think we need to call the FBI," Carrie said. "And a congressman Jazz knows. If Willie is here and like this, what has happened to my friend?"

CHAPTER 81

At 6:30 a.m. when the sun began to rise over Reef Key, Jazz heard the key turn in her door. She hadn't slept more than an hour the entire night, waiting for this, waiting for the attempted escape to begin. Today it would be over, one way or the other.

Venta peered in to see if she was awake. The click of the door caused her to sit up. She had worn her clothes to bed. Venta seemed surprised to see her dressed and ready to go. He pointed to the monitor then put his two hands together and tilted them by the side of his head, making a motion for her to pretend to be asleep. As she lay back down, she saw him take a knife and cut a wire in the back of the set.

"I don't know if he'll check when he gets up," Venta said. "He is still in pain from the fall. I am hoping he will sleep late. The doors to your friends' rooms have been unlocked. You can take the knife and cut their monitor cables too. The keys and supplies are in the boat. It's hidden in a grove of trees on the south side of the beach. That would be the farthest point from the bright house. You must be careful, the rest of the partnership arrived yesterday. Gary always gets up early. So does Arthur. They could be walking on the beach."

Jazz took the knife then held his hand. "Thank you Venta. I won't forget you."

"I won't let you. I brought something for you to sign." From his pocket, he took a rumpled piece of white notebook paper. In a childlike scrawl he had written: "I promise to get Venta Morex the $5,000,000 reward money. Signed _____." He handed Jazz a pen. She signed it and squeezed his hand again. "Thank you. You are a good man."

" I am not a good man. I have done many bad things. I am just tired of all this. And I want the money for my family."

"If I get out and bring back help, you will get it."

"Be careful leaving here. Ralph is sleeping in one of the rooms. I think with Spring. I warned him that Sebastian will find out. But he doesn't listen. To get to the beach, stay off the cart path. If they discover you are gone, they will look there." He quickly left the room.

She picked up her shoes and waited a minute before opening the door. The hallway was quiet. It looked like a hotel with doors facing each other. But what had happened behind those doors, she didn't want to think about. She walked to Chris's room and tried the handle. It turned. As she opened the door, she saw a figure in bed. It wasn't stirring. She flattened herself against the wall and attempted to sneak over to the monitor. Chris popped out from behind the door, and Jazz almost screamed. Chris put her finger to her lips signaling "sssh" and pointed to the bed. It appeared as if she was asleep. There was no reason to cut the monitor cable. Jazz nodded in understanding then motioned for Chris to take off her shoes and follow her out.

Jeff's door opened as easily. Again Jazz peered in and saw a figure in bed. This time she looked behind the door. Jeff was crouched there. She signaled for him to follow her and take off his sneakers.

Carrying their footwear, they raced down the hall and up the stairs to the outside door that Jazz knew from all the times she had returned from the bright house.

The cold night air was beginning to warm up from the rising sun. Not a cloud invaded the Florida sky. The day would be clear. A good omen, Jazz thought. They put on their shoes and ran to the edge of the woodland. For a second Jazz hesitated, then she pointed right. They headed into the woods, toward the other side of the island.

When they were far enough from the house, Jazz spoke. "Venta told me the whole partnership is here, so we have to be careful. The boat is on the south side of the beach."

They proceeded slowly through the brush, keeping the golf cart path in view. Jeff led the way, cutting a trail with the small knife Jazz handed him. It was taking longer to move through the woods then they planned. In a golf cart it took only fifteen minutes to travel from one side of the island to the other. But making a path was tedious. A half-an-hour passed and Jazz estimated they were only halfway there.

Neither Chris nor Jeff had ever left the confines of the dark house. The vegetation and sights were new to them. They depended on Jazz's sense of direction. She was going by the sun. She knew the sun rose over the dark house and set in the west over the bright house, so she told Jeff to head west. With the thick tropical foliage, they weren't always certain the sun was behind them. They tried to keep the golf cart path in view, but with its twists and turns, and their detours around swampy areas, at times they weren't sure in which direction they were headed.

The sounds of their labored breathing and the breaking of branches were the only noises until they heard the puttering of an engine. It was coming towards them. They froze. What was it? Who was it? Nearer it came. "It's a golf cart," Jazz whispered, "probably coming from the bright house." Jeff signaled for them to go deeper into the woods and crouch down in the undergrowth.

The cart appeared in one of the small clearings. They could see a man driving as it passed. They recognized Gary. It was well out of sight before they moved on.

"Why do you suppose he is going to do at the dark house?" Chris whispered.

"I don't know," Jeff said. "But he could find us missing. Let's go."

They tried to move faster through the vegetation. Staying further from the trail made it even more difficult. Brambles and thorns scratched their arms and legs. Jazz was getting eaten alive by the mosquitoes and no-see-ums.

How much longer? It was taking too long, she thought. They heard the cart again, this time coming back from the dark house, this time moving faster. They just had time to fall flat and hope they hadn't been seen. Jazz lifted her head as the cart passed. Ralph was driving, with Gary at his side. Gary was holding a big stick. As the cart disappeared from view, Jazz realized it wasn't a stick. It was a rifle.

"They know," she said. "Gary had a rifle."

Jeff saw it too. "Maybe we shouldn't head out to the beach," he said. "How much farther do you think it is, Jazz?"

"Not much more," She said, and hoped.

A sense of urgency propelled them through the last hundred feet of undergrowth. They could see the edge of the beach.

"Finally!" Chris cried. She gave Jazz a high-five. Ahead of them, Jeff had reached the edge of the woodland. He stopped. Instead of giving them the victory sign, he gave them a halt sign, then crept back.

"Ralph and Gary are stopped at the edge of the beach where the golf cart path ends. They both have rifles. They must be looking for us."

Jazz's heart sank. It was over. To find the boat, they had to pass in open view of the cart.

"We could hide in the woods until they come looking for us," Chris suggested.

"But by then the rest of the partnership would join them," Jazz said, "and you saw what a good shot Ben is."

"There is really only one thing we can do," Jeff said. "One of us has to be a decoy and pull them away from the beach."

"No!" Chris said. She knew Jeff was willing to sacrifice himself. "We vowed to get out together."

"Sometimes vows don't work, Chris. Think of everybody else. We are their only hope. And I'm not crazy. I'll pull Gary and Ralph away from the beach and then double back. If you see me when you reach the sailboat, wait for me. But don't go out on the beach until you have to. Stay in the woods and head south. I'll bring them north."

"Please Jeff, there must be another way."

"There is no other way." He hugged her. "For so long, I've wanted so to touch you, alone, with nobody watching." He looked at Jazz. She turned away. "It will have to wait." He hugged her once more.

"I love you," he said. And then he was gone.

Chris and Jazz watched as he ran to the edge of the woods. He intentionally started a few feet towards the beach until he drew the attention of Ralph. "I see them!" Ralph shouted.

Jeff ran back into the woods cutting behind their golf cart. Gary and Ralph left the cart and raced into the woods after him. The women heard shots. "Oh Lord please help him," Chris whispered.

"We've got to go," Jazz said. "This will be our only chance."

CHAPTER 82

They started running. The underbrush slashed at their legs. Sandspurs burrowed into their feet. Finally they headed out onto the beach. They were a quarter of a mile from the house. Where was the boat? Jazz wanted to go to the right. Chris said it had to be to the left, perhaps near that grove of Australian pine trees. The sun showed that was south.

"All right, all right let's just go," Jazz said. She didn't know how much time they had. Had Jeff held their attention? Had Ralph first radioed Sebastian that the three were missing?

In his psychopathic state, Sebastian would be gleeful. He would gather the partnership and begin the hunt. Chris had told her how much they loved their demented game of cat and mouse. They played it with Jessica Lawrence. And she wasn't the first. They had taken a girl from a poor area of Miami. After bringing her to the island and taking turns abusing her, they set her free. The freedom was short-lived. Now they would be doubly pleased. Chris and Jazz had to be killed, and quickly. They couldn't be trusted to talk to the others.

Only a few minutes had passed since Jeff left, but Jazz felt as if it had been hours. Where was the boat? Venta promised he would leave it near the edge of the water. Chris was running faster now. She was about twenty yards ahead. Did she see something? She turned and waved excitedly. Oh yes, thank you, God. She had found the boat. She was already pulling it out from behind a tree when Jazz arrived. The keys and supplies were under the tarp as Venta promised. "Venta, I will make you the lead of my story," Jazz said. Chris smiled. They were going to make it.

Together they pushed the boat to the water. Jazz jumped in first and reached for the starter cord on the small outboard. Chris gave an extra push, jumped in and they made it out over the first wave. But the engine wouldn't start on the first pull, or the second.

"You're flooding it," Chris shouted.

"I don't know what I'm doing," Jazz shouted back. "Get the paddle, start paddling as I keep pulling." The engine choked and stalled as Chris tried steering with one paddle into the breaking waves.

They didn't notice the men running towards them until they were nearly adjacent to them on the beach. "Chris, look they're here," Jazz shouted. "Use both oars." The women desperately tried to paddle out to sea as Sebastian dove in the water. Ben followed. There would be no mercy from him now. Two other men were swimming towards them. The engine continued to cough. It would start then stall. The waves were carrying them back to shore, not out. Sebastian had made it to the boat. He grabbed the side. Chris whacked him with an oar. Jazz grabbed a flashlight and hit Ben's hand as he tried to grab hold of her arm. Gary and Ted had reached the boat too. The women kept trying to bat them away. For a second Jazz had a crazy thought of the arcade game where you whack the alligator heads that keep popping out, until more and more come and finally—Whack! She hit Ben's hand again, then Sebastian's. But Gary had made it into the boat from the other side. He grabbed Chris. She stood up to fight and they both went over. The movement caused the boat to tip. Jazz fell into the water, too. A few feet away Chris was struggling with Gary and Ted. Jazz still had the flashlight in her hand. She hit Ted with it. She tried to get to Gary when Sebastian grabbed her.

Her head went under. She came up gasping for air. A loud noise sounded from above. What was that? She went under again. She fought like a mad woman. When she was able to come up again, she flailed with the flashlight and kicked until Sebastian let go. The noise grew louder and louder. For some reason Sebastian stopped grabbing for her. She saw Gary holding Chris under and she started to swim towards them. But the noise above was deafening. She looked up. Three huge black shapes hovered over her head. Helicopters! It looked like *Apocalypse Now*. Still holding Chris's head under, Gary looked up too. He didn't see Jazz. She clubbed him with the flashlight. He floated away. Jazz grabbed Chris's limp body and tried to keep her head out of water. One of the helicopters hovered above her. The other two headed towards the island. The roar was deafening. "Live! Oh please live!" she shouted at Chris who lay limp in her arms. She felt something touch her back. A rope had come down from the helicopter. Sliding down it was a man in a black wetsuit. He jumped into the water and attempted to tie the end of the rope around Jazz, but she motioned towards Chris. They both worked the rope around the chest of the unconscious woman, and with a signal, the man and Chris headed up towards the helicopter.

Jazz kept treading water. But she was no Olympic swimmer. "I've got about a minute left before I'm going under for good," she thought. The rope came back down. Before she could grab it, she heard popping sounds. Oh God, gunfire.

Ralph was on the shore with his rifle. He was shooting at her and the helicopter. Oh God, please. She reached for the rope. There was no time to tie herself. She grabbed it and yelled, "Go!" She wasn't even sure who she was yelling at. The helicopter started moving up and away as the rope was brought back into the cargo area. Jazz was hanging like a stuntwoman. Pop. Pop. More gunfire. She felt a sudden burning in her thigh. She had been shot. The pain was excruciating. She felt faint. She was going to let go of the rope.

"Hold on Agatha Jasmine!"

She heard her mother's voice. Where was it coming from? Was she in the helicopter? "Don't die on me!" Delilah's face floated in front of her. "Just a few more seconds. Hold on to that rope."

Jazz's hands clutched the rope more firmly. She was almost up to the helicopter now. But the pain was too much. She felt too weak. She was going to let go. "HOLD ON JAZZ, HOLD ON!" She heard a male voice. It was Wit's voice. Was he in the helicopter with her mother? She looked up. Wit really was there. He and the man in the wet suit were hanging over the cargo area with their hands outstretched. Wit grabbed her hand, pulling her in. She made it. But she didn't know it. She had passed out as his hand reached hers.

"Oh Annie," he whispered looking at the crumpled figure laying on the helicopter floor. "Please somebody take a look at her." Two paramedics had just finished checking on Chris.

"Is my sister okay?" Wit asked, as one of them came over to Jazz.

"She'll be fine," the paramedic said. "She's regaining consciousness."

"What's all this blood around Jazz?" Wit asked. The paramedic rolled her on her side. "She's been shot. She's lost a lot of blood. I'll put a tourniquet on it. We'll go straight to a hospital."

"We can't," an FBI agent shouted from the front of the helicopter. "The rifle fire must have hit a fuel line. We have to land. Captain says we're going to land on the beach."

As the tourniquet was being applied, Jazz regained consciousness. "Is that really you Wit?"

"Yeah, it's me. You're safe."

"Where's my mother?"

"What? Jazz, your mother's not here."

"But I heard her. Are you sure? Is Chris all right?"

"She's fine, thanks to you. I saw you trying to save her. You are something."

"What about Sebastian and the others? And the captives?"

"Graham is in one of the other helicopters. He's got two FBI teams landing by each of the houses."

"How did you know about the two houses?"

"When Carrie found Willie, we knew you were in danger. And we—."

"Willie's alive?"

"Yes. He was in the Bronx. And he was pretty sick. But he's going to make it."

"Sebastian told me he was dead."

"I'm sure Sebastian told you and the others a lot of things. I suppose he did a lot of things too." He looked at Jazz, then Chris. Chris was sitting up, trying to focus on her surroundings.

"I'll be right back, Jazz." He rushed over to his sister. "Hi baby, remember me?"

"Oh Wit, oh," she hugged him hard. "I'd knew you'd come. Is it over?"

"Yes, it's over. We've got you."

"What about the others? What about Jeff?"

"The FBI is here. They'll find them all."

"Tell the FBI they are in the dark house in the basement. Tell them Jeff is somewhere in the woods trying to keep the partnership away. Tell them I heard shots. I don't know if he's all right. "

"We'll find them, Chris. It's over, you're safe."

"How is mother?"

"She's okay." He looked at Jazz. "She's as feisty as ever."

Their helicopter landed next to another that had already discharged a rescue team. Men in black were swarming the beach.

One was pulling something out of the water.

"We've got a body!" the agent shouted.

"Whose body? Who is it?" Chris cried. "I've got to see it." Before Wit could stop her, she was out of the helicopter and stumbling towards the corpse.

"It's Gary," she yelled. Then she kicked the body. Jazz pulled herself over to the opening at the side of the helicopter. Although she was too weak to walk, she could see everything from that vantage point. "I think I killed Gary," she said to Wit.

"Good," he replied.

The pilot was talking on the radio to Graham who had landed on the other side of the island. "He says there's a fire in the other house. They don't know if they can go in."

Voices cracked over two-way radios.

"Get the helicopter out of here!" someone shouted. "We'll go in by foot."

"We may need the helicopter to get out of here!" someone else shouted. "Three agents are in the house. The fire is on the other side of the building. I don't know how long they have."

In the meantime agents were rushing the bright house. The invasion and surrender did not take long. Jazz saw four men being escorted out with their hands over their heads—Ralph, Ted, Clorio and Ben.

Where was Sebastian? Had he started the fire in the dark house? Venta was missing too.

Chris had returned and was standing by the helicopter. "I smell smoke," she said.

"The dark house is on fire," Jazz said. "But look, they've got Ben, and some of the others."

"Ralph's there," Chris said. "He went after Jeff. He should know what happened to him." She started towards the group, but before she traveled a few yards, two agents came out of the woods carrying another man.

Jazz couldn't see his face. "Chris, is that Sebastian?" she called. Chris turned to look. "Oh no!" she raced towards the unconscious man. "He's been shot," one of the agents said. "We don't know if he's a bad guy or a good guy."

Chris touched his head. "Oh he's a good guy, a very good guy," she said. "This is Jeff Worthington. Please, you've got to help him." They carried him to the helicopter where Jazz waited. The paramedic, who worked on her, took a look at him. "Gunshot wound in the lower back," he said. "We've got to get him to a hospital. And her too." He pointed to Jazz.

"Can we switch helicopters?" Wit asked the pilot.

"You'll have to," he said. "I'm not sure I have enough fuel to get to Key West, let alone Miami."

The sound of a helicopter approaching made everyone look up. It was the helicopter from the other side of the island.

It landed between the other two. Two agents in black jumped out from the open side, then turned as if to help others out. Everyone stared as one by one the remaining A-list captives got off the helicopter. Kensington Washington led the way followed by Spring Bellingham, then Fanee.

"Was everybody alive all this time?" Wit asked Jazz.

"No, some didn't make it. Eva committed suicide a month after she got here. And Jessica Lawrence was killed a few weeks ago."

"Eva gone? Oh Eva—," his voice trailed off. "And Jessica Lawrence, the movie star? I thought she died in a plane crash."

"No, Sebastian faked it. Look, there's Tracey Wise, the singer. She's okay too." Hobbling on one foot, Tracey was leaving the helicopter assisted by an agent.

"And Paine—remember Paine Hayes who started this all for me? Oh Wit I found her. But she was killed just a few days ago. I saw it happen."

"I can't believe it. He really had all of them. Where is that bastard?"

"I don't know. He's still missing and so is Venta his employee. Venta is the one who helped us escape."

"Yes, we saw part of that. Two days ago Graham convinced his superiors to use satellite imagery. We saw golf carts moving from one side of the island to the other. And a guy hiding a dingy. This morning we saw some people running through the woods and that's what made us come. We wanted to wait until tomorrow and land under the cover of darkness."

"If you had waited until tomorrow night, we all would have been dead."

A FBI agent came running over from the other helicopter and yelled to the pilot. "The fire is starting to come this way. We're going to have to take off soon. I don't know what we're going to do about Graham and the other agent, Gerron. They are still out there. They saw the guys who started the fire and they went after them."

"I've got a lot to tell you about Graham," Wit said to Jazz. "I was wrong about him. He's really a good guy."

As if on cue, a golf cart lurched out of the woods. Graham, his face covered with soot, was driving. Seated next to him was Venta. In the back sat Gerron holding a gun on the fourth passenger. It was Sebastian.

Two groups formed on the beach. The captives stood in one cluster surrounded by FBI agents. Their abductors stood in another group also surrounded by an armed guard. In between was where the golf cart stopped. Several agents rushed over to help Graham. He handed them the guns he had taken off of Sebastian, and he explained that Venta told him he had helped free the captives. If it was true, Venta was to be given special treatment.

Graham led Sebastian to the group where Ben was standing.

"Well Luvana, it's a pleasure to see you again," Graham said. "We have a lot to talk about."

He turned to Sebastian. "And you, well your father already had a lot to say about you this morning when we arrested him for the stolen art. We told him what you were doing on this island. Armando was very upset. He said something like "that little shit can't ever be satisfied."

A few of the agents laughed.

"I have something to say!" Sebastian shouted. The laughter died down. All eyes focused on Sebastian. "I just want to say—" he turned to the captives, "I just want to tell you, all of you, that you were great pieces of ass." He smiled his "I am a Guyera—so much better than you" smile. It was the last expression he would make. As he raised his hand to blow a kiss to the captives, a shot rang out. The bullet tore through his heart. He was dead before his face hit the sand.

Shocked eyes that had focused on Sebastian now looked for the killer. She wasn't hard to find. While everybody was watching Sebastian she had taken one of the guns from the golf cart. She was going to kill him regardless of what he said. She was going to kill him for taking her soul, her self-respect, for turning her into one of them. Fanee hadn't dropped the gun. It was now pointed at the ground. She stood as if in a trance. An agent came over and took the gun out of her hand.

Everybody understood why she did it. Many were relieved she had. No court would convict her of murder in her temporary, or perhaps permanent, state of insanity. Little was said as Sebastian's body was placed in a black plastic body bag and carried to a helicopter. Following behind, handcuffed together, were the rest of the partnership. All except Luvana. Graham personally escorted him.

As they passed by the helicopter where Jazz sat, Ben waved. "I'll miss you, and your body," he shouted, then winked at Wit. Wit started to jump out of the helicopter after him, but Graham waved him off, pushing Ben along. Then Graham yelled back to Jazz. "Your mother sends her love."

"What is all that about?" Jazz asked as the group boarded the other helicopter.

"It's a long story," Wit said. "It turns out Graham was a friend of your father's in Viet Nam. He's been talking to your mother almost every day."

"Have you too?"

"I've got my own mother to deal with."

As the smoke drew nearer, four agents brought stretchers and transferred Jazz and Jeff to the other helicopter. Wit and Chris boarded with them. Already seated on the floor were the surviving A-list captives. Tears streaming down her face, Tracey was signing an autograph for the sister of the agent who bandaged her foot. Kensington and Spring grasped each other's hands. Fanee stared off in space. Although the ordeal was over, the memories would never end.

The sun was turning into a red ball on the horizon as the helicopter lifted off and headed towards Miami. Jazz clung to Wit. "Are we heading off into the sunset together?" she asked.

" Yes," he said. "And we're going to live happily ever after."

She smiled up at him. "At least," she said, "until our mothers meet."

THE END